W.A.NOBLE

BEASTSPEAKER 4

DEAD MAN'S FINGERS

STONE TABLE BOOKS

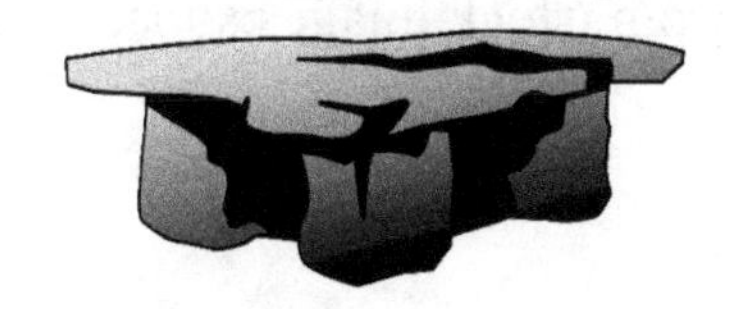

Beast-Speaker 4 Dead Man's Fingers

Stone Table Books
An Imprint of Wipf and Stock Publishers
199 W, 8th Ave., Suite 3
Eugene, OR 97401

PAPERBACK ISBN: 978-1-6667-5406-3
HARDCOVER ISBN: 978-1-6667-5407-0
EBOOK ISBN: 978-1-6667-5408-7

Cataloguing-in-Publication entry is available from the National Library of Australia http://catalogue.nla.gov.au.
This edition first published in 2022

Typesetting by Ben Morton.
Cover art by Ben Morton
image sourced from istock images:sqback

Dedicated to:

This is for Jeff, my companion on the journey, and to all the healers dedicated to the health and welfare of others.

Acknowledgments:

Dr Mark Worthing and the staff of Stone Table Books, for their expertise and wisdom.

My fellow Kapunda writers – Rosanne Hawke, Nancy Johnson and Patricia Gordon-Stevens – for their encouragement, helpful suggestions and wonderful afternoon teas.

Dr Marshall W. Anderson (USA) MD, MPH, FACOEM, for discussion and advice re possible causes of skin infections and poisons.

Fellow author Matthew Edwards for introducing me to the Wulver of the Shetland Islands.

My husband for his continued, enthusiastic support and Rex the Wonder Dog for protecting the house from aliens, pigeons and the postman.

To see a picture of a singing stone, in the American Museum of Natural History, try this link:

https://tumblr.amnh.org/post/651075069204971520/its-baaack-this-massive-block-of-vibrant-blue

To hear the song that Maraed sings to the Old Healer, Google: YouTube/Unst Boat Song/Ezmay Grace: Oldest song in the Shetland Islands.

Contents

One

Mac

They came riding in on dragons. It had been so long since I'd seen one of those creatures that I thought they'd become things of legend. But there they were, riding the thermals above the valley, skimming the air like giant birds from the beginning of time. I watched them from the mouth of my cave but they didn't see me.

Some of the dragon-riders were armed but they didn't seem as though they were looking for trouble. There's a certain set to the mouth, the angle of the shoulders, that tells if a person is looking for a fight. The riders were alert but relaxed. The last time people came looking for me they pretended to be peaceful, but they had weapons hidden under their cloaks. The wolves dealt with them.

One of the riders had a servant of Rafnagud, the raven god, sitting on his shoulder, uncaged and untethered. Dragons and ravens. These weren't ordinary folk.

There was an old grey-hair and some females as well. They were wise to be on guard in these hills. Most creatures protect their females. If they're gone, so is the species. That's why I think I might be the last of my kind. I haven't seen a female since before silver frosted my pelt. Long before the township down below was built. Long before there were wolves in the valley.

From my home in the hill, I watched the dragons swoop over my lake, then set their riders down on the path that leads into the town. Two of the younger ones lifted the grey-hair down and placed him in the arms of the tall, armed female. I thought the old man might have needed my help. He didn't seem well. Then they set off towards Wulverstane.

Their humans gone, the dragons circled back and plonked themselves down into the water on the edge of the lake. I wanted to shout, 'Be off with you! You'll scare the fish.' But I stayed hidden in the shadows and kept my peace. Eventually they took off and found a perch in the hills, closer to town. I hoped they wouldn't burn the place down. Dragons can do that, you know.

When I first moved into this place there was just me and the fish, but it was too good to last. People started to visit the valley and then, one day, a couple of families built houses. Then more came. Eventually, there was a whole town. For a long time, I hid in my cave and only went out in the moonlight to sit on my rock to fish but, as time passed, the people and I learned to get along. I left them alone and they didn't bother me. I've even taken fish to families that were struggling to feed their young. I can't bear to watch littluns go hungry.

Many turns of the sun ago, a werewolf passed through the valley. I knew what he was as soon as I smelled him. I'm always a little sad for the creatures. The poor things can't help themselves. Usually, they don't know what they're doing until it's done. The stranger was on his last legs and, if the moon hadn't been high and full, he probably would have died without causing any damage. But fate is fickle. A couple of the townspeople found him lying in a field. When they tried to give him aid, the wolf took over. He didn't kill them, he was too weak to do that, but his claws and teeth still did some damage.

There have been wolf-people in the town ever since. Some families even choose to keep the wolf strain in the family, initiating their child at the full moon once he or she has thirteen years.

When the changes first began, and people were killed, they came to me for help. I suppose they thought I'd found a way to master the wolf. They didn't understand what I am. I couldn't fix them – once a werewolf, forever a werewolf – but I did my best to help them learn to live with it and to gain some control. I know something about healing. You don't live this long without learning a thing or three. So, I became their healer and when anyone tries to give me trouble, the wolves take care of it. They treat me with respect.

When the dragons came, carrying their riders, I hoped they'd be sensible. Most of the dragon-riders were quite young and deserved to live a full, long life. I didn't want anyone torn limb from limb.

Two

Seeger

As we made our way through the palace I asked Asher, Record-Keeper of Seddon, if he knew why the Commander had summoned us.

'No idea, Seeger,' he said. 'I don't know whether to be intrigued or worried. It's rare for anyone, other than the Commander's family, to be invited to visit his living quarters. Most unusual. Very odd.'

The guard at the door saluted Asher and inclined his head toward me. 'Go straight in, gentlemen,' he said. 'You're expected.'

It was like our gathering room at home but much bigger, with thick carpets on the floor and colourful tapestries on the walls. There were a lot more chairs scattered throughout the room, as well as several small tables, and a huge cabinet and some bookshelves at the far end. The Commander was seated on a velvet couch; a tray with cups, a jug and a plate of cakes were on the table in front of him.

'Make yourselves comfortable, men,' he said, waving his hand at the chairs on the opposite side of the table.

As Asher and I sat down, the Commander poured us all a warm drink of milk laced with cinnamon and honey. I noticed that the Commander's fingertips had a faint tinge of blue but I didn't say anything. I didn't want to be rude.

He offered us each a cake. I declined but Asher happily took the largest one on the plate. Then we sat in awkward silence. I had a mouthful of my drink – my goodness the honey was strong! – and decided I'd just take polite sips of it now and then.

'Commander,' Asher said, wiping crumbs away from the sides of his mouth, 'why are your fingertips blue?'

'That's why I've asked you to come here today,' he said. He put his cup down and rubbed the back of his head. As he turned his head away to stare at a painting of boats out on the harbour, I swear I saw unshed salt water in his eyes.

'Sir?' Asher said. The Commander didn't move. 'What's wrong?'

We waited. I sipped my drink for something to do and immediately regretted it. Eventually, the Commander sighed and turned to face us.

'I'm gravely ill. This you see here,' he held his hands up, 'is just the beginning. It's Dead Man's Fingers.'

'What?' Asher said. 'Like the mushrooms?'

'I think that's how it got its name,' the Commander said.

'Have you eaten any lately?' Asher said but then he shook his head. 'What am I thinking? They're not poisonous. Kieran and I ate a pile of them on our last trip and we didn't have a scrap of trouble. I ran to the privy a lot but that was probably because –'

'It's called by the same name because it looks like the fungus,' the Commander said, cutting off Asher mid-sentence. 'The fingers go pale blue first and then the colour darkens the longer it's on the body. It's just like the mushroom, which is blue when young and then darkens as it ages. Eventually, my skin will harden into large scabs that look like bark.'

'Yes, I see now. Those mushrooms eat away dead tree branches and they're quite fibrous when they're older,' Asher interrupted.

The Commander continued. 'Eventually, the patient dies.'

'Oh. Right,' Asher said, his cheeks reddening.

'Are you sure?' I said. 'That's just awful.' My left leg began to jiggle. 'Oh my goodness! Have the healers seen you?'

Asher put his hand on my arm and I stopped talking. 'You've seen this before, sir?' he asked.

The Commander nodded again. 'When I was just a boy. It was General Rickard, my father's friend. Pa brought him home to care for him. It was a terrible thing to watch. I've never forgotten it.'

'Do you know what causes it?' Asher asked.

The Commander shook his head. 'At the time there was talk of a curse. Some said it was poison. Others said it was Sed's punishment. And then there were people like my father, who said it was just bad luck. Who knows?'

'No one knew of a cure?' Asher asked, putting his cup back on the tray. I quickly put mine down as well.

The Commander shrugged. 'The healers tried all sorts of things but in the end they had to admit they had no idea. An old hag visited us one day. She told us the name of the disease and said a cure could be found in the hills towards the east. She mumbled something about an old healer and wolves. I can't remember everything she said. I was just a lad and she was scary. She was bent over and there were hairs sprouting out of her chin and ears!' He shuddered.

'Did anyone agree with her?' Asher said.

The Commander shook his head. 'The healers said father should ignore her. They said she was just a crazy old woman whose mind had begun to fade. Even so, some of the general's men went searching in the east but they never returned.'

Asher rubbed his forehead. 'Dear oh dear,' he said.

The Commander leaned forward. 'Please find that cure.'

I squirmed in my seat. 'Err … sir?' I said. 'Why did you ask for me?'

The Commander looked at me and smiled briefly. 'I have enemies. Perhaps one of them has done this to me. I want to keep my dilemma secret for as long as possible. When soldiers were sent for a cure, they failed. I thought it would be safer if people thought you and Asher were setting off on another of your little jaunts.'

Asher bristled when his information-gathering expeditions were described as 'little jaunts' but, for once, he held his peace.

'Also,' the Commander continued, 'you are strong in the art of beast-speaking and I thought it might help you on this mission. Perhaps the dragons have heard of such a thing?'

'I'll ask them, sir.'

'And I want you to take my daughter, Tiffany, with you,' the Commander said.

Asher frowned. 'Why?'

The Commander sighed. 'I don't want her to see what I will become and, if this is the work of an enemy, she'll be safer out of the city with you.' He studied his blue-tipped hands for a moment, then straightened his back and smiled ruefully. 'It will also provide a reason for your attendance here today in case I'm being watched.'

'How old is she?' I said. I didn't like the thought of some strange girl, probably a spoilt little brat, coming with us. I'd never met her, so I had no idea what we'd be dealing with. I mean, what sort of name is Tiffany?

'She has fourteen years. She'll have a chaperone with her, of course,' he said.

Oh no, I thought, *we don't want some old granny trudging along with us.*

'This chaperone …?' Asher said.

'Will be a trained bodyguard,' the Commander said. 'Don't worry. No special favours. Treat my daughter as just one of the team.'

Asher stood up, so I did too. 'It might take a while to find the information,' Asher said, 'but we'll begin work straight away.'

'Let me know when you're leaving and I'll make sure Tiffany will be ready,' the Commander said. 'Time is of the essence, Ash. I've probably only got two seven nights, at the most.'

The lump in my throat nearly choked me. Asher patted the Commander's arm. 'We won't let you down, sir.'

Two

As we were leaving the palace, Talia the Well-Keeper passed us in the entrance hall. 'Asher!' she said. 'What brings you here?'

He bobbed his head in respect and said, 'Greetings, Talia.' I nodded as well but didn't say anything.

'Seeger and I are off on another trip,' Asher said. 'The Commander has asked us to take his daughter with us this time. He wants her to see a bit of the world.'

Talia smirked. 'I'm sure Seeger will teach her a thing or two.'

Asher shook his head. Talia waggled her eyebrows at me and walked away, laughing.

'Come along, Seeger,' Asher said. 'Things to do.'

'What's her problem?' I asked.

'Who knows, dear boy,' he said. 'Who cares?'

We left the palace and headed back down the hill to Asher's house. We walked for a while in companionable silence but it wasn't long before Asher picked up speed as we began to head down the hill. He said, 'Where's Joffre this fine day?'

I kept pace with him. 'Boyd and Rimini are leaving tomorrow with Rog, Riff and a few others, to search for new water sources. Joffre wanted to spend the day with Rimini as he won't see her for a while.'

'Lovely. Lovely. For a raven, he's quite a sweet bird.'

He was almost at jogging pace by the time we could see his street. Finally, we turned the corner and saw his house straight ahead. 'Will they go east?' He was short of breath. 'They could … come with us.'

'No, they're going to search the mountains in the west.'

'That's … a shame.' He stopped at his front door and leaned against it, sucking in deep breaths.

'Are you all right, sir?' I asked.

He sucked in another breath. 'Yes. Yes.' He heaved in another lung full. 'Haven't done any dancing for a while. Doesn't take me long to lose condition.'

Once he was breathing normally, we went inside.

I said, 'You realise Joffre will want to come with us?'

'Of course!' Asher said. 'When has he not?'

That was true. Ever since we had found Joffre hanging upside down in a tree and brought him back to Seddon, he made sure he came with me wherever I went; usually perched on my shoulder. He liked Rimini because she spoiled him but he seemed to think he was my personal bodyguard. Even though he was a small bird with a big ego, I admit there were numerous occasions when he proved his worth.

Kieran, Asher's assistant, came into the room from the direction of the kitchen. 'Are we off on another trip?'

'That's right, lad,' Asher said, pushing up his sleeves, which promptly fell back down his skinny arms. 'But first we must head to the archives. We've got lots of work to do.'

I began to sidle towards the kitchen where I hoped to find Maraed, Kieran's sister. 'You won't be needing me, then.'

Asher shook his head. 'This time, it's all hands on deck.'

'What does that mean?' Kieran said.

Asher shrugged. 'I'm not sure exactly. I read it in an ancient manuscript once and I liked the sound of it.'

Kieran looked at me but I just frowned and shook my head. 'Why would you want everyone to put their hands on the deck?' he said. 'Unless it means something gruesome like, once you've cut their hands off, throw them on the deck. Is that what it means?'

Asher shrugged. 'At the time I read it, I thought it meant that everyone had to help, but you've got me thinking, now.'

'I don't see how putting your hands on a deck,' Kieran said, 'or even throwing someone else's hands on a deck, could be helpful.'

Asher stared off down the passageway. 'Why *would* you put your hands on a deck? Maybe it means, everyone has to help *lift* the deck?' Then he shook himself and said, 'No time for that now. Grab a light, lad, and meet us in the back room.' Kieran hurried away. 'Come with me, Seeger. You're in for a real treat.'

I'd never seen inside Asher's archives, so I knew I should feel honoured, but I wasn't really that interested in old papers. I followed him reluctantly down the passageway.

'Is Maraed going to help, too?' I asked.

'She's at the temple, today.'

'Oh. Right.' Maraed was having music lessons from the Choir Director at the temple. I don't know why, because she could already sing like a bird and knew more about music than I do about … well … most things.

We waited outside the room until Kieran arrived with a candle. Asher opened the door and I peered in over his shoulder. The room was as dark as a moonless night. I didn't dare take more than a couple of steps. Kieran bustled about lighting lamps and, as the glow spread, I saw shelf after shelf full of labelled boxes.

'It's the middle of the day, Asher,' I said. 'Why don't you have some windows in this room that'll let the light in? You wouldn't have to waste your oil.'

He shook his head. 'I forget there is still far too much to teach you. Tell him, Kieran.'

Kieran lit the last lamp and then blew out his candle. 'Daylight damages the scrolls and fades the ink.'

I frowned. 'But –'

Asher sighed. 'The whole point of the archives is to keep the acquired knowledge for as long as possible.'

'Well, I realise that but –'

'Some of the scrolls in this room have existed far longer than any of your dragons. Hundreds of turns of the sun, Seeger.'

'Oh my!' I said. I'd always known that Asher was the Records-Keeper of Seddon but I just thought of him as 'the man who knows lots of stuff'. I'd never really considered the 'records' part. 'Are these all the records of Seddon?'

'Don't be silly, lad.' Asher swept his arm out and flapped his hand at the boxes. 'These are just a few. Most of the records are kept in Seddon's Record Depository, where the other record-keepers work. I just have a few here. They're either things I need for my own research or some of the older ones that I've found and have kept in my care. They'll go to the Depository when I die.'

'If there are so many in the Record Depository,' I said, 'then perhaps we should look there?'

'This is as good a place to start, as any,' Asher said.

'What are we looking for?' Kieran asked.

Asher told him about the Commander's problem. Kieran's response was a low whistle and a shake of his head.

'Yes, quite!' Asher said. 'We're looking for anything labelled ancient cures, strange maladies, poisons, wolves, or anything pertaining to the hills in the east. Off you go.'

Asher began searching the shelves near him so Kieran and I went to opposite ends of the room. I read slowly and carefully, terrified I'd miss something important. At first, I was fascinated by the topics listed on the box labels – weapons, magical creatures, ancient waterways, extinct fruits – but after a while I stopped taking a moment to daydream about the contents and just kept reading. I did pause once to ask Asher, 'What's a pygmy?' but he just flapped his hand in the air and said, 'Not important now.'

We stopped for a short break to visit the privy and to eat some toasted bread that Kieran prepared but otherwise we searched all afternoon. My back ached (I'd fallen off the stable roof the other day – a long story, Joffre's fault) and, to give it some respite, I sat on the floor while reading the lower shelves, just scooting along when I could no longer see the writing clearly. Occasionally our hopes were raised by something that looked possible but, after a quick perusal by Asher and a shake of his head, we moved on.

I got excited when I found something labelled, 'Wolves' but it turned out to be a study of their mating habits.

Kieran found several references to 'Ancient cures' but they were about healing wounds incurred in battle, or inflammation of the eye, or the treatment of warts, but nothing about strange infections that turned a person into a tree stump.

It was frustrating! I'd given up hope there was anything in that room and just went through the motions to keep Asher happy. I weighed up the wisdom of suggesting that he put all the record-keepers to work searching the Depository but decided to hold my peace.

I thought about the Commander, knowing his terrible fate and yet staying so calm and brave. I also wondered who would take his place as our leader once he was gone. I hoped it wouldn't be Talia.

Then, as some of the lamps had begun to sputter, and I was thinking about finding the privy again, Asher said, 'Well, well, well. I think this might be it.'

The box was labelled, 'The Wisdom of Delia'. This was typical of Asher. It wasn't any of the things he'd told us to look for. When I pointed that out, he seemed surprised. I looked at Kieran who smiled ruefully and shrugged.

'What makes you think this will be helpful?' I asked.

Two

He carried the box of scrolls closer to one of the better lamps. 'I remember Delia. She was from a town in the east. She was already advanced in years when the Commander was just a boy and I was still a young man. In fact, she did flit through my mind when he was describing the old woman. She wasn't quite as ancient as he remembers but she certainly looked it. She had a lot of problems with her back and it had quite a curve by the time I met her. It all fits.'

'Is she still alive?' I asked.

'Oh no, lad,' Asher said. 'She died ages ago. I'll just have a quick read of one of these, just to make sure, but I've got a good feeling about them.'

He got Kieran to hold the box while he read one of the scrolls. 'Yes, yes, I can feel it in my waters,' he said. 'Bring the box with you, lad, out into the front room. It'll be easier to read these in the daylight.'

I dealt with the lamps and then ran out to the privy. As soon as I left the house, I realised the night had arrived while we were still fossicking in the archive. There was a light on in Maraed's room, so she'd come home while we were searching. By the faint glow that shone from her window, I could just make out the privy door.

When I ran back inside, I saw that Kieran had put the box down on the table and was lighting the lamps. Asher stood in the middle of the room, twisting his hands together. 'I had no idea it was so late,' he said, looking at me with concern etched all over his face. 'Will your mother be anxious?'

I sat down. 'Father will have told her I'm with you. Don't worry.'

Asher stopped the hand wringing and sat down next to me, the scrolls in front of us both. 'Lovely. Lovely. I don't want to cause the dear lady any concern. I suppose we should have something to eat but I'd really like to get stuck into these. The sooner we find what we need, the more time we'll have for our mission.'

Maraed strolled into the room. 'There you are!' she said. 'Where have you been?'

I sat up straight, my painful back no longer important, and smiled at her. 'Hello, Maraed,' I said. 'You're looking lovely today.'

She blushed. 'Thank you. What have you been up to? Have you eaten anything yet?

'We've been searching in the records,' Asher said. 'We haven't eaten but I don't want to soil these scrolls with greasy fingers and –'

Maraed smiled and suddenly the room was even lighter. 'I made tuber and leek soup while I waited for you. I can heat it up and serve us all some in beakers,' she said. 'Oh, and I could make some syrup puffs to go with it. How does that sound?'

I hadn't had syrup puffs in ages. They're simple things to make. Even I can do it. It's just a matter of ground wheat, milk, butter and syrup, stirred together and then dropped a spoonful at a time into hot nut oil. The heat makes them puff up. My mouth began to fill with dribble as I thought about them.

Asher clapped his hands. 'What a clever girl you are. Yes, please.'

Maraed nodded and headed for the kitchen.

'Are you going to tell her?' Kieran said.

'Only if she's coming with us,' Asher said. 'Otherwise, no. We promised to keep this secret.'

Kieran nodded. He turned to me, 'Don't weaken, Seeger. She only has to smile at you and you turn to mush.'

I bristled at the suggestion. 'I do not! I can keep a secret as well as anybody.'

Asher pulled the box towards him. 'Let's get stuck into these while she's busy in the kitchen.'

I gave Kieran a menacing stare and he crossed his eyes at me, but then we both picked up a scroll and began to read.

Three

At first, I thought the scroll I took was a waste of time. It was all about Delia's early life growing up on a farm. Her mother had died while Delia was still a child, which was sad, but what possesses a person to write a memory scroll about being frightened of spiders, only having a bath once every lunar cycle, and learning how to milk a goat? Why do people think that someone else would be even remotely interested in that sort of drivel? I told Asher, thinking he'd say try another one, but he just said, 'Keep reading.'

Kieran said, 'In this scroll she's describing how she joined the Healers' Guild. Most of the other healers were men and they made life difficult for her.'

'How?' I asked.

'They called her a 'hick from the sticks' and rubbished any ideas she had. They wouldn't send her out to a patient unless there was no one else free to go. They played mean tricks on her. It goes on and on.'

'I knew she was looked down upon by many of the older men but how is that helpful to us?' Asher said.

'She says that she only stayed in Seddon because, and I quote, "the Old Healer believes in me, and he knows more than all the Seddonese healers combined."'

Asher leaned forward; his eyes alight. 'Does she say anything more about this person?'

'Well, that's the thing, Asher. She's a bit mysterious about him. She says he was living in the hills since before her grandparents were born. That can't be right, though. She probably just meant he'd lived there for as long as she could remember.'

'He's got to be dead by now, then,' I said.

'Anything about wolves?' Asher said.

'Just once. She says … Let me find it so I can read her exact words.' He quickly scanned the scroll. 'Yes, here it is. She says, "So many times I was tempted to unleash the wolf on those ridiculous know-it-alls but the Old Healer would be proud of my self-control. And, to give them their due, there were many occasions when they did help people. So, I kept the wolf at bay."' He looked up at Asher. 'Did she have a pet wolf?'

'Not that I know of,' Asher said. 'That's odd. You'd think I'd remember something like that. Anything about the general's strange infection?'

Kieran shook his head. 'I haven't finished yet.'

We kept on reading. Then it was Asher's turn.

'I found it! Listen to this. "The Chief Healer sent me to the bedside of General Rickard. The others had done their best with lotions and poultices. All a waste of time. I could see I was probably too late. The bark had already coated his four limbs and was making its way up his back. If only those smug, self-righteous idiots had called me sooner. I'd seen this infection many, many years before. It's a thing of the earth and only the earth itself could have cured him."'

Looking up from the scroll, Asher said, 'Blinking heck! Why does she speak in riddles? Silly old woman!'

'It's typical old wisewoman-talk,' Kieran said. 'We've got one back home and she's always coming out with that sort of thing.'

'It's not helpful!' Asher said. He kept reading. "I told his friend to send a messenger to the Old Healer telling him the general had Dead Man's Fingers."

Asher looked at me and shouted, 'HA!' I nodded.

Kieran said, 'The mushroom?'

'No,' I said. 'Just named after it.'

Kieran shuddered. 'Creepy looking things.'

Asher studied the scroll. 'Where was I? Oh yes, here we are. "...The Old Healer would know what to do. As soon as I saw the patient, I knew it was probably too late but while life is still present there's always hope. However, the men never returned. I suppose the wolves got them. That was always the risk. The general died a terrible death. I think I know how it was done and I have a good idea who did it, so I must be careful."'

'My goodness!' I said. 'Do you think anything happened to her?'

Asher checked the date on the top of the scroll. 'This was written in the year that she died, so it's possible.'

My mind began to spin. 'So, it's likely that someone has done this to the Commander?'

'It seems so,' Asher said.

Kieran said, 'Does she say any more?'

Asher shook his head. 'That's the end of the scroll.'

I sighed and slumped in my chair. 'That Old Healer would be long in his grave by now.'

'Yes,' Asher said, 'but usually healers pass on their knowledge to their apprentices, so we may still be in luck. We just have to find them.'

We sat in silence for a while. I wondered who cursed General Rickard with such a terrible disease. Then I wondered who would do the same thing to the Commander. He was a good leader, compassionate and fair. Not knowing what else to do, I kept reading and finally found something.

Just as I said, 'Hey, I found her hometown! It's –', Maraed walked in carrying a tray laden with beakers of soup and a platter full of syrup drops.

Asher turned to Maraed. 'Thank you, dear. Just put it down there and make yourself comfortable.' He nodded at me. 'Carry on, lad.'

I thought we were going to keep things secret from Maraed but if Asher said it was all right then I wasn't going to argue with him. 'She grew up on a farm outside a town called Ballyfaol in the Mac Tire mountains. Where's that?'

Asher scratched his chin and stared up at the ceiling. 'Hmmm,' he said. 'I know the Mountains – by the way, it's pronounced Mac Cheera – but the town … Ballyfaol, you say?'

I nodded as I chewed over the fact that a word was spelled T. I. R. E. but pronounced CHEERA. How weird is that? I also kept reading just in case she said anything else about where she was from.

'Who is this woman?' Maraed said, reaching for one of the syrup drops.

'A healer called, Delia,' Asher said. 'You wouldn't know her.'

She shrugged. 'You're right. I've never heard of her but I do know what the name of the town means, if that'll help.' She popped the sweet treat into her mouth and chewed.

Asher put his scroll down and turned in his chair so he could stare at Maraed. 'You what?' he said.

She swallowed the drop and reached for another. 'It might not mean the same to the people living there now but in the old language bally means place and faol is an old word for wolf.'

'Kieran, fetch a map of our region please,' Asher said. Kieran did as he was told. Asher rubbed his hands together. 'So, Ballyfaol means, 'place of the wolf'?'

Because her mouth was full of the syrupy pastry, Maraed simply nodded.

I grabbed two of the drops while there were still some on the plate. I'd been waiting to finish my soup first but no one else had done that and the sweets were disappearing faster than ice on a hot kettle. Before he'd been sent to get the map, Kieran had been shovelling them into his mouth as if his life depended on it.

Maraed swallowed and said, 'Mac Tire is an old name for wolf, too.'

Three

'That can't be right,' I said. 'Not if faol means wolf. Those two words are nothing like each other.' I folded my arms across my chest and smiled smugly.

Asher agreed with me. 'He's correct, there, Maraed.'

She shook her head. 'I hate to pop your smug bubble, Seeger, but Mac Tire means 'son of the earth', which is a title given to wolves.'

Asher and I looked at each other, our mouths open. He recovered first. 'Well, that's interesting. I must make a note of that,' he said.

I went back to reading Delia's scroll and that's when I saw it. 'Oh hey, she and her father moved to Wulverstane when she was still little, after her mother had died. When she had thirteen years, she became an apprentice to the Old Healer.'

Kieran came back with a map, handed it to Asher and grabbed three more of the drops. *The pig!* Asher pushed the platter to one side – closer to Kieran and Maraed – and spread the map out. I found myself on the wrong side of the table. I gazed longingly at the last few syrupy puffs of pastry as they disappeared. I slowly picked up my beaker and finished off my soup.

Asher leaned over the map, searching the area east of Seddon. I could see Zenda, where Boyd's friend Idris had come from, but no other large towns. I'd gone with Boyd over a turn of the sun ago, to visit Idris's parents. It took us nearly a full day to ride there, so we stayed at a hotel that night. In the morning, we went to their home and Boyd gave them a portrait of their son that Riva had painted. They invited us to stay for the midday meal and in the afternoon, Idris's cousins and aunts and uncles came to the house. It was quite an emotional day.

After studying the map with eyes squinted, I finally saw the towns that lay past Zenda. They were too small for me to see them at first. I could, however, see a range of mountains further along from Zenda, probably another couple of days ride from there. I assumed they were the Mac Tires.

Asher's finger traced the road to Zenda and then moved it in the direction of the mountain range. He muttered to himself, 'Hmm. There's Carrig. They're renowned for growing tubers.'

He looked up at Maraed. 'Does Carrig mean anything?'

She thought for a while and then said, 'I think it's something to do with rocks or a rocky place? Something like that.'

Asher nodded. 'Makes sense,' he said, and went back to searching the map. He'd obviously been over it many times before because it was badly stained in places. He muttered, 'I'm sure it was here. No, no, nope.' He shook his head and sighed. 'I don't think …' he said. 'No. Wait! Yes, here it is. Ballyfaol. Well, well. Just a flyspeck of a place.'

Kieran leaned over for a closer look. 'Is there anything else that hints at wolves?'

Asher shook his head. 'I don't think so.' Maraed coughed politely. 'Hmm?' Asher said, not looking up from the map.

'I might be wrong,' Maraed said, 'but there's Wulverstane.'

She pointed to a tiny spot on the map. I hadn't noticed it before she pointed it out. It was a little way up into the Mac Tire mountains.

'And?' Asher said.

'I think it means, the wulver's stone,' she said.

'Learned all this in music class, did you?' I asked.

She smiled and tucked her hair behind her ears. 'As a matter of fact, I did. Corban, the Choir Director, has been teaching me some of the old language. It helps me better understand the stories in the ancient songs, as the old words are often used in them.'

'Good old Corban,' I said.

I wasn't happy that Maraed spent so much time in his company. He had many more years than me, as well as being taller. In fact, he was far too old for her. The past year, since she'd been having lessons, things had grown a little cooler between us. It was all, 'Corban this' and 'Corban that'.

'Well then, Miss Smartypants,' I said, 'what's a wulver?'

She shrugged. 'No idea but it sounds a bit like wolf.'

She put the now empty beakers and the empty platter onto the tray, and then took them to the kitchen. She and Kieran had eaten most of the syrup drops. I'd only had two!

'Do you know what it is, Asher?' Kieran said.

Asher pursed his lips. 'I have a faint recollection… I read something once… I'll have to do some more research but we're on the right track. We'll get some supplies together and we'll leave the day after tomorrow. I'll send a messenger bird to Dirven first thing in the morning. The dragons can meet us somewhere along the road, preferably near the town of Carrig.'

'Why?' I asked.

'The terrain gets too hard and rocky for the camels after there,' he said. 'We're going to have to find somewhere to keep them while we're further up in the hills.'

He rolled up the scrolls, put them back in Delia's box and laid the map across the top. 'Put these in the cupboard, Kieran. I want to keep them close by. Seeger, will you organise the camels with your father and see if he has an idea what to do with them once we've reached Carrig?'

'Of course,' I said. 'What about Tiffany?'

Asher groaned. 'I'd forgotten about her.'

Maraed came back into the room. 'Tiffany?' she said.

Kieran stared at Asher and then at me, and then back at Asher. 'What sort of a name is that?' he said.

'The Commander's daughter,' I said. 'She's coming with us.'

Maraed moved in a little closer and put her hands on her hips. 'Is she now? I don't think that's appropriate.'

Asher rubbed his eyes with the heels of his hands. He looked tired. In fact, he suddenly looked like an old man. Of course, that's what he was but he was so full of life and enthusiasm that it was easy to forget he had many years. I looked at him with his grey hair hanging around his shoulders but now thin on top, and his straggly grey beard, and the lines on his face, and I suddenly thought, *He's probably not got many more adventures left in him.*

I decided to answer for him. 'She's going to have a bodyguard come with her, so it's all above board. The Commander asked us to take her on the trip. It's not as though we could refuse him.'

She stood glaring at me. Then she turned on her brother. 'I suppose you think it's acceptable for a young lady to travel about with strange men, while they're on a wolf hunt?'

He threw his hands in the air. 'This is the first I've heard of it!'

She sniffed. 'Corban will be disappointed. We've been working on a performance for the winter solstice. Still, it can't be helped. I'm coming, too.'

Asher smiled at her. 'That's kind of you, dear, but it really isn't necess –'

'It most certainly is necessary!' she said. 'I don't know what you were thinking. I'll stop by the temple first thing tomorrow morning to give Corban the news and then I'll go to the markets to buy supplies. If you have anything you'd like me to pick up, write a list and leave it on the kitchen table. Some money to help pay for the goods would be appreciated. I'm off to bed. Goodnight.'

She left the room, clutching her disapproval around her like a warm blanket.

'She seems a bit annoyed,' I said. 'Anyone would think we'd invited Tiffany, just to ruin her life.'

Kieran shrugged his shoulders. 'She'll get over it.'

Asher sighed. 'Now that she's coming with us, I'll explain the situation to her tomorrow. Kieran, in the morning please send a message to the palace to let the Commander know our plans. All right?'

'Yes, sir,' Kieran said.

'Off you go now, Seeger. Make sure you have whatever you need for the journey and we'll see you outside Kane's office, first light, the day after tomorrow.'

Joffre was waiting for me on the roof of our home stable. He fluttered down onto my shoulder as I led Bruce inside and settled him for the night.

Hello, bird, Bruce said. *Still hanging around like a bad smell?* He yawned, his lips pulling back from his enormous teeth.

Shut your gob, fleabag, Joffre said. He fluttered over and perched on Bruce's head, while I removed the saddle and leads.

I patted the camel on the neck, he humphed and then sank down onto the straw. *See you in the morning, Bruce,* I said.

Nighty night, Brucie, Joffre said. *Don't let the bedbugs bite.*

Don't turn into pillow stuffing, Bruce replied.

The bird cackled as we walked across the yard. *I like him. He makes me laugh.*

Did you have a good day with Rimini? I said, as we reached the back door.

She gave me pumpkin seeds and slices of goat meat.

Mother was sitting in our kitchen, polishing our cutlery. 'Have you eaten?' she said as I walked in.

'I had some soup at Asher's house. Were you waiting for me?'

'No, no,' she said, 'you can go where you please.' She gathered up the gleaming knives, forks and spoons and put them back in the cutlery drawer. 'I was having trouble sleeping, so I thought I'd do a job I've been putting off for a while. Your father is snoring like a pig.'

'I think I'll go do the same. It's been a long day.' I kissed her cheek. 'Good night, Mother.'

Joffre squawked and she smiled at him. 'Good night to you both.' Then, as I moved towards the staircase, she called out, 'Seeger?'

I turned around. 'Yes, Mother.'

'Is that old ratbag, Asher, taking you off on another of his wanderings?'

'We're leaving the day after tomorrow,' I said. Joffre rubbed his head along my cheek and I absentmindedly reached up and stroked his chest.

'I thought so,' she said. 'I'm not sure that's a good idea.'

I walked back into the kitchen. 'Why?'

She rubbed the tabletop with her fingers, brushing away imaginary breadcrumbs. 'I know I'm just a silly old woman.' I started to protest and she held up her hand. 'Let me finish. Sometimes I get strong feelings about things. It's as if Sed is warning me. I knew that something terrible was going to happen the night you were taken from us. I knew that something was going to happen to one of you when you went to war against Midrash. Thank Sed it was just Riff losing the use of his arm. It could have been worse.'

I patted her shoulder. 'It's just a knowledge-gathering trip, Mother.'

A fluttering smile tried to settle on her lips but quickly left in despair. 'I have a strong feeling that you will be going into danger. No, no. Hear me out. I can't stop you. I've learned that the hard way. But please, take some weapons with you and be very, very careful.'

'I'll be careful and Asher is sending for some dragons to go with us.'

'Good.' She nodded. 'I don't trust Asher. He's a bit of a silly wheel. But I know the dragons love you and I trust them. That makes me feel a bit better. Sleep well, dear.'

'Good night.'

On the way up the stairs, Joffre ruffled his feathers.

What's up with you, friend?

I don't know why she makes such a fuss about dragons. I'm right here, on your shoulder. I'm a raven, I am! You couldn't have a better bodyguard than me.

I'm so glad you're with me.

He settled his feathers and hunched his head down into his shoulders. *I suppose you'll want me to fly up to Dirven's place to bring the dragons back.*

Asher's sending a messenger bird.

His head shot up, he dug his claws into my shoulder and squawked right in my ear. *Are you suggesting a fat old pigeon can do better than me?*

It's their job, I said. *I'm sure you could fly as far and as fast as a pigeon but let them have the dignity of doing what they're kept for. You have more important things to do.*

A messenger pigeon could easily fly faster and further than him but I didn't want to hurt his feelings.

He settled down again. *You argue well.*

Let's get some sleep now, Joffre. Tomorrow's going to be a busy day.

Four

The well-keepers' expedition left first thing in the morning. I got there just in time to give my farewells to Boyd, Rimini, Riff and the others. Father and I stood with Talia at the stable gate as the team moved out. She stood at attention and saluted but Father and I just waved. I was surprised that Riva wasn't among them.

I found my sister-in-law cleaning the camels' stables, raking the floor and scooping up the dung. Ever since I'd found out she was actually older than me, our relationship had changed. It happened during the wedding preparations. Mother asked Jonathen, the priest, if Riva needed special dispensation because of her young age.

Jonathen said, 'How old is she?'

Mother said, 'She's only just reached fifteen years.'

Riva, who'd been making gooey eyes at Riff, whipped around. 'What?' she shouted. 'Who told you that?'

Everyone turned to look at me. I shrugged. 'Aren't you younger than me?'

'What gave you that idea?' she said.

'Well … you were so skinny and small … I just thought …'

Father ran his hand down his face. Riff shook his head and Mother glared at me, with her hands on her hips.

I pleaded, 'You never said –'

'You never asked!' she said. 'As it happens, I now have seventeen years. You idiot.'

Four

I couldn't believe it. She was older than me! I wasn't the most popular fellow in the room from after that. I even expected Riff to kick me out of the wedding party but I guess he took pity on me because he still let me be his witness. Ever since then, things were a bit prickly between Riva and me. When she has a grudge against you, she nurtures it like a precious child. I'd been trying, for over a full turn of the sun, to restore our friendship.

'Why aren't you going with Riff and the others?' I asked.

She stopped and held the rake in her two hands, angled across her body. Joffre squawked a greeting but for once Riva ignored him. 'I don't have to follow Riff around everywhere,' she said. 'I'm not a well-keeper. I'm employed here.'

I ran my fingers through my hair. 'I know. It's just that you've been on other trips so I thought ...' She continued to glare at me, her fingers turning white on the rake's handle. 'Never mind. Sorry I asked.'

'It's not as if I'm permanently attached to Riff's side, you know. I'm my own person.'

'Yes, I understand.'

I shouldn't have opened my big mouth. Joffre trilled in my ear, *She's in a bad mood, Seeger.*

She continued, 'I don't see that it's any business of yours what I –' She dropped her rake, slapped her hand over her mouth and ran pull pelt towards the privies.

That was odd! I tipped the rake over so that the prongs were facing down into the sand, shrugged and led Bruce to his stall. Joffre preened his wings, inspecting each feather as if they were inlaid with precious stones.

Still got them all, have ya? Bruce said to Joffre. *Ya didn't find any stuffed inside Seeger's pillow?*

Joffre huffed and fluffed his hackles.

What do you think is wrong with Riva? I asked. *Do you think she's cross that Riff's left her behind?*

Why don't ya go ask her? Bruce said.

I'm not following her into the privies. She won't thank me for that.

I swear, I'll never understand women. I told Joffre to stay out in the stable complex while I talked with Father. He began to complain but I told him the geese had just been fed and, without even bothering to say goodbye, he flew off to their enclosure.

Father knew it was serious when I closed the door of his office behind me without being told to. I dragged a chair up to his desk and sat opposite him.

'Father?' I said, 'I have something I need to discuss with you.' I leaned forward, lowered my voice and, in a near whisper, told him about the Commander's illness.

Father's lips pursed. He swallowed hard and said, 'Go on, son.'

'We need to keep our voices low,' I whispered. 'Someone might be listening.'

He nodded. I told him how the Commander had commissioned Asher and I to find the cure and to bring it back before it was too late.

'How are you supposed to –?'

I interrupted him, whispering in an even quieter voice, telling him how Asher, Kieran and I had searched Asher's archives until after the sun had gone to rest. I also told him what we'd found in Delia's papers.

He tipped back in his chair and rubbed his eyes. He sat like that for a while, eyes still closed as he thought about what I'd shared. Then, he leaned forward and whispered, 'Asher thinks someone has done this to the Commander, the same as what happened to General Rickard?'

I nodded.

'That's terrible.' He frowned. 'Who could it be?'

'The Commander said he's got a lot of enemies. Is that true? I thought everyone liked him.'

I glanced at the window but no one was there. I was beginning to hear and see things that didn't exist.

'There are ambitious people in every generation,' Father said. 'There are some who aren't content to wait until the Commander is too old to lead us.' He fiddled with his pens. 'Of course, there may well be personal enemies as well.' He looked up at me and spoke normally. 'You're going to have to be very careful, son.'

I nodded again. 'Asher's sent a message to the dragons, asking if one or two could meet us along the way.'

'Good!' He stood up and went over to his filing cabinet. He took out a map from the large bottom drawer and brought it over to his desk. 'Show me where you're going.'

He spread it out across the desk and stood over it, putting a paperweight on each end to stop it curling back up.

With my finger, I traced the route we were going to take. Seddon to Zenda; Zenda to Carrig; Carrig to Ballyfaol and then on to Wulverstane in the Mac Tire Ranges.

'I've heard rumours about those mountains and the towns in that area. None of them are good. There are bandits in the hills and there are supposed to be wolves up there as well. I'm not so worried about wolves. They're usually peaceful creatures who've been tagged with an unfortunate reputation. Besides, I trust that your gifting would enable you to connect with them. I can't say as much for the wild humans. At least you'll have the dragons with you.'

Then, I told him about Tiffany.

He rubbed his hands through his hair, making it stand up on end. 'What? No, no, that's not good. It's not safe out there. What can he be thinking?'

Whispering again, I explained the Commander's reasoning.

He smoothed his hair down and sat back at the desk. 'I still don't approve but I understand.' He sighed. 'Even so …'

'She's going to have a bodyguard with her and Maraed is coming too. She said it wasn't appropriate for Tiffany to be alone with us men, even though we'd already explained the girl would have a chaperone.'

He studied me for a moment. 'You're not happy about Maraed going with you? Are you two having problems?'

I shrugged and stared at the floor.

'Do you want to talk about it?'

I shook my head.

'So, is the plan for you to fly to the mountains?'

I looked up, relieved that he'd moved on. 'We intend to ride camels as far as we can and then transfer to the dragons when the path grows too rocky.'

I lowered my voice. 'The idea is that once we have the cure, Asher can fly back to the Citadel, while the rest of us can bring the camels home. It'll save a lot of time. The Commander said he thinks he's only got two seven nights at best and, with us not leaving until tomorrow, that's already a couple of days gone.'

He studied the map again. 'You're right. The camels would struggle once you head up into the hills. They'd probably make it as far as Ballyfaol but I wouldn't want you to force them to go any further.'

'Do you know of a safe place to leave them?'

He pulled on his bottom lip while he considered the question. 'I know a chap near Carrig. Pederson. He used to work here in the stables. He only went back there when his parents grew too frail to look after their farm. It's here…,' he said, pointing at a place on the map, '… on the far side of the town near the track that leads to Ballyfaol.'

'Can we trust him?'

'Pederson was gentle with the animals and he's an honest fellow,' Father said. 'I'll write him a letter that you can take with you, asking him to stable the camels on his farm for a few days. I'll also give you some coins to pay him for his trouble.'

He rolled the map up and put it back in the drawer. 'When are you leaving?'

'Asher said to meet outside your office at first light tomorrow. We'll need four camels. The girls can share one and so can Kieran and I.'

Father nodded. 'I'll let you choose them but don't take any females. You know it's breeding season and they're all either newly pregnant or still on heat. Leave Karmal, too. He's the main stud.'

'I know that, Father.' The heat rushed into my cheeks.

'Oh, that's right.' He laughed.

Sudden heat raced down my neck and gave my gut a hefty kick. Unlike in previous years, I hadn't been warned that breeding season was about to start. I won't go into any details but, believe me, I wasn't going to endure that again. Although I was much better equipped at handling the sudden rush of overwhelming emotions from animals, that season I'd been caught out unprepared. It was extremely embarrassing. There are some drawbacks to being a dragon-speaker. Other beast-speakers don't have this problem.

'The older males will be more philosophical about being taken away at this time of the year,' Father said. He suddenly changed the subject. 'Does your mother know?'

I shook my head, the heat receding slowly from my face. 'I told her it's just a regular fact-finding mission. We're taking Tiffany to explore a bit of the world, while we search for the elusive wolf pack of the Mac Tire Ranges.'

Father picked up one of his pens and began to tap it on his desk. He muttered, 'I wish we had some idea who's behind this.'

'It could be just sheer bad luck,' I said. 'There's no proof that it's anything else.'

'True,' he said. 'I hope that's the case.'

'Thank you for listening, Father.' I winked at him.

'Anytime, son,' he said and smiled.

Again, I thought I saw a shadow pass the window so I ran over to look. There was nothing. I smiled ruefully at Father. 'Seeing things,' I said.

When I left the room, Riva was back from the privy and had almost finished cleaning the main floor of the stable area.

'Are you all right, Riva?' I asked.

She glared at me. 'No reason why I wouldn't be.'

She went to hang up her rake and I left her to it. She was obviously in one of her black moods and when she was like that I could never do a thing right. I decided she could find someone else to vent her spleen on.

Father, Joffre and I were the first to wait outside the office. We'd gone to the stables before sun-up to get the camels ready. In the end we took five. Errol got the job of carrying our swags and other supplies. He was a big, moody old grump who got along much better with baggage than he did with people. Ajax, the lead camel, promised to keep him in line. Bruce, Kevin and Bryan made up the rest of the caravan.

Asher, Kieran and Maraed arrived as the sun was peeking over the stable walls. Asher immediately went into a huddle with Father while Kieran, Maraed and I stood with the camels. When some of them sat down to wait, we joined them, leaning up against Bruce's belly. Joffre perched on the stable roof.

Kieran and I both had time to make a trip to the privies and still Tiffany hadn't turned up. Father came to have a final word with the camels, while Asher paced up and down. 'Where can she be?' he said.

'It's no skin off our noses if we waste time,' Maraed said. 'It's her father that's dying.'

'Meow,' Kieran said.

By the time Tiffany and her chaperone had arrived most of the stable hands were already at work and the sun was above the stable roof.

She was dressed just like the rest of us – tunic and pants – but anyone could see they were made of better cloth. Her yellow hair was tied up at the back in a sort of roll, with little bits sticking out here and there. The girls have a name for the style but I never bothered to learn it. She dragged her feet as she walked towards us, her plump lips twisted in a snarl and her grey eyes hooded. I swear I could see a giant chip on her pretty shoulder.

Her companion was tall, with her black hair close-cropped and muscles bulging under her tunic's sleeve. She had vivid blue eyes that were all the more startling because her skin was the colour of cinnamon. Her bow and arrows were slung against her back and in her hands she carried their bedrolls, kitbags and a bag of other goods, which turned out to be contributions to our meagre larder.

She walked up to Asher, put the luggage down and bobbed her head in a short bow of respect. 'My apologies for our late arrival, sir. Tiffany wouldn't leave until her hair had been arranged properly by her maid. I don't know who she thinks will be fiddling with it on the journey but it won't be me.'

Asher nodded. 'Greetings, Tiffany and … err …'

'Call me, Cal,' she said.

'Greetings, Cal,' Asher continued. 'All's forgiven but we need to get moving.'

Tiffany scowled at us as we sat leaning against Bruce's stomach. She pointed and, disdain dripping off every word, said, 'Who are they?'

'Oh, sorry, sorry,' Asher said. 'Kieran, his sister Maraed, and Seeger.' We all gave a little wave when he said our name and then we stood up. 'They're coming with us. We can get to know each other as we travel. I'm keen to get started.'

The Commander's daughter folded her arms across her chest and stuck her bottom lip out. 'I don't want to sit on a smelly old camel.'

Hmph! Bruce said. *We don't want a spoilt brat sitting on us. Tell her to walk.*

Joffre cackled. *Sensible girl!*

She glared at the raven. 'Cal, shoo that bird away.'

'Do it yourself,' Cal said. 'I'm not your servant.'

I think I like Cal, I said, *but this girl is going to be hard work.*

I've gone off her, too, Joffre said. *Just wait until she meets the dragons. She'll probably insult them as well and then she'll be sorry.*

'Is that boy a bit simple?' she said, pointing at me.

Joffre flew down and perched on my shoulder. Tiffany glared at him but sidled back, closer to Cal. Joffre rubbed his face against my cheek. *Don't worry,* he said, *we know you're not simple. Not really. Not much, anyway.*

You'll keep.

Father gave me Ajax's reins. 'Good morning, Tiffany,' he said. 'I'm Kane, Beast-Master, and this is my son, Seeger, Dragon-Master. He was talking with the bird just then. You'll get used to it.'

She huffed and shrugged her shoulders. 'Not your fault he's not all there,' she said. 'Is he taking that ugly bird with us?'

Permission to peck! Joffre said. *I promise I won't put her eye out. Just a quick jab to her cheek to teach her some manners.*

Settle down, mate, I said.

We're not taking her, Ajax said. *She was rude to us. She was rude to you. She was even rude to the bird. She can get lost!*

I dropped Ajax's reins, put my hand on Father's arm and led him away from the girl. Asher came with us. I saw Maraed go over to Tiffany. I wished her luck. 'I'm sorry Asher, Father,' I muttered, 'but none of the camels want her to ride on them.'

Asher started to wring his hands and moan, 'Oh dear. Oh dear.'

Cal had been helping Kieran load the luggage onto Errol's strong back. She came up to us and said, 'Any problem?'

'The camels refuse to let Tiffany ride on them,' I said.

She frowned. 'So? We'll just put her up on one, anyway.'

Father shook his head. 'She insulted them and Seeger. Once they turn against someone, they're very hard to budge. They'll just refuse to move. The only solution is, she apologises to them and does it straight away. The longer she leaves it, the less likely there'll be any change.'

Cal ran her hand over her face and sighed. 'I can tell you right now, that little madam won't do it.'

We stood in a tight circle, gloomily staring at our feet. 'We can't make her walk while the rest of us ride,' Asher said. 'And if we walk, we'll lose valuable time. Ask them again.'

Fellas? We'd really appreciate it.

The rest of you are fine, Ajax said, *but the girl can go take a running jump at herself. We ain't doin' it.*

Father and I shook our heads. Asher groaned. Cal threw her hands up in the air.

'What are we going to do?' Asher said. 'We've already wasted too much time this morning. We need to get going!'

'I'll talk to her,' Cal said.

She strode over to Tiffany and Maraed. As soon as she started talking, Tiffany began shaking her head. Once again, she folded her arms over her chest, stuck her lip out and then stamped her foot.

Maraed looked upset. She glared at me as if all this drama were my fault! I shrugged and spread my hands out in the universal gesture of, 'Don't blame me, I have no idea what's happening'.

Cal came back. 'It's no good,' she said. 'She refuses to apologise to, these are her words, a dumb animal.'

The three of us groaned together. The camels all rumbled and huffed and Errol spat.

'Here's what I think you should do,' Father said. 'Begin the journey with everyone walking, leading the camels out of the city. Give them time to calm down and for you to convince her that they are more than dumb animals. Perhaps the girl is scared and is hiding it with petulance and aggression. It will also give you, Seeger, some time to explain the situation to the camels. They're a good-hearted bunch so I'm sure they'll come around.'

Asher tugged his beard. 'I don't want to begin this way. Every wasted moment is a step closer to losing our Commander.' He looked across at the pouting girl and sighed. 'Fine. Let's go. Seeger, you lead the way with Ajax. Will we need to hold the other camels' reins?'

'Just Errol's,' I said. 'The others will follow in line.'

'Right,' Asher said, 'I'll get Kieran to do that. Thank you for everything, Kane. Let's get going.'

He shook hands with Father, then hurried over to Kieran and the girls to explain what we were going to do. Cal also shook hands and walked over to stand next to Tiffany. I quickly hugged Father.

'Be careful, son,' he said, 'and be patient with the young lady.'

'I'll try, Father. I'll try.'

I still say a good pecking would sort her out, Joffre said. *I'd be happy to do the honours.*

Ajax, Joffre and I led the way out of the stables, through the city and eventually through the Eastern Gate. To be honest, Ajax led the way. I just held his reins loosely and let him do it. Even though I now had seventeen years, I still didn't have a compass in my head.

Kieran walked behind us, leading Errol who was huffing and occasionally spitting. Kevin and Bryan, with Bruce bringing up the rear, followed along behind us. Asher, Cal and the girls walked in a group close to Bruce's shoulders. Bruce wouldn't take a step until Maraed made sure she was the closest one to him, and Asher and Cal walked on either side of Tiffany.

I don't like the new girl, Kevin said.

Try to be kind, I said. *Her father is dying and she's frightened.*

She's got scabby manners, Bryan said, *and she smells.*

Five

Kane

Once Seeger and the others had left, I saddled Karmal and rode up to the Citadel.

I headed straight for the Commander's private quarters but was surprised when the guard at the door said, 'I'm sorry, Beast-Master, but he's in his office.' Back down the corridors I went, wondering if perhaps Asher and Seeger had exaggerated the Commander's condition. I knew that Asher could get carried away at times but it wasn't like Seeger to do that.

I knocked on his door, consumed with curiosity. Would I see a sick, frail man behind the desk? When he called me in, I was pleasantly surprised. He looked fine. The only difference that I could see was that he was wearing gloves.

'Come in, Kane,' he said. 'I thought I might see you today.' He pointed at a chair that stood under the window. 'Pull that up and be seated.'

Carrying the chair over to the desk, I said, 'You're looking well, Commander.'

He smiled ruefully. 'For now. This is what you can't see.'

He peeled off one glove and showed me his blue fingers. I gasped. Seeger had told me that the Commander's fingertips were pale blue. Two days later the colour was already seeping down onto his palms!

The Commander put the glove back on. 'I want to keep working for as long as possible.'

'Won't people wonder why you're wearing gloves?'

He shrugged. 'I'm hoping it'll start a new trend and in another seven days, half the Citadel will be wearing them.'

It was highly likely that would happen. Two lunar cycles ago, he wore an embroidered cloak to his celebration of life party. It was a special event because he had gained fifty years. His aunt had sewed it for him and he didn't have the heart to tell her it was too fancy for his taste. Within a short time, it seemed like every second man in the place was wearing embroidered cloaks. I'd asked Fee for one and she told me that I'd have to pay an embroiderer to do it because she had neither the time nor the inclination to bother with such frippery. I did without.

I said, 'I'm sure it'll catch on.'

'What can I do for you, Kane?'

'I promised Asher I'd keep an eye on you. If anyone asks, you can tell them I'm petitioning you to consider purchasing some donkeys. It won't be a lie because I'd really like to get a breeding pair, to see how we go. They're strong, sturdy beasts and they can travel on hard, stony ground, which the camels can't do. Only the larger ones are good for riding but all of them are excellent for carrying loads. We could expand our trade routes.'

'I assume you want to visit me regularly?' he said.

'Yes, sir.' I smiled.

'Then, for now, consider your request denied.'

The smile slid off my face.

'Of course, I like the suggestion,' the Commander said, 'and I'm rather curious about the beasts but we need to give you a reason to return.' I smiled again. I should have figured that out for myself. 'The less lies we tell,' he said, 'the better.'

I leaned forward. 'Do you have any idea, sir, who did this to you? Or when and how it happened?'

He stared thoughtfully at the ceiling. 'How and when? Good questions.' He looked at me and shrugged. 'I have no idea.' He fiddled with the cuff of his left glove. 'There are a few contenders but I haven't narrowed it down to one as yet. Unfortunately, it means I must treat everyone with suspicion.'

I nodded. 'I understand. However, I assure you that I and my household are loyal and will do everything in our power to help.'

He smiled. 'I guess I'll have to take your word on that. I'm asking Sed to guide your lad to the cure.' He leaned forward. 'Would you please ask your beasts to keep their eyes and ears open and report anything suspicious to you, so you can pass it on to me. They may not understand what is said or done but I trust their instincts so if there's anything that makes them uneasy …'

'Of course, sir,' I said. 'An excellent idea. Most people forget that beasts can hear and understand and therefore are completely unguarded in front of them.'

'Excellent.' He leaned back in his chair and pulled the cuffs of his gloves up his wrists.

'Who else knows about this?' I asked. 'I don't want to put my foot in it with anyone.'

He sighed, staring at the desktop. 'Apart from the group who left this morning, my healer and you, there's no one. I haven't even told my aunt. It's a pity Father died a few years ago because he'd remember what happened to General Rickard. He might have had some insight into my problem.'

'What does your healer say?'

'He's never heard of Dead Man's Fingers. He's trying some creams on my skin but although they feel good when I rub them in, they haven't produced a cure. Perhaps they're slowing it down. I don't know.'

He sighed again. 'I'm just glad my dear wife didn't live to see this day.' He looked up at me, 'I've never said that before. I still miss her terribly. So does Tiffany. Poor child. I haven't given her any details but she knows something is wrong. I hope I've taught her enough over the years to help her get through this.'

'I'm sure you have,' I said. 'She's a strong-willed young lady.'

He grinned. 'Already given you some grief, then?'

I smiled back at him. 'Not me. Just my son and Joffre the raven and the camels and Cal. Nothing to worry about. She's in good hands.'

He tugged on his gloves again. 'She's angry with me for sending her away.' He looked back at me. 'I just couldn't let her see what I'll become. And … I don't know who to trust here.' His eyes were damp with saltwater. 'You're a father. You understand?'

'Of course, sir. You were between a cliff and stony ground. I'm sure you've made the right decision.' I smiled at him. 'She'll have an adventure she'll never forget. Just wait until she meets the dragons.'

He took out a kerchief and wiped his eyes. 'I'd love to be there to see that!'

I stood up. 'I'll come back regularly to see how you are, to pass on any information I might have and to see if there's anything I can do for you. Meanwhile, please keep thinking about donkeys?'

He roared with laughter. 'You're a persistent beggar, Kane!'

I grinned, bowed my head in respect and left his office. On the way down the main stairs I met Talia, who was walking up.

'Good morning, Kane,' she said. 'I saw your lad leading the expedition out of the city. They were moving quite slowly. I suppose little Tiffany was holding them up.'

I said, 'There's no reason for them to rush.'

She tucked her hair behind her ears. 'So, where are they not rushing off to?'

I studied her for a brief moment. She tilted her head to the side, smiling at me. 'You know Asher,' I said. 'He loves finding out stuff. Seeger said something about possibly finding a wolf pack, which is why he's included this time.'

She nodded. 'Yes, dear Asher. Strange little man. So, what brings you here today?'

'I'm petitioning the Commander to consider buying some donkeys. What about you?'

'Ho hum. Boring!' She pretended to yawn. 'It's none of your business, Kane, but it's far more important than some poxy animals.'

'You know, Talia, sometimes you're incredibly rude,' I said.

'And you're incredibly dull,' she said, moving past me up the stairs.

For a moment, I watched her go and then I went on my way. The woman was insufferable, especially in the past few years since she'd been made Master Well-Keeper. It was a wonder she could still balance her head on her shoulders, it had grown so big. Our conversation left me feeling uneasy. I began to understand the Commander's dilemma: who can you trust? Every encounter now had overtones of cunning and treachery. But there was probably nothing in it. Talia had always been nosy.

Before returning to the main stables, I stopped in at the smaller one next to the Citadel. Simpson the Stable-Master, a nervous fellow, thought he was in trouble but I soon put him at ease. I told him I just wanted to have a chat with the animals, to see how they were doing. It was a normal part of my job as Beast-Master. He offered to accompany me. I told him it wasn't necessary but I knew I couldn't avoid taking Marie, the resident beast-speaker, with me. Not if I wanted to keep everything I did there as normal as possible.

Simpson sent a stable hand off to the geese pond to fetch Marie, while he led Karmal to a spare stall. While I waited, I pondered how I was going to handle this without giving anything away. I didn't want Marie overhearing my conversations with the camels and goats. How could I ask them to spy for me, with Marie standing next to me? When the stable-hand returned with the beast-speaker, I thanked him and sent him back to his regular duties. Marie and I headed to the pig sty.

'How are you, Marie? Is life treating you better these days?'

Marie had spent a long time away from work, while she recovered from losing her daughter. Little Mel had died in the arena at Midrash. Marie had already been deep in grief during the many lunar cycles that we all endured while our children were missing. Then, when the children were rescued and she'd discovered that her daughter wasn't among those who returned, her mind had snapped. Eventually, she'd spent a full turn of the sun in the hands of the healers. She'd been back at work for some time but I hadn't had the chance to have a proper conversation with her.

'I'm much better, thank you, Kane,' she said. 'I still have some dark days but it does me good to get out of the house and the animals are such a comfort to me.'

I patted her shoulder. 'I'm so very sorry for your loss, Marie.' I felt her stiffen so I quickly dropped my hand. 'Listen, Marie, I'm –'

'I'm glad you got your son back, Kane,' she said. 'I thank Sed that so many were rescued. I'm just aggrieved that Mel wasn't one of them. I don't think I'll ever fully recover from that but I don't begrudge you your happiness.'

She smiled at me and the prickly awkwardness that had settled around us gently wafted away on the morning air.

'Please remind me of the animals with which you can speak,' I said.

'Geese, pigs and goats.'

'Not camels?'

'No, sir, so I wouldn't have been much use back when the camels' feet were being ruined by the cobblestones,' she said.

I'd forgotten about that! It's probably why Simpson was still so twitchy around me. It's not often I lose my temper but seeing the stable floor covered in those stones had made me see red. I couldn't blame Simpson for it; he was only obeying the Commander. But when I saw the damage done to the poor creatures' feet, well ...

I hastened to reassure her. 'No, my dear. You'd have picked it up soon enough. I'm sure the camels would have told the rest of the animals about their misery. They're very good at complaining.'

We did the rounds of the different pens: pigs, geese, goats and hens. I spoke with the goats and Marie did the honours with the geese and pigs. Neither of us could talk with the hens. There are times when I find myself jealous of Seeger's extraordinary ability to converse with every living thing. Nevertheless, I still inspected their coop, their water supply and their health. They were in excellent condition. I made a mental note to commend Simpson for the good work he was doing.

When we got back to the stables I said, 'Thank you, Marie. You can go about your business now. I can do the camels on my own. Karmal will have talked to them while we were doing the rest of the complex, so it will only need to be a quick check.'

'If you're sure, sir.'

I shook her hand. 'I'm glad you came back into the service, Marie. You do an outstanding job and it's obvious to me that the animals love you. Well done.'

'Thank you, sir.'

I watched her leave the camels' quarters and head out into the sunlight, her head held high. Then, I quickly visited each camel stall and whispered my news and my request for them to keep their eyes and ears open. I swore them to secrecy which, I think, delighted some of them. They loved the thought that they knew things that the other animals didn't know. They were a little peeved when I said they had to let the goats in on it but they grudgingly accepted the situation. With Marie being unable to speak camel, they would have had to get the goats to pass on a message anyway.

Each camel promised they'd be the one that found the clue to who was trying to hurt the Commander. They'd forgiven him for the cobblestone incident. He hadn't realised their feet wouldn't cope with the hard surface. He just thought it would make the stables look nicer. Admittedly, some of them sulked for a few weeks back then but, when I explained how the mistake had happened and their feet had recovered, they got over it. They're complicated beasts. They can be easily offended and are quite touchy about some things, but they're also fiercely loyal to the creatures and people they love.

'I think camels are my favourite animals,' I said as I rode Karmal back down the Citadel's hill, heading towards the town.

What? Karmal said, *Not the dragons?*

'Dragons are certainly fantastic creatures,' I said. 'They're both terrifying and intriguing. However, I'm happy to leave them to Seeger. Camels are more my style.'

I felt satisfaction and smugness from Karmal wash over me, wave after wave, until I began to feel a bit queasy.

'Settle down, now,' I said. 'I didn't say you were perfect.'

Six

Seeger

Having ridden to Zenda with Boyd, I knew how long it took to get there. At the speed we were going, we'd never make it by nightfall.

I tried to lift the pace. I told Kieran what we needed to do and he agreed. Ajax and Errol quickened their stride and the other camels kept up. For a while, so did Asher and the others but eventually they began to lag behind.

Ajax said, *The old man can't keep up with ya, matey. You're gonna have to slow down.*

Time is of the essence, Ajax. We need to keep moving.

Ya keep this up, he said, *and he'll go all doolally on us.*

I called a halt. The camels immediately all slumped to the ground and made themselves comfortable.

'What's going on?' Cal said. 'Why have we stopped?'

I pointed behind her, so she turned around and saw Asher hanging onto Maraed's arm and wheezing as he limped. We hadn't even got as far as the Great Sea Caves yet. We hadn't even got to where the road forks: the main road continuing on to Zenda and the track on the left heading up into the hills.

'It's time to ride,' Cal said.

Ajax blew air between his lips, making them flap. Bruce, Bryan and Kevin grumbled and Errol spat.

'We need to talk about this,' I said. When everyone was gathered in a circle, a little way away from the camels, I said,

Six

'We're not going to make Zenda before nightfall. We'll have to camp out in the open tonight.'

'Don't be ridiculous!' Tiffany said.

Asher shook his head. 'No, we can't have that.' He sucked in a lungful of air. 'That's another day gone.' He breathed deeply again, still hanging on to Maraed's arm. 'We can move faster than this.' He sucked in another lungful. 'Don't worry, lad, I won't let you down.'

Maraed patted his hand and smiled at him.

'Asher,' I said, 'you're not a young man anymore. You can't keep up.'

Asher pushed away from Maraed, his eyes burning as he glared at me. 'How dare you!' Raising his voice, brought on a bout of wheezing and coughing.

Tiffany giggled. We all looked at her. She shrugged. 'He's right. The old man's holding us up. We should leave him behind.'

A thunder cloud descended across Maraed's face. 'You selfish little –'

'Now, now,' Cal said. 'Steady on.'

Maraed pointed at Tiffany. 'It's this little brat's fault that we're walking in the first place!'

'Everyone calm down,' I said. 'Here's what I suggest –'

'Who made you the boss of everyone?' Tiffany said, folding her arms and sticking out that bottom lip. It seemed that was her favourite pose.

Cal nudged her. 'You promised your father.' Tiffany's head dropped but I noticed she kept the pout. 'Asher and

Seeger are in charge of this trip. We'll do what he says.'

'Are you willing to apologise to the camels?' I asked her. She shook her head. 'Very well, then I suggest that Asher rides on Bruce while the rest of us walk.' He started to splutter and protest. 'I'm sorry, Asher, but it's for the good of the mission. Besides, you can check the map and do any other reading you need to, while you're up there.'

He fumed for a little longer but then slowly nodded. He walked over to Errol and untied his kitbag from the luggage pile.

I said, 'The rest of us must pick up the pace.'

Everyone except Tiffany agreed. She just sulked. I heard Maraed mutter to Kieran, 'I don't see why we can't ride and let dear Tiffany run alongside us.' He laughed.

Just then, Joffre flew back and landed on my shoulder. He'd been enjoying a fly around out in the open. *There's a group of men coming up behind us,* he said. *I can't tell if they're friend or foe. Better get a move on.*

I gave them Joffre's report and Cal immediately swung her bow around to her chest and put her hand on her sword. Asher dropped his kitbag and pulled at his beard.

'Oh dear, oh dear,' he said. 'Have I put us all in danger?'

'Don't panic,' Kieran said. 'They might just be merchants or fellow travellers. No one knows why we're out here.'

'Mount up, Asher,' I said.

Maraed helped the old man climb onto Bruce's back. She passed up his kitbag once he was settled.

Six

'Let's get moving,' I said. 'Tiffany, please walk with me for a while?'

Maraed sniffed and glared at me. What was eating her? She chose to walk alongside Bruce and Asher, even though Asher was studiously ignoring her. It would take him a while to recover from us thinking he was getting old.

Tiffany said, 'I thought I had to stay with Cal.'

'I'd like to have a bit of a chat.'

We both turned to look at Cal, who gave a quick nod of approval. Tiffany shrugged sulkily but, once we got going, she moved up beside me. Cal took up a position at the rear of the caravan. I felt better knowing she was there.

As we strode along the road to Zenda, I asked Tiffany what she would have been doing back at the Citadel that day. She told me about her lessons with her tutor – she didn't go to Foundation like other children – and then in the afternoon she would have probably done some practice on her flute and then some bead work with her maid, Ellen.

'Did you tell anyone about this trip?' I asked.

'Just Ellen,' she said.

'What did you tell her?' I waved a persistent fly away. Joffre snapped at it as it flew past him.

'I told her Pa had insisted I go on your little jaunt to see a bit of the world or some such rubbish.' She whined, 'He said it would be good for me.'

We walked on in silence for a while. A thought began to nag at me. 'Err, Tiffany?' I asked. 'Do you know the purpose of this trip?'

She shrugged. 'Not really.' She pulled at that stubborn bottom lip.

'No idea at all?'

'Pa said that if I was lucky I might get to see some wolves. Ha! As if that's something I care about.'

I could feel Kieran listening in behind me. The silence was too intense for him not to be eavesdropping. Not that I blamed him. I'd be doing the same.

'I'm not stupid, you know,' she said. 'Something's bothering Pa. He thinks I'll be in the way, so he's lumbered me with you lot.'

Joffre humphed. *It's the other way round, girlie. We're lumbered with you!*

I suppose the Commander thought he was doing the right thing, not telling her in case she let the secret slip, but I was still annoyed with him. It meant I had the joy of telling her the truth about his situation.

'There's something you need to know,' I said.

I explained what was happening to her father. At first, her hand flew to her mouth and her eyes widened in shock. But then, her mouth tightened, her eyes narrowed and she said, 'So, he expects me to just run away?'

She began waving her hands about as if she were juggling dinner plates. 'Like some scared little kid? Hey? He doesn't think I can handle it?' Her eyes threw poisoned darts at me. She stopped dead-still and folded her arms. 'Well, I'm not going and you can't make me!'

I held her arm and began to pull her along with me. 'We're trying to find a cure for your father,' I said. 'We're not running away from anything. We're running *to* something.' Although, technically, at that stage of the journey we were still just walking.

'A likely story,' she said and pulled her arm away. However, she kept pace without me having to force the issue, so that was an improvement.

'Your father has sent you on his rescue mission,' I said. 'He's trusting us, you included, to find the thing that'll save his life. I can't think of anything more important to do. Can you?'

She chewed on that idea as we strode along. Eventually she mumbled, 'I guess not.'

'It's possible that someone has done this to him and we don't know who,' I said. 'There may be people who will try to stop us. That's why Cal is with us. The rest of us aren't exactly soldier types.'

She giggled. 'That's the truth.'

'Speak for yourself!' Kieran said.

I flicked a smile at him. Then I looked past his shoulder to see what was happening with Maraed. She was still glaring at me, so I quickly looked away. I thought about talking with her the next time we stopped and then I thought, *I've done nothing wrong so she can just get over it.*

Tiffany swung her arms as she walked. 'Can you really talk to the animals?'

I nodded. Joffre squawked. 'And birds, too.'

'Why can't I ride a camel?' She looked up at me and you'd swear butter wouldn't melt in that cute little mouth.

Kieran said, 'I can answer that one.' She turned to him. 'You said you didn't want to ride on a smelly old camel. You hurt their feelings, so they gave you what you asked for.'

'I didn't know animals had feelings,' she said. 'I've never had anything to do with them.'

'All living things have feelings,' I said. 'Have you never seen an animal weep salt water? Or seen an animal mother caress its young? The Most High called them into being, just like he did with us. All Sed's creatures have the same desire to find a partner and create a family. They think and feel. They even communicate. They just don't speak like we do.'

She flapped her hand in the air. 'No need to carry on about it,' she said.

We trudged on in silence. For a while, the road wound along the cliff edges. We'd finally left the Great Sea Caves behind us. The sun glinted on the ocean and a cool breeze lifted off the waves. Joffre flew a short distance in front of us, pooped and then returned to his perch next to my neck. When he first began sitting on my shoulder, my clothes used to get a thick white streak down the back. Maraed used to wrinkle her nose and refuse to hug me and my mother made me wash my own tunics. It was both disgusting and annoying.

Joffre and I had a long conversation about it. At first, he thought I didn't want him to be near me. He couldn't understand what the fuss was about. Birds and animals have a different approach than humans to the business of passing water and poop. Eventually, he accepted it was a quirky foible that we had and he agreed to do his business elsewhere.

At the curve of the road, where it began to pull away from the cliffs and head inland again, we stopped for a quick break. All the humans found a tree, a thick collection of shrubs or a large pile of rocks to give us privacy as we relieved ourselves. Then, after cleaning our hands with a dampened cloth, we made a quick lunch of dried fruit and cheese. As we were finishing off the last few pieces and drinking from our water flasks, Tiffany stood up.

'I'd like to say something, please,' she said.

We all stared at the girl in front of us, the sun gleaming on her yellow hair, her hands restlessly pulling at the sides of her tunic.

'I didn't know about my Pa. I didn't know why we were out here. I didn't know that animals have feelings. I'm sorry.'

She turned to look directly at the camels. 'I apologise for being rude to you. You're such big, strong beasts and – I admit it – I was a little scared when I first met you. Please let me ride on you?'

The camels rumbled their approval of her speech but she, not knowing camels, thought they still weren't happy with her.

'Please?' she said. 'My father is dying. We have a chance to find a cure for him but it won't do any good if we take too long to get it. Please, let us all ride? I just know, with those long legs of yours, you'd be able to move a lot faster than the speed we're going now.'

The camels honked their approval and she turned to me. 'I don't know what else to say.'

I leapt up and put my arm around her shoulders. Maraed scowled at me but I ignored her. 'They accept your apology.'

'They do?' she said. 'Then why are they making that noise?'

I laughed. 'That's their way of saying, you're forgiven.' I dropped my arm and smiled at the rest of the group. 'We're riding the rest of the way to Zenda.'

Kieran cheered and Maraed smiled. From the way she'd been wiggling, stretching her back and rubbing her feet while we were having lunch, I knew she'd be happy to be riding.

Joffre, who was perched in a nearby tree, said, *Excuse me. What about me?*

I leaned close to Tiffany's ear and whispered, 'Joffre, the raven, would appreciate an apology, too.'

She nodded. 'I'm sorry, Joffre,' she called up to the bird. 'You have the most beautiful feathers. In the sunlight, they have a gorgeous blueish sheen on them.'

Very well, he said, *she can stay.*

He flew down and settled on her shoulder. She yelped in surprise but then she smiled. 'Look at me, Cal,' she said. 'Wait until I tell Pa.'

Maraed came up to me. 'Can I have a quick word, please?'

I nodded. She walked a little way along the road, creating a small space between us and the rest of the group. Then, she lowered her voice and spoke quietly and intensely.

'Listen, Seeger,' she said, 'you need to be careful with Tiffany.'

'I saw you glaring at me,' I said. 'Are you jealous?'

She folded her arms across her chest. 'Don't be ridiculous. That little girl is playing you like a fiddle.'

I frowned. 'What do you mean?'

She put her hand on my arm. 'Believe me, I'm more than happy to finally get up on a camel's back.'

I smiled. 'I saw you rubbing your feet.' She punched my shoulder with her knuckles. 'Ow! That hurt!'

'Good!' she said. 'It's a pity you haven't noticed anything else.'

I rubbed the sore spot on my upper arm. 'Look, Maraed, we're on a tight schedule so get to the point.'

'Tiffany couldn't care less about the camels' feelings. She doesn't care how rude she was to Joffre.'

I shook my head. 'She apologised. And very nicely, too.'

Maraed sniffed. 'They don't matter to her.'

'But she said –'

'She said what she knew you wanted to hear,' Maraed said, 'simply because she's sick of walking.' She shrugged. 'It's all the same to me. We finally get to ride. But I'm warning you to be a little wiser in your dealings with her. She's not all sweetness and light just because she's pretty.'

'I don't know what you're suggesting but –'

She interrupted me. 'I've seen her kind before, Seeger. Trust me. You always take people at face value. Just keep your wits about you.'

I nodded, while once again rubbing my sore arm. 'Very well.'

'Good,' she said. 'Let's go.'

We walked back to the others and I told them it was time to mount up. Joffre flew back to me. Tiffany sat on Bryan behind Maraed. She wrapped her arms tightly around Maraed's waist, her face a mix of excitement and terror.

Finally, we were moving faster than a walking pace! I was most impressed with the big bull camel, Errol. He was loaded up with our swags, kitbags and provisions but he easily kept up with the rest of us.

You're doing a good job, Errol, I said. *Are we going too fast for you?*

Don't be daft, he said.

If I tell Kieran to drop your reins you won't wander off, will you?

He made a rude noise, blowing air through his flapping lips. *Don't insult me.*

My apologies, I said. 'Drop Errol's reins, Kieran. He'll be fine.'

Every now and then, Joffre would take an exploratory flight. He looked as though he was just riding the thermals but he kept a wary eye on the group of men who were further back on the trail.

The camels knew the urgency of our mission so they kept up a good pace. By the time the sun was starting its slide down into the sea, we could see the town of Zenda up ahead. I asked the camels to put on an extra spurt and we made it through the town gate in time.

Shortly after we'd gone through, we could hear a commotion behind us. Kieran looked back and said, 'There are four men arguing at the gate. I think the guards want to shut them out. They've cut it fine getting here so late.'

They're the ones I saw earlier today, Joffre said.

'They're lucky they've been let in,' Kieran said.

I said, 'I thought for a while that we weren't going to make it in time, either.'

'They're not coming our way,' Kieran said. 'They've turned off down a side street.'

We rode through the town, looking for somewhere to lodge. Lamps were being lit. Shutters were being pulled across windows. Zenda was closing down for the night.

I saw a man outside a store locking the doors, so I called out to him, 'Excuse me, sir?'

He turned around. 'Yes?'

'Could you please direct us to a place of lodging?'

He smiled. 'Certainly. Keep going up here,' he pointed straight ahead, 'until you reach a crossroads. Take the road to the south. Halfway down, you'll see The Beggar's Arms. You'll get a good night's kip there and the price is reasonable.'

'Thank you, sir,' I said. *Ajax, did you get that?*

Don't worry, mate. I'll get ya there.

He led our caravan in the direction the man had indicated and a short time later we pulled up outside the hotel. Light streamed out from the big front windows and we could hear a band inside the building, playing a lively jig.

'I'll go in and sort things out,' Asher said. 'The rest of you wait here.'

'I expect a room of my own!' Tiffany called.

Seven

Just before Kieran and I took the camels to the stables, I heard Cal warn Tiffany, 'Stick close to Maraed and keep your mouth shut.' Tiffany put her hands on her hips and out came that bottom lip. 'Don't bother to argue,' Cal said. 'If you don't do as I ask, I'll be marching you out of there. If that means you don't get to eat, that'll be on you.'

Kieran and I grinned at each other. As we settled the camels into their stalls, Kieran began to laugh and I soon joined him.

'Did you see the look on her face?' he said.

'She could have tripped over that lip,' I said.

'Cal certainly has her measure,' Kieran said. 'It's going to be an interesting trip.'

We laughed and laughed. The camels joined in, rumbling and snorting. Joffre sat up in the rafters, preening his feathers.

I think you're being mean to that little girl, he said.

Earlier today, you wanted to peck her, I said. *She says one nice thing about your feathers and you're suddenly her best friend.*

There's no need to be nasty to her.

I sighed. The bird was right. 'Kieran,' I said, 'Joffre says we shouldn't be mean to Tiffany and he's right.'

He nodded. 'I know.' He patted Bruce's neck. 'But the look on her face …' He and the camels laughed again. Joffre turned his back on us.

Inside the hotel we found that Asher was at the bar ordering drinks. The ladies were seated at a table, in the centre of which was a large platter of roasted meat and vegetables and a basket filled with chunks of bread. I love hotel food.

Once Asher joined us, he muttered a quick thank you to Sed for his provision and then we all tucked in. For a while, Tiffany watched us with a look of horror on her face.

Cal said, 'Hurry up, girl, or you won't get any.'

'Shouldn't we wait until they bring us knives and forks?' Tiffany said. We all laughed. She frowned. 'Are you telling me this is it?'

Maraed leaned closer to her and said, 'Look around. This is how we eat in these places. It's good food and you can wash your hands afterwards.'

Tiffany sat there for a while, watching us eat while clenching and unclenching her hands. She looked around at the other hotel patrons and saw they were doing the same as us. Then I guess the aroma of the food and our happy-to-be-eating noises finally enticed her to join in. She tentatively reached out for a slice of meat.

'Here,' Cal said, offering her a piece of bread, 'put it on this.'

Tiffany did as she was told, took a deep breath and then bit into the food. She chewed thoughtfully, closed her eyes and then swallowed. She sat like that for a moment or two and then she opened her eyes, grabbed a large slab of bread, piled meat and roasted tuber on it and shoved it into her mouth.

'Good, isn't it?' Cal said.

'Mmmm,' Tiffany said, her mouth too full to answer any other way.

Towards the end of our meal, there was a tap on my shoulder. It was a lad who probably had as many years as Tiffany, or maybe one or two more. His face was vaguely familiar but I couldn't think where or when I'd seen him before.

'Are you Seeger?' he said. I had a mouthful of meat so I just nodded. 'I thought so. I don't suppose you remember me?'

I gulped the meat down. 'You look familiar but I'm sorry, I just can't place you.'

'I'm Alun,' he said. 'I was one of your escorts the day they tried to burn you.'

I heard Tiffany say, 'What?' and then Maraed began to mutter an explanation.

That morning came back to me in a flash: the warmth of the sun on my back; Boyd's sad face; the singing of my Seddonese guards as we walked towards the arena; the bonfire waiting for me and then, just as I'd prepared myself to die, the dragons coming to save me.

I stood up and grabbed Alun's hand and shook it long and hard. 'I can't thank you enough for the comfort you gave me that day.'

He placed his other hand on top of mine. 'No, it's you who should be thanked.'

He let go of my hand, turned to our fellow customers and shouted, 'Hey, everyone!'

I said, 'Don't make a fuss, mate.'

When he didn't get immediate silence he shouted again, 'HEY, EVERYONE!' That time it worked. 'This here is the dragon-friend I told you about. He's the bravest person I have ever met.'

I shook my head. 'I didn't really –'

He talked right over the top of me. 'I saw him march to his death with his head held high and he was just a kid.'

I tried to stop him. I grabbed his arm. 'Please don't, mate.'

But Alun kept shouting. 'This man is the reason I escaped from Midrash. He's the reason all the missing sons and daughters came home.'

'No, no,' I said, 'it was the army who won the war.'

He ignored me. 'He'll tell you it was the army, and they fought bravely and well, but it was this man and his dragons that brought it all to pass. I owe him my life.'

Everyone stood up and cheered. The hotel owner came from behind the bar and rushed up to our table. He grabbed me into a bear hug, lifting me up off the floor. 'Everything is on the house!' he said, putting me back down.

I looked to my friends in desperation but, apart from Tiffany's bewilderment, the others just grinned at me.

Asher said, 'Thank you, sir. You don't need to do that but we appreciate your kindness.'

The hotel owner raised his hands. 'No, no, no!' he said. 'You've given me my son back.' He threw his arm around Alun's shoulders. 'There are others in this room who got their child back from the hell of Midrash, as well as some who still mourn.' He turned to me. 'I'm Stefan. You're my guests. No. You're family to me.' He pumped my hand. 'Thank you, thank you, thank you.'

Other hotel patrons began to push their way forward to shake my hand or thump me on the back, all the time gushing with praise and thanksgiving. I wished the floor would open up so that I could descend into the cellar and hide away. I gave Alun the death-stare but he just grinned at me. I looked to my companions but they were no help.

I put my hands up and said, 'Please. PLEASE! I thank Sed that so many made it home alive. Now, let's put that behind us and enjoy the evening. Maraed, would you sing something for us?'

She walked over to the band and had a short chat with them. I took the opportunity to whisper to Alun, 'How are you? I still occasionally get the shakes and Boyd had a really hard time of it when he came home.'

He couldn't look at me, so we both stared at the floor for a moment. I looked up at him. 'We visited Idris's parents last year.'

He nodded. 'I heard about that.'

We continued to study the floor for a time, then he sighed. 'I still get nightmares on and off,' he said, 'but I can't complain. There are others worse than me. Those Midrashi sure left their mark. I heard you dealt with Blunt, too.'

'The dragons sorted him out,' I said. 'He found he couldn't argue with gravity.'

He squinted and tipped his head to the side. 'What?'

I held my finger up in the air, then tipped it over and made a whistling noise as my finger plummeted towards the floor. I finished the display by flaring out my fingers and saying, 'Whump!'

He nodded and grinned. 'Excellent!' Then his smile slid off his face. 'The thing is …' He looked at me, his eyes pools of sadness. 'I don't know how to go back to being the inn-keeper's son. You understand?'

'Yes, friend, I do. You're not just a returned son. You're a returned soldier.'

He grabbed my arm. 'Could I come with you, wherever you're going? I don't care what you're doing. I just need a change…something…anything… Please?'

I looked at Asher and thought about his plea. 'Have a word with your father, then join us for breakfast tomorrow and we'll talk about it.'

'Sounds good to me!' He shook my hand again and went back to his friends.

When Maraed's golden voice soared up and over the instruments and out into the room, a hushed awe settled on the hotel's customers. She was magnificent, as usual. Her song choice was perfect: *The Homecoming*.

Home, home to the hills and the sea.
Home to our dear friends and family.
Home to the fields and home to the bar.
Home is the wanderer from places afar.

I sat down next to Kieran and sighed. 'Thank Sed for Maraed.'

He gently thumped my back. He knew I didn't like a fuss. Asher smiled his approval to me and then turned to concentrate on Maraed's song.

Cal nodded at me. 'I was there,' she said. 'You and the dragons were awe-inspiring.'

Tiffany leaned across the table. 'That was Pa's army that freed those kids, not you!'

Cal gently pulled her back. 'It was a combined army of Boroni, Seddonese and Rigoni, plus the kids inside the citadel, plus the dragons. You weren't there, kid. I was.'

Tiffany humphed and frowned. 'It was Pa who sent the biggest army. It was Pa who organised the whole thing. It was his doing.' She pointed at me. 'Not this boy!'

I smiled at her. 'You say true.'

Cal and Tiffany argued some more but I ignored them. I turned away and focused on my flame-haired songbird. When she'd finished *The Homecoming,* everyone stomped and cheered and begged for more. She ended up singing four songs in total. She finished with a rousing jig that got several happy customers up dancing.

Kieran was in the thick of it, of course, tapping and clicking his heels. Those of us watching, began to clap in time. Slowly but surely the other dancers went back to their seats and Kieran was the sole attraction. Maraed stopped singing and joined him in the middle of the room. She lifted her arms above her head and then her feet began to tap and slide, just like Kieran's.

I grabbed Asher's arm. 'I had no idea she could dance like that!'

He grinned. 'All the Islanders can do it. They're taught to dance as soon as they can walk.'

I felt stupid. Why hadn't I learned that about Maraed before now? She flicked a glance at me and blew me a kiss. She and Kieran tapped and twirled and the audience whooped and clapped. The band got faster and faster and Kieran and Maraed kept up with them. They grinned at each other like demented cats. The jig ended with a flourish and the siblings threw their hands in the air and cheered. The applause thundered around them. I glanced at Tiffany, who was staring as if the two dancers had just flown in on dragon-back. Her mouth was open and her eyes glittered. She had her head tilted to the side and was staring at Maraed. I think that meant she'd enjoyed the show and, perhaps, she'd realised there was more to Maraed than she first thought.

Seven

Later in the evening, as we made our way upstairs to the bedrooms, I told Maraed how proud I was of her and how impressed I was with her dancing.

I said, 'Why, you're almost as good as Kieran!'

He giggled but she didn't look as pleased as I'd thought she would.

We were about halfway up the stairs when Asher told us where we'd be sleeping. Tiffany was not happy. 'I said I wanted a room to myself!' she said to Asher, poking him in the chest. 'You seem to forget who I am.'

Maraed stared at me and nodded, as if to say, 'See, I told you.'

Cal pulled Tiffany back from the old man. 'Listen to me. When we're travelling, we take what shelter we can get. Be grateful you'll be sleeping in a bed tonight and not somewhere in the wild, lying on the ground.'

'Huh!' Tiffany said, her hands on her hips. 'As if!'

Maraed joined in. 'You're not home now, kid.' Tiffany sneered at her. 'Your dad told us to treat you the same as everyone else and that's what we're doing.'

'But I'm –'

Cal put her finger on the girl's lips. 'Hush. Not here. Stop acting like a spoiled brat. Now get up those stairs.'

Asher patted Tiffany's shoulder. 'Please, dear girl? We're all very tired and it'll be a long day tomorrow.'

She shrugged off his hand but nodded her agreement. It was the surliest 'yes' I've ever seen. She spun around and snarled at Kieran and me, 'What are you two looking at?'

We shrugged. She stuck her nose in the air and proceeded up the rest of the stairs.

The three ladies shared room four. I gave Maraed a quick kiss as we said goodnight. Cal smiled at us but Tiffany looked as though she'd eaten something sour.

Asher, Kieran and I were in room five. It had a window that looked out over the street. Just after Kieran put out the light and we had settled down to sleep – Asher was already snoring – there was a bit of a commotion outside. I was closest to the window, so I got up and pulled back the edge of the curtain. I could see three men on camelback. A fourth had dismounted and was banging on the front door.

'Hey, Kieran,' I said, 'take a look. Are these the same men who came into town behind us?'

He heaved himself out of bed and joined me at the window. By the time he was peering down at the men below, the hotel owner had come to the door and must have told them the place was closed. The leader of the group was using some very colourful language to argue that a bleeping customer was a bleeping customer, and their bleeping money was as good as anyone else's bleeping money.

'Looks like them,' Kieran said. 'I wonder why they're just turning up now. Where've they been all this time?'

I shrugged. We both kept watching and listening as the men and Stefan argued back and forth. They were eventually allowed inside.

'I think we'd better make sure we leave early in the morning,' I said.

Kieran said, 'Or, we could make sure we leave *after* those men and then we can sleep a bit longer.' He waggled his eyebrows and grinned at me.

'I'd feel a lot happier if I knew who they were and what they're doing here,' I said, climbing into bed and pulling the blanket up.

Kieran sat on the end of my bed. 'I'll give them time to get settled and then I'll nip down and have a chat with Stefan. I'll see what I can find out.'

'I'm sure there's no need for that,' I said. 'Get your rest.'

He patted my foot. 'I can snooze on the camel's back tomorrow if I need to. Don't worry.'

A bit later he got up and cracked open our door. He peeked through the gap for a bit and then carefully closed it again. He tiptoed up to me – I was still awake – and whispered, 'They're in the rooms down the corridor from us, on the other side of the stairwell. I'll give them a bit longer before I sneak out.'

I must have drifted off to sleep because the next thing I knew he was sitting on my bed, shaking my shoulder. I sat up and rubbed my eyes. 'What?'

Asher snorted and turned over, breaking wind in his sleep as he rolled. Kieran and I snickered with our hands over our mouths. When we'd settled down again, I yawned with my mouth so wide I thought I'd split my cheeks.

'I found Stefan,' Kieran said. 'He'd gone back to bed but he came to the door when I knocked.' I nodded and yawned again. 'Stefan says the men claimed to be merchants but he doesn't believe them. He says they look more like mercenaries to him.'

'He must have wondered why we were interested,' I said. 'What did you tell him?'

'I said we were on an important fact-finding mission for the Commander and that the men might be following us. That's all he needed to know. He said he'll wake us up extra early so we can be gone before the men are up and around. I've already told Cal.'

'Can we be sure he'll wake up early enough,' I said, 'seeing as his sleep was disturbed twice?'

'He says he always wakes up before the sun is above the horizon,' Kieran said. 'Habits of a lifetime, I guess.' He stood up. 'See you in the morning.'

'Night.'

He stubbed his toe on Asher's bed as he walked past it. He clutched his foot and hopped up and down, madly hissing, 'Shoot! Shoot! Shoot!

'Are you all right?' I asked.

'Yes, yes.' He stopped hopping and sat on the end of his bed, rubbing his toe. 'Go to sleep.'

Asher snorted again and then said, 'Settle down, lads. A man can't sleep with all these shenanigans going on.'

I considered telling him about the men, and I'm sure Kieran did too, but I just said, 'Sorry, Asher. Good night.'

Eight

When Kieran shook me awake the next morning, it was still dark. Once I was up and moving, he went to do the same to Asher. The old man muttered, 'Yes, yes' but within a moment he was snoring again. When we finally got him awake, and we were gathering our things together, he demanded to know why we were up before the crack of dawn.

'Those men from yesterday followed us here,' I said. 'We're making an early start so they won't know where we've gone.'

Asher rumpled his hair so that it stood up in spikes. 'Isn't that a little overcautious? They could be innocent merchants.'

Kieran handed Asher a wide-toothed comb and pointed at the old man's head. Asher began to pull the comb through the spikes. 'Stefan said they look like mercenaries,' Kieran said, 'That made Seeger and me nervous.'

Asher gave the comb back to Kieran and sat down to pull on his boots. 'I take your point,' he said. 'Has anyone roused the women yet?'

'Stefan has,' Kieran said. 'If we hurry, we can have a quick breakfast in the hotel's kitchen with him before we leave.'

'Lovely, lovely,' Asher said. 'Come on then.' He grabbed his bag and hurried to the door.

'Move quietly,' I said. 'The men are only a few rooms away.'

Out in the corridor, Cal and Maraed were tiptoeing towards the stairs, followed by a rumpled and surly Tiffany. Asher started to whisper, 'Good –' but Cal put her finger across his lips and shook her head. She pointed down towards the ground floor and once we'd all nodded to show we understood, she led the way downstairs.

Half-way down, Tiffany said, 'Why'd we have to get up so early?'

All five of us said, 'Shh!'

'Don't shush me!' she said, even louder than before. 'It's a reasonable question.'

Cal leaned into Tiffany and whispered, 'I'll tell you in the kitchen.'

I was sure I heard movement in the rooms above us. Cal must have as well because she grabbed Tiffany's arm and hurried her the rest of the way down the stairs. Kieran questioned me with his eyes and I pointed up towards the mercenaries' room. He nodded, nudged Asher, and we all picked up our pace.

In the kitchen, Stefan already had milk warming on the stove, eggs in a pan and was cutting up some bread. 'Sit you down,' he said, pointing to the table in the centre of the room. 'Breakfast is nearly ready.'

'This is kind of you,' Asher said. 'Thank you.'

'Not a problem dear chap,' Stefan said.

He put a platter of sliced bread and a tub of butter onto the table. He handed a knife to Cal, who began buttering the bread. Stefan hurried back to the fire. He scooped the fried eggs out of the pan and slid them onto a big plate, which he set down next to the bread. 'Fresh from under the chickens' bums,' he said. 'Eat up. I'll get you something to drink.'

Eight

Tiffany stood at the end of the table with her hands on her hips. 'Is someone going to tell me why we had to get up before the sun and why everyone keeps shushing me?'

Stefan brought Asher and Maraed beakers of warm milk.

'Sit down, Tiffany,' Cal said. 'Have your breakfast.'

The brat's voice rose another decibel. 'I demand to–'

'Good morning,' a male voice interrupted. Through the doorway came the leader of the merchants, followed by his companions. 'We're looking for some breakfast.'

Stefan, who'd been pouring milk into beakers, said over his shoulder, 'If you seat yourselves at a table in the front room, I'll be with you in a moment.'

The man smirked. 'We were hoping we could squeeze in here.'

Tiffany slid into the last empty chair next to Cal. Stefan turned around, holding a tray of beakers. 'Sorry,' he said. 'Guests eat in the front room.'

'What about them?' the man said, pointing at us.

'They're family. Otherwise, they'd be out there as well.' Stefan smiled. 'I'll just give them their drinks and then I'll be out to get your order.'

He put the tray on the table and handed the rest of us our drinks. We thanked him, he nodded and then turned to look at the men who hadn't moved. The one who was just behind the leader's right shoulder, kept his gaze fixed on Maraed. It made me nervous. I shifted closer to her.

'Thank you,' Stefan said to them.

The men ignored him. 'We were looking forward to your company,' their leader said.

Asher said, 'Sorry about that, friend, but we're nearly done here.'

'Where are you off to on this fine day?' the man said.

'We're looking for wolves,' Tiffany replied. Cal nudged her. 'What?' Tiffany said. 'That's what we're doing. It's no secret.'

The man moved a step closer and grinned. 'Going hunting, hey?'

Kieran shifted in his seat so that he could look the man in the face. 'No, sir. We're just going to observe them. We don't kill anything unless it's to defend ourselves. What about you? What's *your* mission on this fine day?'

'We're hunting, too,' the man said. 'We've been commissioned by the Slave-Master of Forabad to recapture a runaway slave. The tavern-keeper of the Rusty Anchor is keen to have his property returned.'

I felt Maraed stiffen next to me. I held her hand under the table and squeezed it.

Stefan said, 'You told me you were merchants!'

'Did I? It must have been the lateness of the hour,' the man said. He graced us all with an oily sneer.

'No slaves here, friend,' Asher said.

'Good to know,' the man said. 'You might have met this one on your travels. She's a singer.'

Tiffany opened her mouth but Cal cut in before the brat could say anything. 'Lots of people can sing. We'll need more than that to go on.'

'She has flame-coloured hair,' he said and smiled at Maraed.

His cohorts chuckled and I squeezed Maraed's hand again. It was wet with fear. Stefan wrung his hands in the washcloth and flicked his gaze back and forth between the strangers and us.

Asher smiled at the man. 'Lots of people have hair that colour,' he said, 'especially down in the Islands where my wards come from.' He nodded in Kieran and Maraed's direction.

'Your wards?' the man said.

'I say true,' Asher said. 'They've lived with me for many turns of the sun.' He smiled at Kieran and Maraed, who nodded back at him.

'That's nice,' the man said. 'You know it's your duty to report any runaway slaves to the authorities.'

Asher shook his head. 'I know it's different in Forabad but we Seddonese don't believe in slavery. Sed teaches that no person should own another. Don't count on us to assist you in your quest.'

The man glared at Asher, with his arms folded across his chest. His companions standing behind him, smirked at us and each other. One snickered as if Asher had said something deeply amusing. I found myself wishing the dragons were waiting in the courtyard.

'Just run off, did she?' Cal said.

'A bunch of ruffians attacked her owner and stole her,' the man said, sweeping his gaze across all of us.

'What happened then?' Cal said.

'We think she's joined their gang,' he said.

'That's all very interesting,' Asher said, 'but of no importance to us. As you can see, we're respectable people at this table.'

'You need to look elsewhere,' Stefan said.

Asher said, 'I wish you a good day.'

He picked up his beaker and began to drink his milk. The rest of us copied him, ignoring the watching men and finishing our breakfast. I heard the camels asking me what was wrong and I filled them in on the situation.

We thought there was something wrong about those fellas, Bryan said. *Their camels are scared to death of them.*

They don't smell right, Errol said.

Don't worry, I said. *The dragons are meeting us a bit further up the road.*

They can't get here soon enough, Ajax said. *The bird wants to know what's going on. I'll fill him in. Stay safe in there!*

'What's wrong with your lad?' the man said, tapping his forehead. 'Is the attic empty? What a shame. Such a nice-looking young man, too.' His companions laughed.

I stared at him with my mouth open. I've learned over the years that sometimes it pays to let others think less of me.

Cal said, 'That was rude!'

Eight

There was an awkward silence for a moment but then Stefan said, 'Please, gentlemen? Through here, thank you.' He ushered them out into the dining room.

As soon as they'd left, Cal whispered to Tiffany, 'Next time if I ask you to be quiet, you be quiet. Got it?'

Tiffany frowned. 'I don't understand.'

Cal, still whispering, said, 'Those men are soldiers for hire. They're dangerous. We don't want them following us.'

Tiffany pouted. 'You don't have to be so bossy,' she said. 'They're only looking for some old slave.'

Maraed put her hand on Tiffany's arm but she shrugged it off. 'I'll explain a few things once we're on the road,' Maraed said, 'but it's also possible they've been hired by the person who's poisoned your father.' Tiffany's mouth formed a perfect O.

Stefan bustled back in and began to bang pots and pans around. Asher looked around the table at all of us and said, so quietly we could just hear him, 'Ready?' We all nodded. 'Let's go. Quietly!'

We stood up from the table, making sure our chairs didn't scrape on the kitchen floor. Asher shook Stefan's hand and whispered a thank you to him. I put my arm across his shoulders and gave it a squeeze.

'Please apologise to Alun but we can't wait,' I whispered.

He leaned his head back and said, 'I'll tell him. And don't fear, I won't mention last night.' He looked at Maraed and then smiled at me. 'Which way do I tell them you're going?'

I looked to Kieran, who said, 'North.'

Stefan held his thumbs up and then went back to cooking the mercenaries' breakfast. We tiptoed out the back door and raced over to the stables to get the camels and Joffre. After we'd packed our gear onto Errol's strong back, we left through the rear gate so as not to be observed by the men sitting in the front room of the inn. We were soon on the main road heading towards Carrig.

As we made our way through Zenda, Joffre regaled me with his morning activities. On the scrounge for something to eat, he'd left the stables while it was still dark. He'd found a couple of tasty mice and he'd had a pleasant rummage through the discarded kitchen scraps at the back of the inn. It was a little unfortunate for the mice that they happened to be scavenging the same rubbish at the time Joffre turned up.

I said, *That's fascinating, Joffre. Thanks for sharing it with me.*

Not a problem, pal, Joffre said. *I like to keep you well-informed. You'll never guess what I saw on my way back to the stables. Go on, guess.*

There doesn't seem to be any point in trying, Joffre.

You're right! You'd never guess it. I saw one of those fat birds.

I gave him a moment to elaborate but, when there was no more information forthcoming, I said, *There are a lot of plump birds in the world.*

I saw one of those pigeons that thinks it can fly faster than me. I asked it what it was doing flitting about before dawn and it said it couldn't stop and talk because it was on a mission to Seddon.

Oh, it was a messenger pigeon! I said.

I suppose so. It didn't look any different to all the other smug pigeons in the neighbourhood, so it was hard to tell.

Where did it come from?

One of the bits of clear wall up near the roof of the inn.

A window? I asked.

That's what I said, didn't I? Wake up, son!

How interesting, I said.

I knew you'd want to know about it.

He fluffed his feathers and began preening them. For a while I thought about what he'd just said: a messenger pigeon, sent towards Seddon. Perhaps Stefan was using it to order more supplies. Or, he could have family in Seddon. Or, it might have been sent by the slave-hunters. I couldn't remember if I'd seen any pigeon boxes amongst the men's luggage. I'd been too focussed on the men themselves to notice much else. I decided to have a quiet word with Cal the next time we made a stop.

Before we reached the eastern gate, we could hear someone hailing us from behind. It was Alun. 'Wait for me!' he called. When he'd caught up with us he said, 'I'm sorry I was late to breakfast. Can I join your expedition?'

'We haven't really had a chance to discuss this, Alun,' I said. 'Those men turning up last night, made things more complicated.'

'I'll be useful,' he said. 'I've been trained as a soldier and I know this area well. I reckon you could use another able-bodied person. Plus, I've always wanted to see wolves in the wild.'

I looked to Asher to send Alun home but he stroked his beard, turned to Cal who nodded, and then he said, 'How many years do you have, son?'

'Sixteen, sir.'

'Has your father given his permission?' Cal said.

'He has,' Alun said. 'I might be young but I survived Midrash's army. I can look after myself.'

Asher said, 'We're honoured to have you. However, I must warn you, our mission's not just about wolves.'

Alun grinned. 'That's fine with me.'

'I see you're an archer,' Cal said.

It wasn't hard to figure that out, seeing as he had a longbow and a quiver slung across his back.

'One thing I'll give the Midrashi, they teach you how to fight,' Alun said. 'I've worked on my skills since I got home and, if I do say so myself, I'm a pretty good shot.'

'This mission could be dangerous,' Asher said.

Alun nodded and flashed another grin at us. 'I was hoping it would be. Life's a little dull in Zenda. I can hold my own with the bow … and with a long knife if it comes down to it.'

'One question,' I said. 'Did your father send off a messenger bird this morning?'

Alun shook his head. 'We don't have any. Why?'

'Doesn't matter,' I said. 'We're glad to have you. Let's get moving.'

Once we'd left Zenda, Maraed told the story of her time as a slave. It seemed that neither Tiffany, Cal nor Alun had heard of the problems in the Outer Islands, with the crooked Mayor of Marella and the fraud that he and some men from Forabad had conducted. They gasped when they heard about the sacrifice of the maidens to the dragon and how it was all fake. I heard a guttural growl from Alun when Maraed explained that the mayor shared the gold offered to the dragon with the Forabadians, and the maidens were taken to Forabad and sold into slavery.

She also told them how she'd been displayed in the slave market and bought by the owner of the Rusty Tavern. Then, how she was kept in a small room and only allowed out at night to perform for the tavern's customers. She'd initially been spared any inappropriate contact from her owner but she knew the day was approaching. He'd become more and more familiar with her as time had passed. Cal stiffened in the saddle and her frown was fierce.

Tiffany said, 'Oh my goodness!' and put her hand over her mouth.

Alun slowly shook his head and said, 'It seems the Midrashi aren't the only monsters in the world.'

For a while we rode in silence. The camels spoke to me of their sadness for Maraed and their desire to kick anyone from Forabad that they might meet. They hadn't heard the story either because we didn't take camels with us on our rescue mission. Shortly after getting Maraed back, we were in the fight with Captain Blunt and the Xanthi and I guess no one got around to telling the camels of Maraed's story.

They all promised to protect her from the evil men who were following us.

Kieran took over and told Tiffany and Cal a short version of our rescue mission into Forabad to steal Maraed back.

Cal laughed. 'So, you were the band of ruffians?'

'We had help,' Asher said. 'Felix was with us, as well as Seeger's special friends.'

Joffre insisted I recount his role in Maraed's rescue. When I'd finished, Tiffany said to the bird, 'You were so brave!' She made a friend for life at that moment. When Kieran told them how Rimini had whacked the tavern-owner between the legs with a frying pan, Cal cheered.

Alun said, 'That's our Rimini. You don't mess with her.'

Kieran and I nodded and said in unison, 'You say true.'

'Do you think they know it's you they're looking for?' Tiffany said to Maraed.

She nodded. 'I have no doubt they'll be back on our trail very soon.'

'Can we beat them in a fight?' Tiffany said. She turned around to look at Cal, who shrugged. 'But we've got Alun with us now! He's not useless like the other men.'

Maraed gasped. Asher sniffed and said, 'I beg your pardon?'

Kieran and I didn't say anything but we gave her the death-stare: eyes squinted, lips thinned and pressed together, brows furrowed and thoughts of pain and mayhem flying towards her at breakneck speed.

Cal said, 'Our chances are definitely better than before.' She smiled at Alun, who dipped his head at the compliment. 'I'd still rather not have to be in that situation.'

Tiffany said, 'Couldn't we set up an ambush and deal with the men once and for all. After all, there are only four of them.'

Asher shook his head. 'So far the men have done nothing wrong, nor anything that is life-threatening. We don't just kill people because they're a nuisance.' He then muttered under his breath, 'More's the pity.'

'Pardon?' Tiffany said.

'Certainly dear,' Asher said. 'You're excused.'

'I didn't quite hear you,' Tiffany said.

'YOU'RE EXCUSED!' Asher shouted.

Tiffany rolled her eyes and gave up. I didn't dare catch Kieran's eye because I knew we'd both burst out laughing if I did. I heard him snort but I didn't turn around.

'What are we going to do?' Tiffany said.

'We keep going,' I said. 'We're meeting up with some strong allies on the other side of Carrig and then we'll be fine.'

Alun grinned. 'I hope they're who I think they are.'

Tiffany frowned and started to say, 'Who are –?'

'You'll see,' Maraed said.

The dragons will soon show those fellas a thing or two! Ajax said.

Yes, I said, *but we must get to them first.*

Nine

Kane

The next morning as I headed to my office, I heard someone retching in the privies. I waited for them to come out so I could offer my assistance. It was Riva!

I said, 'Are you all right?' She said she was but she looked pale and her eyes were red rimmed as if she'd been crying. 'Do you need a healer?'

'I'm sure it's just something I ate,' she said. 'I'm fine.'

'Very well,' I said, 'but if you feel you can't keep working today, you're free to go home.'

She shook her head. 'It's just a bit of an upset stomach. I can manage.'

'That's good but if you stay unwell, let me know.'

'DON'T FUSS!'

Taken aback by her tone, my eyebrows shot towards my hairline.

'Sorry. Sorry,' she said. 'I say true, I'm fine. Everything's fine. Nothing to worry about. I need to muck out the camels' stalls. Is that all right with you?'

'Of course, dear,' I said.

My goodness! Seeger often complained of Riva's temper but I had always thought that was just a thing between the two of them. I decided to discreetly keep an eye on her for the rest of the day. However, by midday she'd cleaned the camels' stalls and had moved on to the goats' pens. Whatever had been bothering her earlier in the day seemed to have worn off.

Nine

Early in the afternoon, I left Karmal with Simpson while I visited the Commander.

He was at work in his office signing some order forms for the army. A young soldier was standing at ease in front of his desk.

'Sit you down, Kane,' the Commander said. 'I'll be with you in a moment.'

I sat in the chair below the window and watched him work. He seemed to be fine – despite wearing gloves – writing his name and the occasional message on the order slips. I wondered if his hands were any bluer. I studied his face. Was he more pale than usual? Did he seem a little tired?

Eventually, the last bit of paperwork was done. The soldier saluted, picked up the papers and left the room.

'Bring your chair up to the desk, Kane,' the Commander said. 'I'm glad you came today as I've something to tell you. But first, what can I do for you?'

'Are you interested in purchasing some donkeys, sir?' I asked.

He laughed and leaned back in his chair. 'You're a persistent fellow, Kane. Well done.'

'How are you today?' I asked. 'Is there anything I can do for you?'

He sighed and tugged at his gloves. 'My hands are now completely blue. So are my feet. I'm tired but otherwise I'm doing well. It hasn't yet interfered with my work.'

'I'm glad to hear that,' I said. His lips twitched into a half-smile. 'What I mean is, I'm glad it hasn't stopped you working but it's not so good that the blue is still creeping forward.'

He nodded. 'Every day it's a little further on from the day before.'

'Has anyone said anything about the gloves?'

He shook his head and smiled. 'No, but a couple of the young officers that frequent the Citadel were wearing some this morning.' We grinned at each other. 'I need to tell you something.'

I shuffled forward a little in my seat. 'Yes, sir?'

'I had some visitors here yesterday morning, shortly after your visit. Four men. They were making enquiries about a runaway slave.' I felt my heart lurch in my chest. 'I suppose we were a little naïve to think we could get away with rescuing Maraed, without any repercussions.'

I put my hand up. 'That was nothing to do with you.'

He shook his head. 'I'm the Commander of Seddon. Everything that is done in the name of Seddon is my responsibility.'

I slapped my hand on his desk. 'No! That was purely down to Asher, Seeger and others. Private citizens.'

He leaned forward. 'Who were accompanied with my blessing by Felix, a member of my personal guard.'

That was correct. I'd forgotten that Felix couldn't have gone with the team if the Commander hadn't given his permission. I backed down and the Commander leaned back in his chair again.

'Not many people in Seddon know that Maraed was a slave,' I said. 'We just let people assume she'd come to be with her brother. Asher treats them as if they were his children. We've never told the tale of her rescue.' I shook my head. 'She's been doing so well with her singing lessons at the Temple.'

I rubbed my hand across my forehead and then down over my eyes. 'This is the last thing we need right now.' I looked up at the Commander. 'What did you say to them?'

'I told them they were free to search the city but I doubted they'd find such a person here in Seddon,' he said. 'I also told them that we don't practice slavery here because it is against the teaching of Sed. They found that amusing. They're not nice people.'

'I would imagine one must have a hardened heart to be involved in such a life-destroying practice. What happened after that?'

He tugged his gloves again. 'They described the slave for whom they were searching. It's definitely Maraed. They know exactly who they're looking for and where they'll find her. When it was obvious I wasn't going to tell them anything helpful, they left. I had them followed. They went straight to Asher's house. Finding no one at home, they conferred quickly among themselves and then left the city through the Eastern Gate, heading in the same direction that Asher's team took.'

Something was niggling in the back of my brain. 'How did they know where to find Asher's house? How did they know to immediately set out on the eastern road, instead of searching the city?'

'Exactly!' the Commander said. 'Someone is feeding them information. I think our little band of rescuers are in trouble.'

My heart had begun to race. I left my chair and paced back and forth. 'What can we do?' I asked. 'Asher and the lads will be no match against those men. Even with Cal doing her best, I can't see her holding off mercenaries on her own.'

'I agree,' he said.

'Is there any way I can contact them to warn them?'

He shook his head. I paced some more and said, 'I'll beseech Sed that they reach the dragons before anything happens to them.'

'You say true,' the Commander said. 'Also, we must try to discover who it is that is giving them information. I wonder if it's a coincidence that they've come here at this particular time, when my life is under threat?'

'Do you think the person who did this to you also called in these men?'

He slowly nodded. 'It wouldn't surprise me.'

I stopped pacing and sat down again. 'This is diabolical,' I said. 'Where do we even begin? It could be anyone.'

He shrugged. I thought about it for a while. 'Surely there must be some who are contenders and others who can be discounted?'

'You would think so,' he said, 'but I have no way of knowing. Everyone in my position has political rivals. That comes with the territory. However, there are so many random possibilities. Someone I may have unwittingly offended or upset. Someone who is avenging perceived wrongs I may have done to a loved one in the past. There is nothing to guide us in our search. We must distrust everyone.'

So now not only was my Commander under serious threat to his life but also my son and his girlfriend, my friend and his ward, and the Commander's daughter and guard, and there didn't seem to be anything I could do about it.

When I returned to the stables, I saw Riva down near the grivens' pen talking with Trevor and Harvey. The griven-keeper came out of the storage shed, carrying buckets of oats to put into the feeding trough. As he walked past me, I called him over.

'Yes boss?' he said, taking the opportunity to put the buckets down.

'I won't keep you long, Paddy,' I said. 'Does Riva seem all right to you?'

Paddy gazed across the yard at Riva and the griven. He pursed his lips as he thought. Then he said, 'She's not quite been herself this past week. I'd put it down to Riff's going away without her. But now that you ask, she's also complained about the smell of the animal's dung – says it makes her feel sick – and it's never bothered her before.' He shrugged. 'You know women. It could be anything or nothing.'

'I suppose so,' I said. 'Thanks, Paddy.'

He picked up the buckets and headed over to the griven's pen. I watched him go while I thought about Riva's recent behaviour. In the end I decided to have a chat to Fee about her.

Ten

Seeger

By mid-morning, Joffre could see the men in the distance behind us. They were keeping a steady pace and didn't seem in too much of a hurry to catch up. Why did they bide their time? Perhaps what Asher said at breakfast gave them some doubt? Perhaps they were waiting for something else – Sed knows what – before making their move.

Asher said we should move faster but Cal wouldn't have it.

'We don't want to look as though we're running from them,' she said. 'We're on a mission to find wolves, remember? If we run, it'll confirm to them that Maraed is the one they're seeking. If we act as if we're not bothered with their presence on the road, that will create some doubt in their minds.'

Therefore, we plodded along at a medium pace and every so often I searched the skies for my leathery friends. Occasionally I'd try to call them but, when it was clear that they couldn't hear me, I knew they were still a fair distance away.

At midday we stopped for a break under a cluster of needlewood trees, which were growing near the side of the road. After cadging a chunk of dried goat from me, Joffre flew off to spy on the slave-hunters.

While we were eating, Asher said, 'Tell me, Alun, have you heard anything of an old healer up in the hills of Mac Tire?'

He slowly shook his head. 'People in those parts keep to themselves. I suppose they'd have to have a healer of sorts up there.' He frowned and nibbled on his thumb nail.

'And what about wolves?' Asher said.

Alun brightened up immediately. 'Now I've definitely heard some rumours about them. Oh yes. Wolves and wolf-people alike. They say those hills are riddled with them.'

'Really?' Kieran said. 'That many?'

'So the rumours go,' Alun said. 'Mind you, it's mostly tavern-gossip and you know how those stories grow over time.' He grinned at us. 'Still, I reckon they must be based on truth or why would the stories be there in the first place?'

'What do you mean by wolf-people?' Maraed said.

'Old Jeb used to farm out near Carrig before moving to Zenda when he got too old to push a plough,' Alun said. 'He swears there were people living up in those hills that were either half person and half wolf, or that they turned into wolves when the moon was full. He was a bit vague on the details. But he won't back down from it, even when we all tell him he's full of it and perhaps he should lay off the strong stuff, seeing as his brain is addled. He just shakes his head and tells us that one day we'll all know he was speaking true. Funny old codger.'

Asher sighed and tugged at his beard. 'I wish I'd known of this fellow last night. I would have loved to have had a chat with him.' He sighed again. 'Too late now.'

When everyone was packing up the campsite, I led Cal away from the group and told her about the messenger bird. 'What do you make of that?' I asked.

She rubbed her chin. 'It was probably sent by the slave-hunters,' she said, 'but I'm surprised the bird was heading to Seddon and not Forabad. I don't like the sound of that.'

'Neither do I. Do you think it's possible –'

'I do,' she said. 'It's possible and that makes me uneasy. How much do you trust young Alun?'

I thought about that for a moment. I didn't really know him. However, he was a member of the guard chosen to escort me to my execution. That told me Boyd trusted him.

'He was stolen from his home and forced to do things that have seared his soul. He'll have no sympathy for slavers. Also, the Commander sent the army that rescued him and the other children. I can't see Alun being willing to cause him any harm.'

She nodded. 'I agree. I'll explain to him the true purpose of our mission, mention our suspicions and make sure he's on guard.' She grinned, 'I'll also warn him about Miss Tiffany. She's too pretty for her own good, that one.'

First Maraed and then Cal! Both women were comfortable in their own skins so I knew it was not a matter of jealousy because of Tiffany's beauty. Maraed was always harping on about me taking people at face value but I couldn't see how there was any other way to do it. You can't run around suspecting everyone of serious nastiness. You'd never make friends and you'd never sleep well, with your head spinning like that.

Alun's camel had been welcomed by Ajax and the others into our caravan. His name was Lenny. He was a nervous young chap, who'd never been far from Zenda before.

Alun just ran into the stable and grabbed the nearest camel and that was me! he said. *I tried to tell him to take Jerry instead but he doesn't talk camel. So here I am. I heard the old fella say it was going to be dangerous. He was joking, right?*

Nah, Bruce said. *It'll be danger all the way.*

What sort of danger? Lenny said. *Spiders? Rats? I hate spiders and rats.* His eyes rolled in fear as he whispered, *Please tell me there won't be spiders!*

Who knows? Probably all that and more, Kevin said. *But don't worry, matey, we've got your back.*

Stop teasing him, I said. *There's nothing to worry about, Lenny.* But then I realised I had to warn him. *However, there is one thing that I feel I should mention.*

Yes?

Sometime soon we'll be joined by a dragon or two.

He literally bleated, just like a frightened goat. I don't think I've ever heard a camel make that noise before. The others laughed at him, which was a little mean of them.

Monsters? Lenny said, dancing on the spot. *There's going to be monsters? They* eat *camels!*

They're friends of ours so you'll have nothing to worry about, I said. *They only eat the ones they don't know. You'll be fine. I promise.*

Alun said, 'I think Lenny's feet are bothering him. I'd better check.'

'Don't bother,' I said. 'I've just told him who'll soon be joining our group and it's made him a little nervous.'

Alun reached forward and patted his camel's neck. 'I'll take care of you, Lenny,' he said.

I told him not to take me, Lenny said. *But would he listen? Nooooo.*

'Who'll be joining us?' Tiffany said.

'You'll see soon enough,' Maraed said. 'They want to surprise you. Let them have their little fun.'

'Hmph!' Tiffany said, flipping her hair back over her shoulder. 'I think that's a bit childish.'

Kieran, Alun and I flicked grins back and forth between us.

Joffre circled overhead before landing on my shoulder. *They're still back there,* he said. *One of them pointed up at me and another one* shot *at me. What a cheek! I dodged the arrow but can you imagine it? Me, a handsome raven, shot by a dirty arrow from someone like that? I deserve better, I tell you.*

He fluffed his feathers, raised his hackles and rumbled disgruntledly as he remembered the insult to his birdhood. *Let me tell you, my hackles are up, Seeger. Up!*

I'm glad the arrow missed. What would I do without you, Joffre?

Exactly!

I think it might be wise if you don't go near them for a while. He was going to argue but I said, *We don't want to show our hand. Remember, you're our secret weapon.*

His hackles subsided. *Quite right. You say true. But, Seeger, they were laughing. They're like the men who came with the nets and took my family. They're nasty.*

I told the group that the slave-hunters had shot at Joffre so he wouldn't be doing any more spying that day.

'Wise decision,' Cal said. 'Let them think he's just an ordinary bird.' Joffre squawked his indignation. 'We know he's special but they don't. Let's keep it that way.'

'Joffre, sweetie,' Tiffany said, 'I'm so glad they didn't hurt you.'

I like this girl.

Of course you do, I said.

Apart from Joffre's near-death experience, the afternoon ride to Carrig was uneventful. Cal asked Alun to ride next to her for a while. I heard her explaining the true nature of our mission. When she'd finished, Alun rode up next to me.

'I'm with you, one hundred percent,' he said. He looked as grim as the day he escorted me to the execution arena. 'I owe the Commander my life.'

'Welcome to the team,' I said.

'Those men back there,' he said. 'You think they're part of all this?'

'It's highly possible.'

He pursed his lips and nodded. 'Right,' he said. Then he grinned. 'At least it won't be boring!'

The thought of those men keeping pace behind us was unnerving. What could they be waiting for? I consoled myself with the thought that, with every passing moment, we drew closer and closer to the dragons.

The rest of the trip to Carrig was uneventful. We reached it late in the afternoon. It's a much smaller place than Zenda and there wasn't a town wall or guards stationed at the entrance. We just rode in and made our way to an old inn that Alun had recommended, on the far side of the town.

'The Bearded Man isn't as big, nor as well-equipped as our inn,' he said, 'but it's clean and the food is good. Dad and I always stay in it when we come here for market day.'

That was good enough for us. I heard Maraed say to Tiffany that it would be better than sleeping outside on the hard ground. Tiffany didn't seem impressed but she held her tongue. At least she didn't demand her own room when Asher booked us in for the night.

Shortly after we'd finished our meal and had settled in to enjoy the evening, the slave-traders walked in. Asher suggested we drink up and head for our rooms. Thank goodness Maraed was still at the table and not up near the bar, singing for the locals.

'Not leaving already?' the leader of the slavers said. 'We just got here.'

'Early to bed, early to rise,' Asher said. 'Enjoy your evening.'

He smiled politely at the men. We all dipped our heads to acknowledge their presence but none of us said anything. We began to make our way to the stairs.

'Hey!' the man called. 'Who's the new kid? He wasn't with you last night.'

Asher told the rest of us to go ahead and then he and Alun turned around. 'He joined us this morning,' Asher said.

'Why?' the man said, sneering at Alun and nudging his friend with his elbow.

'We're family,' Alun said.

'Ain't that nice?' the man said. 'The old fella seems to be related to everyone in these parts.' He looked at his men, his eyebrows raised and his eyes wide in pretend shock. 'Why, the inn-keeper in Zenda told us the same thing.' The men laughed.

'The inn-keeper is my father,' Alun said. 'So, it's not that surprising.'

The men stopped laughing.

'We bid you goodnight,' Asher said.

He put his hand on Alun's shoulder and they walked over to the rest of us. We'd been waiting for them at the bottom of the stairs. The owner of The Bearded Man hurried over.

'Everything all right, Alun?' he said.

Alun smiled and, with his back to the slave-hunters, said, 'After I've spoken, laugh as though I've told you a great joke.' The innkeeper nodded. 'The men who've just come in are slave-hunters. They've set their sights on one of my companions. They've been following us. We're doing our best to avoid them.'

We all laughed as if Alun had just told a brilliant joke. The innkeeper threw his head back and roared. He slapped Alun on the back. 'That's a good one,' he said. 'Sleep well, everyone.' He leaned in and muttered, 'Me and the boys'll keep an eye on them.'

Alun laughed and nodded. 'Thank you, sir,' he said quietly. Then, much louder, he said, 'Good night.'

We all headed up the stairs. I held Maraed's hand. She was trembling. Cal looked stern and Tiffany didn't say anything, which was most unlike her. When we reached our rooms, before going in for the night, Cal said quietly, 'Make sure you wedge the door shut with something heavy. Even if it means pushing a bed against it.'

Kieran gestured for us to be quiet. He smiled but at waist level his finger was pointing back towards the stairs. I chanced a quick look and saw a flicker of movement.

I whispered, 'Someone is listening.'

Asher tugged his beard and then said, loud enough for any lurkers to hear, 'Before you settle down for the night, join me for a team meeting in my room. I want to go over a few protocols for observing wildlife.' He opened our bedroom door. 'We may be lucky enough to encounter some soon.'

We all filed into the room. Cal positioned herself by the door. She left it open, just a crack, so that she could see if anyone came close.

'What are we going to do?' Maraed said. She clasped her hands to stop them shaking.

'I have an idea,' I said.

I put my finger to my lips and gestured for them to gather in closer. We were soon a tight huddle in the middle of the room, at the foot of one of the beds, our arms draped around each other's shoulders.

'Once the inn has shut down for the night,' I said in a near whisper, 'I say we sneak out, get the camels and ride to Pederson's farm. Even if they expect us to try to leave earlier than them, they won't know about that detour.'

'Why Pederson's?' Alun said.

'He used to work for my father,' I said. 'Do you know him?'

'Yes, Dad buys his tubers and onions. He's a good man.'

'It's an excellent idea,' Asher said. 'Cal?'

She nodded as she risked a quick peek outside the door. 'When we leave, take your boots off,' she whispered, 'and no talking going down the stairs.'

She glared at Tiffany, who had the grace to look embarrassed. Then she peeked out the door again and waved her hand at us. She pointed at the door and moved her fingers like someone walking. We all strained to listen and, sure enough, I could hear a few creaks and groans, which sounded like someone trying to creep up the old staircase without being heard.

She put her eye to the crack in the door and was as still as a statue. Then she nodded and held up four fingers. I guessed that meant that all four slavers were coming upstairs. We all held our breath as we waited. Finally, she pushed the door so that the crack was gone and pointed at it, then pointed emphatically at her feet. She stared at us, frowning and continuing to point at the door and then at the floor. We nodded to her once we got the message: they were just outside the room!

Asher stroked his beard and then said, at normal volume, 'Is that clear, everyone?' We all murmured our agreement. 'Excellent. We'll meet downstairs for breakfast, at first light. Now let's get a good night's sleep.'

Cal nodded, made her fingers walk again and then pointed out in front of her. They were moving away.

'It's going to be a long day, tomorrow,' Asher continued, just in case they could still hear him. 'Go quietly. We don't want to disturb the other guests.'

'Yes, Asher,' we all said.

'But, what about those men?' Tiffany said and winked at us.

'What about them, dear?' Asher said. 'They're nothing to do with us.'

'But they keep turning up,' she said.

'I'm sure it's just a coincidence,' Asher said. Then he leaned in, patted Tiffany on the arm and whispered, 'Good show, young lady.'

She smiled, looked at Maraed and me, and tipped her nose in the air.

'Good night, ladies!' Asher said.

Cal ushered the girls across the passageway to the room opposite ours. We watched them go and only shut our door when we saw they were safely inside. Then we sat down on our beds, took our boots off and waited until it was safe to leave.

Eleven

Asher rummaged in his kitbag and finally, after removing everything, he pulled out a folded map.

'Seeger,' he said, handing it to me, 'show me on here where Pederson's farm is.' I began to search it. 'Kieran,' Asher continued, 'please pack my bag again for me. You're better at it than me.'

Kieran, looking less than pleased, huffed his way over to the mess on the floor and began repacking the kitbag.

I found Carrig on the map and then, following the directions my father had given me, located the farm near the track that led up into the mountains, towards the village of Ballyfaol. I showed Asher the path we'd have to take and studied it for a while, so that I could show the camels where they would need to go.

Asher pointed to a blue line, which ran between Carrig and the farm, coming down the hill and heading towards the sea. 'That's a watercourse,' he said, 'but the road seems to go straight across it. I don't see any bridge. Do you?'

Alun came over and studied the map for a moment. 'That's Disappointment Creek,' he said. 'The road cuts straight across it because it's usually bone-dry. It hasn't had any water in it for the past six years.'

'So, we can ride the camels straight across?' Kieran said.

Alun nodded. He sat down next to me and sighed. 'I hate waiting. Don't you?'

Eleven

Asher said, loud enough for any listening ears to hear, 'Goodnight, lads.' Then he blew out the lamp and we sat waiting in the dark.

After a while, Kieran whispered, 'Are you sure it'll be safe to ride across that creek tonight, Alun?'

'Positive,' Alun said. 'All we have to do is stick to the road.'

Asher lay back and was soon snoring his head off. The noise helped to keep me awake. I was afraid that if I let myself doze it would soon become a deep sleep and we'd miss the opportunity to put some space between us and the slaver-hunters. I spent the time rehearsing each step we'd have to take along the track to the farm.

Eventually we could hear someone scratching on our door. Alun opened it up and Cal quickly stepped into the room. When the door was closed again she said in a low voice, 'Are you ready? Maraed and Tiffany are already on their way down to the stable.'

I poked Asher in his side and he woke up with a snort. 'I'm not awake!' he said. We all snickered. He said, 'What's so funny?'

'If you're not awake,' Kieran said, 'then you must be talking in your sleep.'

'What are you on about?' Asher said.

We kept giggling.

'Oh shut up!' he said. 'Things to do, lads. Chip, chop!'

He moved over to the door and we followed him. Cal waited until we had got ourselves back under control before opening the door and letting us slip through, one at a time.

The inn was deathly quiet, apart from the faint sounds of snoring wafting down the passageway towards us. We tiptoed down the staircase, keeping as close to the wall as possible. It was smart of Cal to make us do that. Usually, a floorboard is more likely to creak if you step in its middle. It's firmer where it's attached to the framework, against the wall.

We made it down the staircase without incident, hurried through the unlit kitchen and out the back door. We pulled on our boots and then raced across the yard to the stable to meet the girls who were waiting in Ajax's stall. They'd already woken up the lead camel, who was less than happy about it.

It's the middle of the night! he said. *What're you playing at, matey? We want to sleep. We're worn out.*

We're tired, too, I said. *We're trying to get a head start on those men who are chasing Maraed.*

Up and at 'em, everyone, Ajax said. *You heard the lad. We've got to save Maraed.*

We threw the saddles on the camels and quickly attached their bridles and leads. Errol and Lenny grumbled but they did as they were told. Out in the yard, we mounted up and headed out into the street. Kieran joined Asher on Bruce. He held the reins while Asher clutched his kitbag. Errol trotted alongside Ajax and me and everyone else was on the same camel as the day before. Joffre fluttered down from his perch on the roof and landed on my shoulder. I showed the camels the route we needed to take and Ajax said we'd be at the farm in no time at all.

The camels ran through the streets of Carrig and we were soon out of the little town and into the countryside. Once my eyes had adjusted to the dark, I could discern important features like the roadway and whatever trees or boulders there were on either side. I kept glancing over my shoulder but there was no sign of any pursuit.

For quite a way the road sloped gently, but persistently, upwards. At last it seemed to level off for a while and then we were racing down the other side of the hill. As we headed towards Disappointment Creek, I began to feel a faint tugging in my brain. I ignored it at first, thinking it was the result of a lack of sleep and too much anxiety. However, as the road levelled off and we were heading towards the wide expanse of dry creek bed, I felt it again. This time it was stronger. I knew that feeling.

Hello, dragons! I called. *Where are you?*

We are on our way, hatchling, the familiar voice of Shadreer said. *What are you doing awake at this hour?*

We've been followed by some dangerous men, I said. *They want to take Maraed back to Forabad and into slavery again.*

We shall see about that! he said. *Are they chasing you now?*

Hopefully, we've left them asleep in an inn in Carrig. We decided to go on ahead, through the night, with the chance that we can lose them. We're going to a farm, near the trail up into the mountains.

Where is this, hatchling?

I pictured the map in my mind, showing the road from Carrig, through Disappointment Creek and then the turn off to the left, into Pederson's farm.

I see it, Shadreer said. *We will be there some time before midday.*

I thought, because I can hear you clearly, you were closer than that.

We still have quite a distance to travel, Shadreer said. *I think you do not realise how much stronger you are in your gifting, hatchling. It keeps growing as you mature. It would not surprise me if you could now speak to the creatures in the sea. When you are fully grown, you will probably be able to hear the worms in the ground and converse with insects. I am so glad we did not let the Midrashi burn you. It would have been a terrible waste.*

Thank you.

We will sleep now and see you at the farm tomorrow. Good night.

Good night, Shadreer. It'll be good to see you again.

I announced to the others, 'Shadreer and a friend or two, will meet us at the farm some time tomorrow morning.'

'Excellent!' Cal said.

'Who's Shadreer?' Tiffany said. 'And how do you know that?'

'You'll see,' Kieran said.

'Keep your silly little boy secrets then,' she said. 'See if I care!'

I smiled and began to imagine what it would be like to talk with worms. What sorts of things do worms think about? Do they think at all?

We rode on through the night and eventually reached the banks of Disappointment Creek. The moonlight was bright enough so that we could see how the ground dipped down towards the creek bed. We could even make out where the ground rose again on the other side. It was a very wide stretch between the two sides.

'I'd like to see this when it has water flowing down it,' Asher said. 'It would be a beautiful sight.'

Joffre flapped his wings. *Something doesn't feel right, Seeger. I don't think you should go into that creek.*

Why not? It's perfectly dry. There's not even a muddy puddle in it.

There's something not right. I'm worried.

Perhaps you should have a fly around and see if you can spot anything.

I'm on it! he said, immediately lifting off my shoulder and flying off up the creek.

'Joffre says he's worried about us going down there,' I announced. 'He's having a look around.'

'It looks perfectly fine to me,' Cal said. 'I don't think we should let the fears of a little bird determine what we do and don't do.'

Asher agreed with Cal. 'Let's get a move on,' he said.

We began to ride the camels across the dry creek bed. Using only the moonlight to navigate by, we didn't make them run in case there were rocks or soft patches that we couldn't see clearly. We let them walk slowly, feeling their way. Alun made Lenny kneel so that he could climb off and lead the camel across. It was a very wide creek, much wider than a road.

'I thought creeks were skinny little things,' Kieran said. 'Are you sure this isn't a river, Alun?'

He laughed. 'People often make that mistake,' he said. 'Creeks and rivers are determined by their length, not their width. You can have very wide creeks and very skinny rivers.'

'Well, I never knew that!' Kieran said. 'This creek could almost be a small field, it's so wide. I was sure it had been mis-named.'

'If water regularly flowed in it, we would call it a stream or a burn,' Alun said, 'but like so many of our creeks and rivers, it's usually dry. If you're looking for water you'll be disappointed, which explains its name.'

We were about halfway across when I heard a strange sound. It was like the far-off rumble of thunder. I looked up but there were no flashes of storm-light and everything seemed calm in the sky. I shrugged it off.

We'd gone a few more paces when suddenly Joffre was streaking towards me, shouting, *RUN! RUN!*

What's he on about? Ajax said.

I don't know, I said. *Joffre? What's the matter?*

Water! Water's coming. RUN!

'Everyone,' I called out, 'Joffre says water's coming and we need to run. Let's go!' I nudged Ajax's sides with my knees and he began to trot.

'Don't be ridiculous!' Tiffany said. 'What water? The creek is dry.'

I could hear that low rumble again and this time I knew what it was: a flash flood. It must have been raining near the source of the creek. 'RUN!' I shouted. 'Come on!'

The other camels began to pick up speed and head towards the other side of the creek.

Ajax, I said, *move! Can't you hear it coming?*

He began to urge the other camels to move faster, as he broke into a gallop. Errol kept pace with us. Bruce was quick to respond, followed by Cal on Kevin.

Bryan said, *I want to run, Seeger, but that rude girl is yanking on my reins.*

'Tiffany,' I called, 'stop holding your camel back. Let him run.' I was nearly at the other side of the creek bed now. Joffre showed me what he had seen. It took my breath away.

'You're being ridiculous,' she shouted back at me. 'I can't see any water.'

'Please do as he asks,' Maraed said to her. I expect she was regretting giving Tiffany a go at holding the reins.

'No!' she said. 'I'm not stupid.'

Bryan, ignore her and run anyway, I said. *Joffre has shown me there's a wall of water, filled with debris, coming towards us just around that bend. Run!*

'Hurry up, it's nearly here,' I shouted. 'RUN!'

Ajax and Errol had gone up the bank and were now safely away from the edge of the creek. I got Ajax to sink down onto his haunches so I could jump off and run back to help the others.

Kieran and Asher rode past me on Bruce, heading towards Ajax and Errol. Kevin, carrying Cal, was close behind them. Bryan began to run, ignoring Tiffany pulling hard on his reins and yelling at him. He would have been hurting but he did the right thing anyway.

The faint thunder had grown into a growling rumble and, apart from Tiffany, the others began to shout to each other, 'Listen to that! What is that?'

Then I realised that Alun was still leading Lenny across the creek bed. The young camel was skittish, spinning around in place instead of running towards safety.

Lenny! I called. *Come on, matey. It's not far to go. Just run to me.*

I'm scared, Mr Seeger, he said. *I can't swim. I want my mum!*

'Help me please, Seeger,' Alun called.

It was easy to forget that Alun was still young. I ran back out into the creek bed, which was already damp under my feet. I could see little rivulets of water racing along the ground.

Come on, Lenny, I said. *You can do this.*

No, no, no. I can't. I can't. I want my mum! I hate water. Mum! Mum!

The camel was overwhelmed with fear. The other camels began to call to him from the safety of the bank. They could now see what was happening. Kieran and the others were shouting at Alun to hurry up. The noise only made Lenny more afraid.

I had to get him to calm down enough to listen to me. How could I do that? While I was standing there, tugging on Lenny's bridle, Joffre flew out and began to swoop over the camel's head.

Come on, pal, he said, *move your butt.*

Mum, mum, mum, mum, Lenny said, trying to pull his head away from me, while dodging the raven. *Ahh! Ahh! I'm going to die! I know it. I know it.*

The water was now swirling around our ankles. That was enough for me. I gave the camel a hard smack on his cheek.

'Hey!' Alun said.

You hit *me!* Lenny said.

'He was hysterical, Alun,' I said. *Len, listen to me. There's a wall of water racing towards us. It's carrying chunks of trees that it's broken off on the way down here.*

Mum, mum, mum –

'Come on, Seeger,' Alun said. 'Do something.' He yanked Lenny's reins. 'Move, you stupid camel.'

'I'm trying to talk to him, Alun,' I said. 'Give me a break.'

Don't make me smack you again, Lenny. Listen! On those branches are spiders, rats, snakes and other creatures that can't swim and are frightened too. They'll jump onto you if you don't get out of here, fast.

Did you say, spiders? Lenny said. *Spiders and rats? Step aside.*

'Drop the reins, Alun,' I said as I let go of Lenny's bridle.

The camel raced towards the edge of the creek, with Alun running beside him. I turned to look upstream before following them and saw the water rushing towards me. For a moment, I was frozen in place.

Then I heard Maraed screaming at me. 'Run, Seeger! Run!'

Water began to swirl around my legs. It had gone from being damp underfoot, to ankle deep, to now halfway up my legs in a matter of moments and it was tugging at me with surprising strength. I leaned forward and strained to reach safety but I could feel my feet slipping on the now wet and muddy creek bottom, as the churning water pulled at my legs.

Just when I thought I'd be swept away Kieran and Cal ran into the water, grabbed my arms and pulled me to safety.

Asher called out, 'Are you all right, Seeger?'

I nodded. Maraed ran to meet us and threw her arms around my neck as I staggered up the side of the creek. It was awkward walking like that but I didn't mind.

The four of us sat near the edge of the bank. Joffre perched on my shoulder and rubbed his face against my cheek, while I sucked air into my lungs.

Stupid camel, Joffre said. *I could have lost you, pal!*

I'm sorry, Mr Seeger, Lenny said. *I was so scared. I thought I was going to die!*

I know, Lenny, I said. *Everyone is safe now and that's the main thing.*

Are you mad at me?

No, Len.

I am! Joffre said.

We should have helped the young camel, Ajax said. *We'll do better from now on. I promise.*

So you should! Joffre said.

Don't worry about it, I said. *Right now, I just want to catch my breath.*

We all watched the water sweep down the creek. It was just as well we weren't perched right on the edge, as huge boulders and small trees were carried along by the surging tide. If we'd been closer, we would have been in danger of being knocked back into the flooded creek.

Kieran said, 'Hey, Alun, I thought you said it'd be safe to cross here at night.'

Alun walked up to us. 'How was I to know? This creek hasn't seen water for over six years. It must have rained up in the mountains. Of all the nights to get a flash flood, hey? One good thing, those men will have to give it a day or two before the flood subsides and they can follow us.'

I gave myself permission to stay seated on the ground for a bit longer but then I started to shiver as the night air played around my wet legs. Maraed hugged me and kissed me on my cheek. That warmed me up a little. I made sure my breathing was calm and my nerves had settled before hoicking myself upright.

I reached my hand out to Maraed and helped her get to her feet. 'Let's get to the farm, shall we?' I said.

'Good idea,' Asher said. 'I could use a good night's sleep.'

'Me, too,' Tiffany said. 'I'm exhausted.'

Twelve

Mac

I can't remember the exact timing of it all but, a few nights before the raven-friends flew into the valley, the heavens had opened and rain was teeming down. The stone had been singing all day, so I wasn't surprised. I stood in the entrance to my cave and watched the storm-light playing along the ridges. The lake began to fill and then water poured off the edges and began to run down the valley.

My little lake is fed by small streams from higher up in the mountains. It's one of the reasons I came to this place when I was still a young wulver. Most of this world is not so blessed with water.

The torrent brought by the storm ran down into dry riverbeds that had been barren for many turns of the sun. The trees out in the wild got a good soaking. They'd recently dropped some of their branches, conserving what goodness they could get from the ground so that they could live until water returned. I care for the ones that live nearby – some of them are as old or older than me – but I can't give water to all the woods and forests around me. When I was a pup, I used to fret that I wasn't doing my job of caring for the world. I have since learned not to worry about that which I cannot change or fix.

Suddenly, I felt the hairs on my neck rise and my ears began to tingle. It had been a long time since I had felt that way but I knew what it meant. I breathed in and out, slowly and calmly, clearing my mind and preparing myself for what was to come. Then I said, 'Who's there?'

Floating in front of me, about three paces away out in the rain but not getting wet, was Delia! My heart leaped within me.

'Oh, my dear,' I said.

She smiled but didn't answer.

I hadn't thought of her for many, many turns of the sun. She was one of my favourites. Such a clever, inquisitive little girl. Always asking questions. I took her on as my apprentice when she had gained thirteen years and had been initiated into the ways of the wolf.

I taught her as much as I could but, eventually, I had to send her away to the big city. I was limited in what I could show her, up in the hills with only a few villagers to work on. She wept copious tears when I sent her away. I was sad for a while, too, but I soon adjusted to life without her. To be honest, it was a relief to be on my own again. I'm solitary at heart.

For many years she sent me the occasional message about her life in Seddon. The other healers were mean-spirited towards her but she held her own. Her mother had died before Delia gained five years and there were no siblings. Her father had moved up to Wulverstane from Ballyfaol before Delia became my apprentice. He would bring her letters up to my cave, huffing and puffing as he climbed the rocky path. I told him not to, as I knew his heart was weak, but he insisted.

When he died, Delia came back to light his death pyre and we had a warm reunion. She spent several days visiting me in my cave, quizzing me about herbs and poultices, writing it all down to take back with her. She said I knew more than all the healers in the city. When she returned to Seddon, the local store-master took over the task of delivering her letters.

Not long after the men with weapons had come, her messages stopped arriving and dread seized me in its cold talons. I sensed, deep in my heart, that something terrible had happened to Delia. Long before the news reached the valley, I knew without a doubt that she was no longer amongst the living. I wept for the loss of such a bright and good soul in the world.

I didn't know why I would be visited by a vision of little Delia, so many years since I'd last seen or heard from her. The villagers in Wulverstane that were teenagers when she left were now old men and women with silvery hair and wrinkled skin.

Behind … no, *through* Delia's transparent body, I saw the storm-light flash and sizzle. I watched the water streaming away downhill and I felt the rumble of the thunder in the soles of my feet. The sky was angry but the earth was grateful.

It's funny how things balance like that, isn't it? Dark and light, dry and wet, hard and smooth, difficult and easy. Everything in its time. Life with its seasons.

Perhaps Delia wants to be avenged? I thought. Perhaps, at long last, she would reveal to me the cause of her demise?

'What is it, dear girl?' I asked.

She stretched out her hands towards me, then spread her arms wide, smiled and began to fade.

'Is that all?' I asked. 'Why visit me if you have nothing to say?'

Her sweet face was gone in an instant and I was none the wiser. At the time of her disappearance, I'd regretted not doing anything about it. I should have left the safety of my hills and gone to Seddon myself. But then, I couldn't imagine the folk in Seddon responding well to a strange being like myself. It would have to be all hats and scarves and creeping about at night, and I just couldn't do it. I chose to remain in the safety of my little cave and to trust the universe to bring justice to Delia in its own good time. I'd been sure she would understand. At least, I had hoped she would.

I refused to accept any more apprentices but I did my best to care for the folk of Wulverstane and Ballyfaol. I tried to teach them how to be canny; how to protect themselves from brutal men. I grieved at their passing, often sitting outside their bedroom windows, howling until I knew their soul had passed over. They seemed to appreciate the gesture.

Back when those armed men came looking for me, I'd wondered at first if Delia had sent them. But I smelled their fear. I saw their disdain for my villagers. I saw the hardness in their eyes and I could see the bulge of their weapons, hidden under their cloaks. They set my teeth on edge.

The store-master, who brought my letters from Delia, had also noticed their weapons as they passed through Wulverstane. Soon after the men had arrived at my cave there was a small crowd gathered outside, curious about the men's mission and ready to protect me.

The leader of the strangers told a tale of a warrior in Seddon who was suffering from a grievous malady that sounded very similar to Dead Man's Fingers. However, the trees that produce that toxin don't grow near Seddon. I didn't believe him. My friends could sense my distrust.

I said I needed time to think and sent them away. The villagers went to their homes and the strangers pitched their tents down the hill, near the lake. During the night, the wolves encircled their encampment and, when the moon was full, they made swift work of cleansing our valley of the intruders.

The next morning, some of the villagers came up with a cart. They loaded up the strangers' camping equipment and weapons and took them away. I have no idea what they did with it all.

The smell of blood lingered on the air for days afterwards. I kept to my cave, aware of how dangerous I would be if I went anywhere near one of my friends. When blood is spilled like that, the wolf half of my spirit takes over and I am no longer a civilized being.

Twelve

I did not howl at the strangers' passing. I did not grieve. I only wish I had asked them if they had heard of Delia, while I had the chance. Still, if wishes were wings then we'd all be able to fly. Soon after, I felt the cold sense of dread that told me of Delia's passing. Did one event lead to the other?

That question had niggled at me ever since. I didn't like the thought that my distrust caused the loss of my apprentice. That idea was unbearable so I chose to ignore it. However, now and then it resurfaced to nag at me and I had to push it away once more.

That night, in the charged atmosphere of a sudden storm, Delia's spirit visited me and I still didn't understand. I stepped out of my cave into the wind and rain and shouted to the air, 'WHAT DO YOU WANT OF ME?'

Then I saw, in the flash of storm-light, a few steps away from the mouth of my cave and sheltered by an old fallen log, a tiny cluster of Dead Man's Fingers mushrooms. I'd never noticed them before. The hairs on my neck quivered and my heart skipped a beat.

'Why now, after all these years?' I asked.

The thunder rumbled. I pointed my snout at the sky and howled into the wind.

Thirteen

Seeger

It wasn't easy to find the entrance to Pederson's farm. I thanked Sed that Alun was with us. Even though he'd been there before with his father, he still had trouble finding the narrow path that led through the trees to the farm gates. He kept saying, 'It all looks different in the dark.' I'm sure part of the problem was that Lenny was in shock after realising he could have drowned. He trembled uncontrollably and would occasionally stumble.

Eventually we rode our weary camels through the gates and onto Pederson's property. As we followed the pathway up to the farmhouse, we passed by a geese pen. They immediately began calling out, *Intruders! Intruders!*

I tried to reassure them. *We're visitors. We don't mean any harm. Settle down.*

But they just kept shouting, *Intruders! Intruders! INTRUDERS!*

Stupid geese, Joffre said. *You can't reason with them.*

'What a racket,' Asher said. 'Can't you get them to quieten down, Seeger?'

'No chance,' I said. 'They're doing their job as guardians of the property.'

Alun laughed. 'They made the same noise the last time Dad and I came here,' he said, 'and he's been visiting the farm for years.'

Thirteen

Up ahead, the house that had been in darkness now had a light on in one of the front windows. Then a figure came out onto the porch, carrying a lantern. We rode towards the house.

'Pederson,' Alun called out. 'It's me, Alun from Zenda. Stefan's son? I'm with friends. We need your help.'

The figure held the lantern aloft and didn't move. He called out, 'A strange time to be visiting, Alun.'

We could barely hear him over the gabbling of the watch-geese. I tried to talk to them, to get them to be quiet or, at least, to stop shouting but I had no success. We were now close enough to see Pederson's face in the light of the lantern. He wasn't smiling. In his other hand, he held a loaded crossbow.

'That's near enough,' he said, raising the bow and aiming at Asher. I nudged Ajax to move a little closer and he swung the bow towards me. 'I said, that's far enough.'

'We're sorry if we gave you a fright, sir,' I said, 'and we apologise for the lateness of the hour. I'm Seeger, son of Kane the Beast-Master of Seddon.'

He kept the bow trained on me and said, 'Kane's son disappeared.'

'Yes, sir, but I came back. I have a letter for you from my father requesting your help. May I get it from my kitbag and show it to you?'

'Go ahead,' he said but he didn't lower the bow.

Ajax knelt and let me dismount. I went to Errol, retrieved my kit and carried it over to the veranda. 'I'm sorry, sir, but I need the lantern's light to find the letter.'

I began to dig through the bag. Why is it that whatever you need to find is always on the bottom?

'How are the crops coming along?' Alun said. 'We heard you'd planted some different things this year. Are you still growing your fabulous tubers?'

'We're trying a few things,' Pederson said. 'We've had more rain than usual.'

'We know,' Alun said. 'We've just come through Disappointment. Narrowly missed a flash flood.'

'You don't say,' Pederson said.

'Nearly lost my camel,' Alun said.

The geese were still gabbling. *Shut up!* I told them. *Give it a rest ... please? Your master is in no danger.* Mercifully, their noise began to subside.

I found the letter. 'Here it is!' I held it out to Pederson who, of course, couldn't take it because his hands were full.

'Let me hold that for you,' I said, holding out my free hand.

He nodded and passed me the lantern. I gave him the letter and held the light close so that he could read Father's message. He seemed to take forever. At one point he stopped reading and turned to stare at Joffre. Eventually he lowered the piece of paper and nodded at me.

'Oh, wait,' I said. I rummaged around in the bag again. I found the pouch of coins and handed them to Pederson. 'Father said to give you this for your trouble.'

'That's kind of Kane,' he said. 'The geese tell me you're a beast-speaker, too.'

'Yes, sir.'

He nodded. 'Take your camels to the barn and then come into the house.'

He pointed to a big shed that was behind us. Once the camels were settled in for the night, we left them there and walked back to the farmer who was still standing on the veranda. Joffre was perched on my shoulder. Pederson didn't say anything about the raven so I assumed he didn't care whether the bird came into the house or not.

When we reached the veranda Pederson handed the lantern to Cal, who was closest to him, and opened the door. He waved us all in, still clutching his bow. Cal was the last of us to enter, followed by our host who closed the front door behind him.

'Put it there,' he said to Cal, pointing to a small table in the middle of the room. She carefully placed the lantern there and then Asher, Maraed and Tiffany sat on chairs, Alun and Kieran found a place on the floor and Cal and I stayed standing. She was on guard and I was uncomfortable in my wet trousers.

A wavery voice called down the stairs, 'Who's there?'

'Go back to bed, Ma.'

'Very well, dear.'

He looked at us. 'My mother,' he said.

We all nodded. Asher said, 'We do apologise, Pederson, but we need your help.'

'Kane said that. He didn't say you'd arrive in the middle of the night.'

'Let me explain,' Asher said.

He proceeded to tell Pederson about the band of men who'd been following us from Seddon. He even told the farmer about Maraed, and the men's plan to return her to slavery. He told him about our trip so far, our attempt to outrun them on the second day, and then our clandestine departure after the men had gone to sleep. He even described our close encounter with the flash flood. He finished by introducing our host to Tiffany, the Commander's daughter.

As Asher talked, Pederson slowly lowered his bow and, at the end, he leaned it against the wall near the door. He then spoke to Tiffany. 'I'm sorry about your father, lass.'

Tiffany thanked our host. The tension in the room subsided. Several of us yawned. Cal said, 'May I suggest we all get some sleep and we can talk more of this in the morning?'

'Agreed,' Pederson said. 'I've got some beds the ladies can use but there's not enough for all of you.'

'Many thanks to you,' Asher said. 'We'll be perfectly fine in the stable with our camels.' He stood up. 'Goodnight, everyone.' He walked to the door.

Tiffany said, 'But –'

Cal grabbed her arm. 'If you would show us to our beds, please Mr Pederson, we won't bother you again tonight.'

Thirteen

Pederson said, 'The privy is outside at the back of the house. I'll leave the lantern with you. The guest room is first on the left up the stairs. Goodnight.' Without another glance at any of us, he left.

Cal picked up the lantern and said to the other two girls, 'Privy before bed. Come on.' She walked past Asher, who was holding the door open, and Maraed and Tiffany followed her.

Asher said, 'Any of you fellas want to go there? I figure there's the side of the barn if we need to pass water. Right? Good.' He ushered us outside, making sure to close the front door when we'd all passed by.

In the barn, we each found a camel to lean against and before long Asher was snoring. I took my wet trousers off and draped them over a railing and Kieran copied me. It was warm and comfortable in the hay and we both scooped some of it over our bare legs. Ajax's breathing was a steady rhythm that soothed my jangled nerves. Joffre bade me a good night and flew up into the rafters. I could feel myself drifting off. I had a nagging thought that I'd meant to say or do something but I couldn't remember what.

In the morning I woke up with a start and shouted, 'The dragons are coming!'

'Huh? What?' Alun said. 'Wake up, men, the dragons are coming.'

Kieran sat up, rubbing his eyes. 'Wake up, Asher! The dragons are here.'

'No, no,' I said. 'False alarm. I just remembered what I couldn't remember last night. I should have told Pederson that the dragons will be coming here this morning.'

I stood up and brushed the straw off my tunic. I took my trousers off the railing and pulled them on and then slipped my boots on. 'I'd better go warn our host.'

Kieran nodded and poked Asher in the side. He groaned but he didn't wake up.

'I'd better warn the geese as well,' I said. 'Otherwise, they'll go crazy.'

'I'll join you,' Alun said.

Want to come, Joffre? I'd like to introduce you to our host.

Nah, we had a little chat last night.

He can talk with you?

Well, obviously! He says he can talk with most things that have feathers.

'Are you talking to the camels?' Alun said. 'You've got that look on your face.'

We walked down the side of the barn and around the back, to pass water.

'I was talking to the raven,' I said. 'Is the look that obvious?'

Alun nodded. We finished our business and strolled down to the geese pen. Most of them were huddled together in the shade of a black spice tree. One of the ganders waddled over to me.

What do you want? he said.

Good morning. I thought I'd better warn you that some dragons will be arriving this morning.

The geese all stood up and hurried over to the fence while hissing and fluffing their feathers.

Nothing to worry about, I said. *They're friends of mine. I promise you that you are all perfectly safe.*

So you say, the gander said, *but we don't know you.*

My name is Seeger Dragon-friend. My friends and I are going to leave our camels here for a few days. We're going to trust you to look after them. It would be nice if you could trust us.

Trust is earned, mate, the gander said. The others honked their approval.

You say true, I said, *but think on this, I didn't have to warn you about the dragons. If I meant you harm, I would have kept quiet about them. I'm now going to give the same warning to Pederson. I hope you have a nice day.*

As Alun and I walked up to the house, I could hear the geese discussing what I'd said. They decided they would wait and see. I listened to their chatter and laughed.

'What's so funny?' Alun said.

'They're debating what would be the best way to attack a dragon if they needed to.'

'You have to admire their confidence,' Alun said.

Kieran and Asher met us on the veranda and Asher knocked on the door. Cal opened it and whispered, 'We're about to have breakfast. His parents are up now, as well.'

'Why are you whispering?' Asher said.

'I wanted to warn you about his parents. They're both very old and a little bit … odd.'

Kieran laughed. 'The same thing could be said about Ash.'

Asher glared at him. 'Sometimes you go too far, Kieran!' he said.

'Sorry, Ash,' Kieran said. Behind Asher's back, he grinned at me.

We followed Cal down the passageway and into the kitchen, which was a large room that stretched across the back of the house. Maraed and Tiffany were seated at a long table, and directly across from them were two white-haired old people, a man and a woman. Pederson was at the fire, flipping pancakes.

'Good morning,' Asher said. 'Our apologies for being late. We slept longer than we had intended.'

Pederson dipped his head in greeting and went back to cooking breakfast.

'Can we assist you in any way?' Asher said.

Pederson shook his head. 'I'm fine, thanks.'

We shuffled over to the table and sat down. Asher turned his attention to the old couple sitting there. 'Good morning. And you are?'

The old man put his hand up to his ear. 'What?'

'Who are you?' Asher said, louder than before.

'Huh?' the old man said.

'WHO ARE YOU?' Asher shouted.

Thirteen

The old man reeled back in his chair. The old woman said, 'No need to shout young fellow and who the blazes are you?'

Pederson said to Asher, 'They're my parents, Bella and Sam.'

The old woman said, 'They're your parents? Which one is Bella?'

Alun, Kieran and I flicked glances back and forth between us. I didn't know whether to feel sorry for the old couple or to laugh.

'No, Ma,' Pederson said, 'they're my friends.'

The old woman pushed her wiry white hair back from her forehead with a hand that was all bones and wrinkled flesh. 'Well, why didn't they say so? And who are you?'

Pederson put a plate of pancakes on the table. 'I'm your son, Ma.'

Bella nodded. 'That's right. Well done.'

Cal put a couple of pancakes on a plate and handed it to the old lady. Then she did the same for the old man. While she did that, Maraed began to serve out the food for the rest of us. Pederson brought over a jar of honey and some forks and put them next to the pancakes. Tiffany smiled at him, which made him blush.

'I must warn you,' I said to Pederson. 'Some dragons will be arriving here this morning. They're friends of mine, so there's nothing to worry about. I've already told the geese.'

Pederson stood still, in the middle of the room, clutching a jug of water. 'What?' he said.

'WHAT?' Tiffany shouted, as she leapt up from the table.

Cal pulled her back down, saying, 'Shush!'

'Don't shush, me!' Tiffany said, yanking her arm away from Cal.

'I'm sorry, sir,' I said. 'I meant to tell you last night but, what with a lack of sleep and the drama of the flash flood, I just forgot about it.' I turned to Tiffany. 'Sorry.'

Tiffany rolled her eyes.

'You forgot about dragons?' Pederson said.

'I apologise,' I said, 'but you won't have to do anything. They won't be staying long. We'll be flying out on them later.'

He put the jug down and stared at me with his mouth hanging open. I smiled at him and then reached for the honey.

'Dragons!' he said.

'Mind your manners, sonny,' his mother said. 'Who are you calling, dragons?'

The old man said, 'What?'

Cal poured some honey on his pancakes and suddenly Sam was no longer interested in the conversation.

Asher looked at our host, patted the seat next to him and said, 'Sit down, sir, and have some breakfast.' Pederson did as he was asked but he didn't relax. He sat on the edge of his seat, ready to leap up at any moment. 'Don't mind our Seeger,' Asher said. 'He forgets that not everyone is as relaxed about dragons as he is.'

Thirteen

'This was the big secret?' Tiffany said. 'I don't think it's very funny!'

Kieran smacked the back of my head. 'Spoilsport,' he said.

I'd forgotten we were going to surprise Tiffany with the dragons' arrival so we could watch her reaction to them. I said, 'Sorry.'

'I don't know if that's good enough,' Tiffany said. 'Why wouldn't you tell me about them?'

'Give it a rest, Tiff,' Alun said. 'He doesn't have to tell you everything.'

She sniffed and, as far as the table would let her, she turned her back on Alun. 'I don't think I should be the only one who didn't know about the dragons. I thought we were a team.'

'What did you say?' Bella, the old woman said.

'Hey?' Sam said, his hand back up around his ear.

'What's going on?' Bella said.

Cal ignored Tiffany, leaned over and patted the old woman's hand. 'Don't worry, dear. Eat your breakfast.'

'I don't understand,' she said. 'Where's Sam? I want Sam.'

'What?' the old man said.

'He's right there, Ma,' Pederson said, pointing at his father. 'Eat your breakfast.'

She looked at her husband, pursed her lips and frowned, as though she was disappointed with what she saw. She looked down at her plate and cut a piece of pancake off with her fork. She held it up and stared at it. 'What's this?'

'Pancake, Ma.'

'Do I like it?'

'Yes, Ma. Eat.'

She put it into her mouth and chewed. Pederson smiled tentatively at the rest of us, his cheeks a deep red.

'Don't worry,' Asher said. 'We understand.'

'We do?' Tiffany said. 'What do we understand?'

Cal rolled her eyes. Maraed leaned in close and began whispering in Tiffany's ear. I smiled at Pederson and said, 'It might be a good idea to keep your parents indoors this morning. There's no need for them to have any unnecessary surprises.'

He nodded. 'True.' He poured some honey on his pancakes and forked a piece up to his mouth. Before he ate, he said, 'Dragons on my farm. Well I never!'

Fourteen

After breakfast, Pederson and I went to the barn to release the camels into a field that was lying fallow. I checked Bryan's mouth and saw bruising in the corners.

I'm so sorry, mate, I said. *Does it hurt very much?*

It's not too bad, thanks.

I had a look inside his mouth but couldn't see any broken skin. *You were very brave and you saved the lives of Maraed and Tiffany.*

I don't want that girl on my back anymore.

I'll tell Cal and Kieran. He tossed his head. *You'll be able to rest up here for the next few days. Pederson will look after you.*

We remember him. We used to see him around the stables. He spent most of the time with the hens and geese.

'Bryan says the camels remember you from your time at the stables,' I told Pederson.

He patted Bryan's neck. 'I remember all of you, too,' he said. 'Don't worry. I'll look after you while your people are gone.'

Lenny called to the others from the far corner of the field. He was lying on his back, waving his legs about. *Come and have a roll, fellas. The ground is nice and warm.*

I gave Bryan a final pat and then let him join in the fun. Camels love sand-baths and they don't often get to have them when we're travelling.

Pederson showed me around the rest of his farm. His main crop was tubers but he also grew onions and leeks. He'd planted some rows of broad beans in a smaller allotment behind the house, as an experiment, and they were almost ready for harvest.

'I'd better make sure your camels don't find their way back here,' he said. 'There wouldn't be many beans left for me to take to market, let alone to fill my cooking pot.'

I laughed. 'You say true.'

We walked past the small family vegetable patch and over to the hen house. On the way there I said, 'What was it like, leaving Seddon and coming back here to the farm?'

He thought for a while before answering. 'It was hard at first. I loved my work in the stables. It's quiet back here on the farm. I miss the hustle and bustle of people coming and going.'

I nodded.

'You have no idea of the mess that the farm was in when I first came home. The hens were running wild, digging up and eating the few crops that my parents had managed to put in. The geese terrorised anyone who came to visit.'

I laughed. 'I can imagine that.'

'You don't want an angry goose chasing you, that's for sure.' He smiled at me. 'The house was a wreck. There were things all over the floor, stacked up against the walls, and on every piece of furniture. It took me weeks to clean it all up.'

'Why was it so bad?' I asked.

'You've met my parents. They weren't much better back then.'

'Did you have any help?' I asked.

Pederson scratched his head. 'Well … not at first. But one day your father turned up with a few of the beast-speakers and they spent the day sorting out the birds and cleaning up. It made a huge difference.'

'How did Father know you were having so much trouble?'

He smiled at me again. 'He said your mother had a feeling I could use some help. He said he'd learned to trust her instincts.'

We'd reached the hen house, so I leaned against the corner post as I stared at the birds. They ignored me. 'My mother's famous feelings,' I said, and laughed. 'I haven't heard about this. When did it happen?'

Pederson rubbed his chin. 'Let me think.'

He let us into the hen coop, closed the door behind us and stood near their water trough. One of the hens came up to him, so he squatted down and the bird moved in for a hug. It tucked its head on Pederson's shoulder and he absent-mindedly stroked its back.

'I think it was around the time you disappeared,' he said. 'I have a vague memory of hearing about you and the other kids who went missing when I rode into Carrig for supplies, shortly after your father's visit.'

'That was nearly three turns of the sun ago,' I said. 'I'm surprised Father didn't say anything about it.'

'He's a private man,' he said. 'I'd better collect the eggs.'

'You stay there,' I said. 'I'll do it.'

The hen clucked her approval and settled even further into Pederson's embrace. I checked the roost to see if there were any eggs. There were, so I unhooked a bucket that was hanging from the ceiling and began to collect them.

'Where did you disappear to?' Pederson said.

'The Midrashi were stealing children from lots of cities and towns to turn them into child soldiers.'

Pederson put the bird down and stood up. I handed him the bucket of eggs and went to check the hens' feed trough. It needed topping up so I lifted the lid off the closed barrel full of seed that he had near the door of the coop and scooped some grain out.

'Alun was stolen, too. Didn't his father tell you?'

Pederson shook his head. 'I didn't know the lad was missing. Stefan never said a word.'

'Wasn't there a celebration when the children came home?' I asked.

'If there was, it was in Carrig and I didn't hear about it out here on the farm,' Pederson said. He opened the hen-house door and we went out. 'Surely they didn't make the kids fight, though?'

I stopped walking and looked at him. 'You can't imagine the sort of things they were made to do.'

Pederson said, 'You've been through some tough times.'

'The soldiers had the worst of it,' I said. 'Because I could speak to the dragons, I was sent to work in the stables instead but it wasn't easy there, either. The man in charge was a bully. He enjoyed beating me. He was mean to the animals, too. In the end, one of the dragons killed him.'

'Did they?' Pederson said. 'Are these the same dragons who are coming here today?'

'You don't have anything to worry about,' I said. 'My friends are their friends.'

'That's good to know,' he said.

We walked over to the geese's enclosure. Some of them were swimming in their pond. Others were settled under the black spice tree. The gander I spoke to earlier in the morning, waddled over to greet us.

'Good morning, Albert,' Pederson said. 'You've met Seeger, I hear.'

It's nice to be formally introduced, Albert said. *We mustn't forget our manners.*

A pleasure to make your acquaintance, Albert, I said.

Did he speak truth when he said that dragons were coming here? the gander said.

'I believe so,' Pederson said. 'There's nothing to be concerned about. I have Seeger's assurance that the dragons won't harm any of the flock.'

He looked at me and I nodded. 'Thank you for being alert last night,' Pederson said.

We consider it our sacred duty, Albert said. *How are your old ones this morning?*

'No better but no worse,' Pederson said. 'Thank you for asking.'

Albert honked and bobbed his head and then waddled back over to the rest of the flock that were sitting in the shade. We turned to walk back towards the house.

'When do you expect the dragons to arrive?' Pederson said.

'Any time now. In fact, I'm surprised they're not already here. I'll see if I can contact them.'

I sat on the veranda and pictured the Flight in my mind. Then I began to call to them. Pederson took the bucket of eggs inside the house. At first, I could hear the sounds of people moving about and talking inside the farmhouse but, eventually, they began to fade into the background. Finally, I made a breakthrough.

Hatchling! Shadreer said. *Are you well?*

Where are you? I thought you'd be here by now.

We came across a herd of wild griven and satisfied our hunger. Then we thought we would see if we could find the men who were following you.

Any luck?

It took us a while because we were unsure where to begin our search. We flew a grid pattern between the township and the creek. Did you know it is full of water?

There was a flash flood. It nearly swept away one of our camels. I got a little wet, too.

If only we were there to help you!

We made it through without loss of life.

Thanks be for that! Shadreer said. *We found a small group of men encamped not very far from the flooded creek. It is not safe for them to cross the creek yet, but the water is rapidly abating. It might be a different story later in the day.*

Then they're not very far away from us!

It makes no difference. We will be at the farm in a short while.

See you when you get here.

Pederson returned and sat down next to me.

'The dragons will be here soon.' I smiled. 'Wait until you see them. They're amazing.'

Cal and Alun came out of the house, carrying their bows. They said they were going to practice and asked Pederson where it would be safe for them to set up a target. Kieran wandered out, chewing on a piece of toasted bread. He and I followed the archers and Pederson over to a spot behind the barn and then we sat down on the ground, ready to watch. Pederson helped Cal put up a target on the barn's back wall and then he went back to the farmhouse.

I told Kieran that I'd always admired the skill of archery, especially the talents of our old friend, Felix. 'He can kill a fly at thirty paces,' I said.

'So he claims,' Kieran said.

'You don't believe him?'

He shrugged. 'I'd like to see him do it.'

We watched Alun and Cal take it in turns to fire their arrows at the target. Both of them consistently struck the centre, or so close to it that it didn't make much difference.

When they'd finished, Alun said, 'Have you ever been taught how to use a bow?'

'Nah!' Kieran said. 'We don't need to know how. He uses his dragons and I use my wits.'

Alun laughed and walked over to the target to collect the arrows. Cal took her share and headed back to the house. Alun took his gear into the barn and then joined Kieran and I on the farmhouse veranda.

'I hate waiting around,' Alun said.

Kieran nodded. 'I expect Asher's starting to get twitchy, too.'

He had no sooner said that than Asher and the women came out onto the veranda, followed by Pederson.

'How much longer?' Asher said.

'Not long,' I said. Then I felt their nearness and stepped off the veranda so that I could study the sky. 'In fact,' I said, 'I think that's them now.' I pointed up.

The others joined me, off the veranda and a few paces away from the farmhouse. It took a while but eventually we could see the bird-like specks that were heading our way. I called to Ajax, to ask him to keep an eye on Lenny as he'd never seen dragons before.

'They don't look very big,' Tiffany said.

'Don't they?' Alun said.

As the dragons drew closer, Tiffany said, 'Obviously, they're a bit bigger than I first thought. It's because they were so far away.'

'You don't say,' Alun said. 'They might even get bigger.'

She poked her tongue out at him and then stepped forward so that she couldn't see him. Her movement had a ripple effect on the rest of us and we all began to stroll down towards the field of tubers. It seemed the dragons were aiming for that area.

They landed just as we reached the gate that opened onto the paddock. As I hurried forward to greet and hug the dragons, I heard a screeching noise behind me. I turned around and there, racing towards us with surprising speed, wielding a frying pan and looking determined was Bella, closely followed by Sam. For such old people, they were moving fast.

'Out of my way!' Bella shouted. 'Lizards on the farm. Big lizards! I'll get 'em.'

'Stop the blizzards!' Sam shouted.

Pederson groaned. Asher patted his arm, saying, 'Don't be upset, friend.'

Tiffany laughed.

Who are these people? Shadreer said. *Should we be concerned?*

No, I said, *they're old and confused. They're the parents of the man who is looking embarrassed. They're harmless.*

We do not want them to hit us with that weapon.

I'll do what I can to stop them, I said. *Please don't retaliate?*

Very well.

I turned to Pederson. 'Grab your parents and stop them before they reach the dragons. They've made them nervous.'

He stood in his mother's way, with his arms outstretched. She was still yelling threats and waving the frying pan. 'Stop, Ma, please?' he said.

Bella ducked under his arm and kept running towards the dragons. Joffre swooped in calling, *Don't worry dragons. I'll save you.* He fluttered about the old lady's head but she brushed him aside as if he were an annoying insect. Her hand connected, he squawked and flew up onto Shadreer's head. From that vantage point, he proceeded to shout some very rude things at the old woman.

Cal ran up to her, threw her arms around Bella's waist and lifted her up off the ground. She received a clunk on the head for her effort but it did mean the dragons were no longer in any immediate danger. She spun around so that the old lady was facing towards the farmhouse. Bella immediately calmed down.

Old Sam reached his wife's side and leaned over, his hands resting on his knees, wheezing and sucking in air.

Cal asked Maraed to collect the frying pan, which she did. When the old lady couldn't see the dragons, she was calm and amenable.

'We'll take them back to the house,' Cal said.

She guided Bella back towards the gate. Maraed took Sam's hand and led him along behind Cal and the old woman. I heard her saying – to be honest, we all heard her shouting – 'LET'S GO PUT THE KETTLE ON AND HAVE SOMETHING TO DRINK.'

Sam said, 'Yes, please.'

Bella said, 'Who are you? Where are we going?'

Cal replied, 'We're going to have something to drink.'

'Oooh, lovely,' the old woman said.

Pederson ran his hands through his hair, his cheeks bright red. 'I'm so sorry.'

'No need to apologise, friend,' Asher said. 'Come and meet the dragons. You, too, Tiffany.'

Tiffany, who hadn't stopped laughing, suddenly went quiet. She stared at the dragons, biting her bottom lip. 'Not to worry,' she said. 'I'm in no rush.' Joffre flew down and settled on Tiffany's shoulder. He rubbed his head against her cheek.

Alun gave her a little shove. 'Go on, then,' he said. 'You're not scared, are you? I, for one, can't wait.' He strode towards the dragons. 'I remember this one,' he said. He looked at me. 'That's the one that saved you from the arena.'

'You say true,' I said. 'This is Shadreer, the leader of the Flight. The red one is Fitzee.' Asher was already stroking Fitzee's cheek. 'And that one is Hizaree.'

'Greetings,' Alun said. 'Thank you for saving us from Midrash.'

The dragons all lowered their heads in a little bow at Alun's greeting.

'This is Tiffany, the Commander's daughter,' I said, taking hold of Tiffany's hand. She immediately yanked it back. Joffre fluffed his feathers and chirruped to the girl. 'And this,' pointing with my other hand, 'is Pederson, who owns the farm. He's going to look after our camels for us, until we've finished our quest.'

Again, the dragons bowed. Then Fitzee gurgled and nudged Asher, who obligingly began to scratch behind the red dragon's ears.

I said to Alun, 'Hizaree also likes having his ears scratched.'

I didn't have to say anything more. Alun ran up to the young dragon and began to fondle his ears. Hizaree's eyelids lowered to half-closed and he sank down so that it would be easier for Alun to reach.

I turned to Pederson and Tiffany, who were both still standing back a little. 'What do you think? Aren't they magnificent?'

Pederson nodded. Tiffany stared at the dragons for a moment and then said, 'They're all right, I suppose. I was expecting something a little more intimidating.'

Shadreer immediately raised his head and blew a plume of flames. Tiffany went pale.

Joffre said, *Show off!*

Fifteen

Kane

Fee could tell that something was worrying me. 'Something is on your mind, Kane. What is it?' I was determined not to tell her about the predicament that Seeger and the others were in. When our son was taken to Midrash, she fretted so badly that I feared she would completely lose her mind. As it was, she lost a huge amount of weight, refused to leave the house and spent most of her days either god-speaking, crying or sleeping. It was a nightmare. She said that would never happen again but I wasn't so sure.

To keep her from the truth about Asher's mission and the mercenaries following them, I told her that I was concerned about Riva. After all, that was true. However, being Fee, she immediately made me hitch a camel to a cart and take her to Riva and Riff's quarters in the Well-Keepers' compound. Riva, of course, was surprised to see us.

'Hello,' she said, holding the door open. 'What brings you here at this time of night?'

Fee hugged her and then strode past her into the small kitchen. 'I've been concerned about you,' she said, 'being here while Riff is away.' She turned and smiled at Riva. 'It's your first time living on your own, isn't it?'

Riva nodded. That had never occurred to me! Good old Fee. She had a way of seeing through to the heart of a problem.

'I apologise, my dear,' Fee said. 'I should have thought of this sooner. How about you pack up some of your things and come back with us? You can stay in your old room until Riff comes home.'

Riva said, 'Are you sure I won't be in the way?'

'Don't be ridiculous!' Fee said. She looked at me. 'Tell her, Kane.'

'We'd love to have you,' I said and smiled at her.

She thought for a few moments and then said, 'Thank you. That would be wonderful. I won't take long to pack a few things.'

'I'll help you,' Fee said, heading towards the bedroom. 'Come along.'

The two women went into the bedroom. I was left in the kitchen. I pulled out a chair and sat at the table, presuming I could be there for a while. Women who are choosing clothing seem to enter a different time zone.

On the ride home, Fee sat with Riva in the back of the cart and they chatted about her work in the stables. I wasn't surprised to hear her tell Fee that her favourite animals were the grivens. She'd been able to communicate with them for nearly two turns of the sun by then and she'd always thought she'd only ever be able to speak with camels.

Then Riva told Fee that lately she'd found it difficult to cope with the smell of the animals' dung. She'd never been bothered before.

Fee said, 'Is that so? Hmm. That's interesting.'

Fifteen

I could almost hear the cogs whirring in Fee's brain, so I made a mental note to talk to her about it later.

The next morning, I told Riva I'd see her at the stables later on and then I rode up to the Citadel. I was shown straight into the Commander's office. He wasn't alone. A man I'd never seen before was hunched over the Commander's hands and, from what I could see, was smearing an ointment into his skin.

'Good morning, Kane,' the Commander said. 'This is Sarosh, my healer.' I smiled at him. 'Kane is our Beast-Master,' the Commander explained.

The fellow looked up from his work, his eyes black and piercing. He nodded at me and then finished what he was doing. Once he was done he stood up, screwed the lid back onto the jar of ointment and pulled his gloves off, throwing them into his bag.

The Commander reached for his gloves and as he did so, I noticed that the colour was now beginning to creep past his wrists.

'I will return this evening,' Sarosh said, 'to massage your feet.'

'I'd appreciate that,' the Commander said.

Sarosh collected his things and I hurried to the door to hold it open for him. He mumbled his thanks as he swept out the room. He was obviously a man in a hurry.

'Sit you down, Kane,' the Commander said.

I pulled a chair up to his desk. 'I see the colour is on the move, sir.'

'I'm not surprised,' the Commander said. 'My prayer is that Asher and company won't be too late.'

I nodded and said, 'Every day I ask Sed to protect my son and his friends, and to reward them with success.'

'From your lips to Sed's ears,' the Commander said. He smiled. 'No, I don't want any donkeys. Any other business?'

'Please reconsider, sir.' We laughed. 'Does Sarosh's ointment help at all?'

'It seems to sooth it for a while but it's not a cure.'

We both sat in thoughtful silence for a while. Finally, I broke the stillness with another question. 'How did you meet Sarosh?'

'He came here from Boron, about four lunar cycles ago, with a letter of recommendation from the Boroni School of Healers.'

'Do you trust him more than our own healers?' I asked.

The Commander sighed and picked at his gloves. 'The truth of it is, I don't know who to trust. But I figure that a Boroni will have fewer reasons to assassinate me than a Seddonese.' He shrugged. 'He came highly recommended. What could I do?' He smiled ruefully. 'He seems to know what he's about.'

'I understand,' I said. 'The circumstances have made me suspicious of everyone. I'm sure he's a very fine healer.' I shifted in my chair. 'I don't suppose you've had any news from Asher?'

The Commander shook his head. 'All we can do is put our trust in Sed.'

Fifteen

I stood up and dipped my head in respect. 'I must get to the stables. I'll look in on you tomorrow, sir. Stay well and may Sed keep you.'

'Thank you, Kane. You're a good friend.' The Commander smiled at me, tugging on his gloves and pulling his sleeves down a little more.

I made my way down the long corridor and then onto the sweeping staircase. When I was still at the top of the stairs, I saw the Boroni healer walking out the main door. As he turned to the right, and his face was in profile, I thought to myself, *I've seen that face before!* I couldn't for the life of me remember where. It niggled at me all the way to the stables. Then I became enmeshed with the business of the day and I stopped thinking about it.

However, at the dinner table that evening as I was enjoying the meal and relaxing at the end of a busy day, Fee turned to me and said, 'What are you thinking about, Kane?'

I hate it when she asks me that. She's never happy when I answer, nothing.

She sighed. 'It can't be nothing. Your mind can't be empty of thought.' She turned to Riva. 'Is your mind ever empty of thought?'

Riva shook her head.

'Of course not,' Fee said. 'Mine is always thinking. It sings some of my favourite songs, or remembers things that have happened in the past, or it's chewing on a problem. Your face, Kane, tells me you're thinking about something.'

She put her hand on my arm. 'You can tell us. We're family. What are you thinking about?'

My mind was blank. I was enjoying *not* having to think about anything. I looked at her earnest, determined face and thought, *I'm going to have to come up with something or she's going to decide I'm keeping something from her and it'll get complicated.* Then it came to me. 'I saw a fellow today who looked familiar but I couldn't work out where I'd seen him before.'

'I knew it!' Fee said. 'Tell us more. Where'd you meet him? Who is he? Where's he from?'

I flicked a glance at Riva who smiled sympathetically at me. She was no help. 'I saw him up at the Citadel this morning,' I said. 'I went there to ask the Commander to consider purchasing some donkeys.'

'What a great idea,' Riva said. 'They're hardy animals and surprisingly smart.'

'That's what I thought,' I said. 'You know I was wondering whether –'

Fee wagged her finger at me. 'Don't get side-tracked, Kane. Who was the man?'

I'd taken a mouthful of baked fish as soon as Fee interrupted, so I took my time chewing while I pondered how much I could tell Fee without giving anything away.

'He's a healer who is relatively new to Seddon. I think he's a Boroni. He gave the Commander some ointment or something. I only saw him in passing.'

'I see,' Fee said. She pushed her plate away and leaned her arms on the table. 'Something about him must have sparked your interest.'

'It really isn't that important, Fee,' I said. 'Let's not make too much of it.'

'You thought you knew him, even though he's new to Seddon. I think that's important. Why did you think that?'

I thought it over. She was right about one thing: why would I think I knew someone whom I hadn't yet met? I pictured his face with the piercing stare and then the glimpse I got of his face in profile as he left the building. Nothing came to mind.

'I don't know, Fee,' I said. 'It was just as I caught a glimpse of his profile that I had a sudden conviction that I knew him, or that he reminded me of someone. It was fleeting.'

'And yet,' Fee said, 'it was enough to nag at you through the day.' She smiled at Riva. 'I knew he was thinking about something.'

I put my empty plate on top of hers. 'Nothing gets past you.' I stood up. 'If you'll excuse me, ladies, I'm going to finish some paperwork before bedtime.'

'I shall ask Sed to reveal the truth to you even as you sleep,' she said.

'That's nice,' I said. Riva had sagged a little in her chair. 'How are you feeling, dear? You look tired.'

'I'm fine,' she said, straightening up again. 'I'll help you with the dishes, Fee, and then I might take a bath before having an early night.'

Fee stood up. 'Don't be silly, dear. You go ahead and organise your bath. I expect Kane works you too hard at the stables.'

'But –'

'Don't argue, dear,' Fee said. 'Off you go.'

Riva looked as though she was about to do the opposite of what Fee wanted so I left them to it. I went into my work room and shut the door behind me. Sitting at my desk, I shuffled the papers in front of me but I didn't register anything written on them. All I could think was, *Where have I seen that face before?*

Sixteen

Seeger

Shadreer, Fitzee and Hizaree, had a nap in the paddock while we got ready for the trip north. I had a long chat with the camels, explaining why they had to stay behind on the farm. At first they were indignant that they wouldn't be travelling any further with us.

I thought I was going on an adventure, Lenny said. *This isn't fair!*

I'm sorry, I said, *but the rocky terrain would wreck your feet. Pederson will look after you. Think of it as a little holiday.*

What's that? Ajax said.

It's a break from work. You can relax, have dust baths, sleep in and take it easy. It'll be fun.

Are you leaving that girl behind, too? Bryan said.

No, she's coming with me.

Bryan said, *Small blessings, fellas!*

Errol rumbled his approval and the other camels agreed with him.

We'll only be gone for a day or two, I said. *Meanwhile, please keep an eye out for those men who were following us. Keep the farm safe.*

We're on the job, boss, Ajax said. *Be careful with those big lizards. They're a fire hazard, ya know.*

Pederson and Maraed organised some food for us to take on the journey. Kieran and Tiffany refilled all our water canisters. Alun and Cal checked our weapons and I helped Asher sort through Errol's load of baggage. Joffre chatted with the geese.

After a hearty meal together, and the two old people had been settled down for an afternoon sleep, Pederson came out to the field with us to say goodbye. I shook his hand and thanked him for his generosity.

'No need, son,' he said. 'I still haven't repaid your father for all his kindnesses to me. I hope you have a successful mission. The Commander is a good fellow.'

Cal said, 'Keep a watch out for the men who were following us. I would hate for them to hurt you or your dear parents. The creek would have subsided by now, so they'll be on the move.'

'You'd be surprised how many people pass by our farm without ever knowing we're here,' Pederson said. 'I deliberately keep the entrance confusing so that only friends will know where to go. I think we'll be safe. Anyway, if you're flying on the dragons, you shouldn't be gone too long.'

'You say true,' Cal said. 'Even so…'

Pederson smiled. 'You're not the only person who's competent with a crossbow, and my mother is pretty handy with a frying pan.'

We all laughed. We then took it in turns to shake his hand before finding our seats on the dragons. Alun was delighted. The smile on his face would have lit up a darkened room. Tiffany, on the other hand, was terrified but tried to disguise it by acting as though she couldn't care less.

Hizaree gleefully told the other dragons and me, *The little one is so afraid, her paws are sweating. Shall I do some swooping to see if she disgorges her last meal?*

Be kind, Hizaree. She's still a child, I said.

She's my friend, Joffre said, *and it's* hands, *not paws.*

I would not hurt her, Hizaree said. *I just thought it might be fun.*

It would not be fun for the hatchling, Shadreer said.

Besides, Fitzee said, *what if she disgorges her meal all over your back? You would not think that was fun.*

You say true. Hizaree sighed. *I will have to think of something else.*

We made a circle over the farm as the dragons gained height. I could see Disappointment Creek in the distance. There was no sign of the raging torrent we'd experienced the night before. There were a few small pools of water here and there but most of it was mud and stones. Looking at the creek the day after, I wouldn't have believed the flood had happened if I hadn't seen the water racing towards me and felt it's pull on my legs.

Then Kieran tapped me on the shoulder and pointed down. Four small figures on camelback were picking their way over the mud. It wouldn't be long before they passed by the entrance to Pederson's farm. I hoped they would miss thc turn-off and continue up the road towards Ballyfaol. Surely they would assume we had continued along the road? They had no knowledge of our plan to leave the camels and fly with the dragons. At least, I hoped they didn't know.

Shadreer swung away to my left, with the others following behind. *We will make sure that those men do not see us,* he said.

We flew over some rough and rocky terrain. There were no farms below us but, looking at the barren land, I wasn't surprised. I could no longer see the track that led to Ballyfaol but Joffre assured me that he could see it and we were heading in the right direction.

The Mac Tire ranges were in the distance. Although the ground below was merely rock and dirt, I could see a green haze on the distant hills and assumed that meant trees.

It wasn't long before Ballyfaol was below us. There wasn't much to see: just a short main street with the usual assortment of buildings, one of which looked like a tavern, and another like a temple. I was surprised to see a place of worship in such a small town and assumed that the locals were particularly religious. However, as we dipped lower, I could see that half the roof was missing and one of the walls was leaning dangerously. It hadn't been used in many years.

Kieran shouted in my ear, 'Do you think it's worth our while going down there? It's looking mighty empty.'

I shrugged. 'It's up to Asher.'

I asked Fitzee to pull up alongside us so I could talk to Ash. When the two dragons were flying next to each other, I called across the gap, 'What say you, Ash? Is it worth going down there?'

He cupped his ear and shouted back, 'What?'

Maraed spoke to him and then he nodded and called back to me, 'I think so.'

Sixteen

Shadreer began to bank to the left and circle lower until he found an abandoned farmstead not far outside the little town. We didn't want whoever lived in Ballyfaol to see the Flight. They'd probably be terrified. Besides which, we didn't want them informing our followers about the dragons.

When we'd landed, Cal gathered us together and said, 'Those men will be riding their camels hard to make up lost ground. Whatever we're here for, we need to be quick about it.' She looked at Asher who was gazing around him. 'Asher?'

'Hmmm? What?'

'We need to be quick,' she said, 'or those men will be upon us.'

He nodded. 'You say true.'

'So, why are we here?' she said.

He stared at the ruined farmhouse. It looked as though a strong gust of wind would probably blow it over. Joffre had gone for a quick flight and was circling over the house.

There's no one here, mate, he said. *Even the mice have given up on it.*

'Delia originally came from a farm in this area,' Asher said. 'Someone might know her. This might even have been her old home.'

Kieran rubbed his forehead. 'Err, Asher … Delia and her father moved to Wulverstane when she was still a child. I doubt we can learn very much about her here.'

Alun nodded vigorously. 'I agree. The town looks as though it's been abandoned for quite some time. Why don't we just fly on to Wulverstane?'

Asher frowned. 'I like to be thorough when I do my research. Seeger and I will walk into town and see if we can find anyone. The rest of you should wait here.' He turned to me. 'Come along, Seeger.'

He began heading towards the road without looking back. I suppose he wanted to get started before the others forced him to forget about Ballyfaol. He was a stubborn old man.

I looked at the others and shrugged. 'We'll try not to be too long,' I said.

Cal wasn't happy about just the two of us going into town on our own but I told her that we would look suspicious if we were accompanied by an armed bodyguard. 'Besides which,' I said, 'the dragons will come to my aid if I need help.'

Kieran said, 'I've seen them do that plenty of times.'

Cal reluctantly agreed and I quickly ran after Asher. I also god-spoke to Sed, to ask him to keep us safe from the slave-hunters. I looked back just as we reached the road and saw that the dragons were already curled up together in the field. Cal and the others were exploring the dilapidated buildings.

I will be listening, hatchling, Shadreer said. *All you have to do is call me.*

Thank you!

I'll keep an eye on things, Joffre said. *You never know when you might need my help.*

Joffre flew off, while Asher and I strode down the road towards the little township. There didn't seem to be anyone in the place. We could hear our own breathing, interspersed with our footsteps. Joffre flew around the town, perching on one building for a while and then fluttering over to another one. He'd send occasional updates. *Nothing … Oooh yum there's a rat ... Can't sense any two-legs* etc. Finally, he alerted us to the fact that an old man had come out onto the veranda of a building halfway along the main street. The man had sat himself down on a "chair that moves".

If I squinted, I could just see the fellow gently rocking back and forth in the distance. I pointed him out to Asher.

'There doesn't seem to be anyone else around, Ash,' I said. 'So, I guess we'll speak with him?'

Asher nodded. 'I'll do the talking.'

As we got closer, I could see the old man had a small crossbow on his lap. 'He's armed, Ash,' I said. 'Be careful.'

Joffre flew overhead. *Do you want me to swoop him?*

Keep a safe distance, Joffre.

Very well but if he gives you trouble I'll put his eye out. That Alun fella has followed you into town. You won't see him. He's very good at hiding.

Keep an eye on him for me.

I was so annoyed that Alun had disregarded our wishes that, if I'd seen him, I'd have torn strips off him and then made him return to the farm. I thought, *Don't tell me I've got a male version of Tiffany on my hands!* As it was, I had no idea where he was hiding and it would look very odd if I suddenly shouted at an invisible man, in the middle of a deserted town. I kept walking down the main street next to Asher and said nothing.

Joffre flew on down the street and landed on the roof of a sagging veranda. We stopped in front of the old man. His skin looked as though it needed a good ironing. His eyes were a faded watery blue but they were alert and wary.

'Greetings, friend,' Asher said.

'Afternoon,' the old man said. His right hand tightened on his bow, which was loaded and ready to fire. Although it was smaller than a regular crossbow, I guessed it could still do considerable damage.

'I'm wondering if you might recall an old friend of mine,' Asher said. The old fellow shrugged. 'Delia? I remember her saying that she came from here.'

The old man shook his head. 'Don't know her.'

Asher persisted. 'It would have been a long time ago. I was a young man when I knew her and she was already a good age.' The old fellow shook his head again. 'I think her family had a farm a little way out of town. When her mother died, her father took her up to Wulverstane.'

The man paused. 'Wait. Delia? That was a long time ago. She left here when she was still just a kid.'

'That's right,' Asher said.

The old man's hand tightened on his bow again. 'Why are you really here?'

'Delia was a good woman,' Asher said. 'I'm going to write a memoir about her and I was hoping I could learn a few details about her childhood to include in my writings.'

Sixteen

The old man leaned to the side and spat a gob of something disgusting onto the ground. 'Aren't you a nosy beggar?' he said.

Asher shifted his weight from one foot to another. 'I was just hoping I could learn a bit more about someone I cared about in my youth. If you don't have anything you can tell me, I won't bother you any longer.' He looked around at the empty street with the seemingly unoccupied buildings and said, 'Is there anyone else left in town?'

The old man raised his bow. 'Now we're getting down to it.'

Asher frowned. 'I mean, is there anyone else here who might remember Delia?'

The man aimed the bow at Asher's leg. 'I won't kill you but I'm happy to maim you. Then you can drag yourself back out of town. Get going, mister, before you force me to shoot.'

Asher spread out his hands. 'I don't know what I've said or done to make you so hostile but I apologise for disturbing your day. Come along, lad, we won't waste his time anymore.'

Asher turned to head further into the village and I stepped up alongside him. We began to move away but suddenly Asher yelled and sagged against me. There was an arrow sticking through his thigh! I turned to look back at the old man. He was reloading his weapon.

'Why'd ya do that?' I yelled. 'What's wrong with you?'

He raised his weapon. 'Go back the way you came.'

I heard Joffre screeching so, as I helped Asher turn around, I quickly spoke to him. *Get back to the farm. I'll bring Asher.*

I want to poke his eye out!

Please, Joffre? He could shoot you, too.

I could bring the dragons to burn the place down.

Just get yourself to safety.

The bird flew off, mumbling to himself. Then Shadreer spoke. *Hatchling, do you need me?*

I don't think so. Asher's been hurt. We're on our way back.

I put my arm around Asher's waist and we began to move off. He was limping heavily and his breathing was shallow. I wasn't sure whether I should pull the arrow out or leave it in but I decided I should wait until I could get Ash some bandaging. I wondered where Alun was.

'Come on, Ash,' I said. 'Let's get out of here. The old fellow is mad.'

Asher nodded and bravely stumbled on. He leaned heavily on me. It was going to take us a long time, at that rate, to get back to the others. We shuffled on down the street.

We obviously weren't moving fast enough because an arrow went whizzing past my head! The old man must have gone doolally living on his own for too long. I tried to get us moving faster because the crazy old fool might shoot us again. Asher struggled but did his best.

Then I heard a scream come from behind us. We both turned to look. The old man had dropped his bow and was pulling an arrow out of his forearm. Alun walked out of the building opposite and shouted at the old fellow.

'You'll live. Just give the wound a wash and bind it up nice and tight.' The old man said something that I couldn't hear and then Alun shouted, 'Just be grateful I didn't shoot to kill.'

The old man tried to lift his bow again.

'I wouldn't do that,' Alun said, pointing his loaded bow at the fellow. 'Go fix your wound before you bleed to death.'

Once the old man had gone inside the building behind him, Alun put the arrow in his quiver and swung his bow around onto his back. He then ran up the road to us, stopped on the other side of Asher, put his arm around him and said, 'Let's go. He might have friends.'

As we moved on, I said to Ash, 'How are you?'

He groaned. 'I'm a bit woozy, lad. My leg is killing me. At least, the pain in it is. I hope it's not literally killing me. It's an interesting sensation. I've never been wounded before.'

He was a tough old bird but his face was drained of colour and I was worried. I glared at Alun. He probably saved our lives but I was still annoyed with him.

He smiled. 'That felt great,' he said.

'Really?' I asked.

'Let's face it,' he said, 'that man was as crazy as a bag of cats. I was going to let him go but when he shot at you again, I had to do something to make him stop.'

'He missed me!'

'He wasn't going to stop, Seeger.'

'He was an old man.'

Alun nodded. 'You say true but I saved your lives.'

Asher wheezed, 'Thank you.'

I looked at Alun, his chest puffed with pride, and shook my head. His smile slid off his face.

'What?' he said.

'Next time, obey orders.'

I asked Shadreer to meet us on the edge of town, so he could fly us back to the farm. It would have taken Asher a long time to hobble back there and he needed to get his wound attended to.

The others ran to meet us. When Maraed saw the blood streaming down Asher's leg she turned on me. Her hands were on her hips, so I knew I was in trouble.

'What were you thinking?' she said. 'How could you let this happen?'

'There was no way of knowing,' I said. 'It was an old man. How were we to know he had bats in his belfry?'

She clicked her tongue and turned her back on me. Alun and I jumped down off Shadreer's back and then we turned to help Asher down. We settled him on the ground, leaning against Fitzee's huge belly. The red dragon curled his neck so that he could rest his head on Asher's lap. Ash draped his hand between the dragon's ears. Kieran had already got the first aid kit from his bag and was ready to help.

Joffre was perched on Hizaree's head. He made it clear he was cross with me. According to the raven, I should have let him defend us.

Sixteen

All I'm saying is, a good poke in the eye and he wouldn't have shot at you.

I didn't want you to get hurt.

He ruffled his feathers. *I'm not happy with you, Seeger.*

No one is happy with me, I said.

Cal looked at Kieran and said, 'Scissors.' Kieran handed them over. Cal cut up Asher's trouser leg to just past the wound. I knew Ash was in a bad way because he didn't complain.

Cal said. 'I need a roll of bandaging and some wadding to press on the wound to stop the blood flow.'

Kieran dug into the first aid kit. Alun, Tiffany, Maraed and I stepped back out of the way but I made sure I was still close enough to keep a watch on Asher. He was an awful colour. His head was tilted back against Fitzee and his eyes were closed.

'Knife,' Cal said. Kieran handed her his hunting knife and she cut the feathers off the end of the arrow.

'We need to turn him slightly on his side,' Cal said, 'so we can get at both ends of the wound.'

Fitzee lifted his head while Cal and Kieran adjusted Asher's position. The old man groaned deeply when they moved him but he didn't open his eyes.

Fitzee pressed his head up against Asher's chest and said, *I am deeply concerned for my old friend.*

I'm sure Cal knows what she's doing, I said.

You mean, you hope she knows what she's doing, Joffre said.

'Cut the wadding in two,' Cal said. 'Once I've pulled the arrow through, Maraed, you shove that wadding against the wound on top of the leg. Kieran, you do the same on the bottom half and both of you press down hard.'

As Kieran cut the wadding in half, Alun stepped forward. He put his hand on Maraed's shoulder. 'Let me,' he said. 'I've had more practice at this.'

Maraed nodded and moved back next to Tiffany and me.

Tiffany whispered, 'Is the old man going to die?'

I shook my head. 'We won't let him.'

'Ready?' Cal said. The two lads nodded. 'Here we go.'

She grabbed the tip end of the arrow and pulled hard and fast. Asher shrieked as the weapon was dragged through his leg and out the other side. Then his head flopped back. Blood gushed out of the holes in his leg but Kieran and Alun immediately shoved the wadding in place and pressed down on it. It was a good thing the old fellow had such skinny shanks. I hate to think of how difficult it would have been to push that arrow through a fat and muscled thigh.

After Asher's breathing had steadied, Cal untied the roll of bandaging and began to wind it around his leg, leaving the wadding in place. 'This will have to do for now,' she said. 'We need to leave the farm. We don't know when those slave-hunters will get here.'

When Asher had regained his wits, we all climbed back on the dragons. Alun and I helped the old man up onto Fitzee and Cal held him tight.

Sixteen

We flew off towards the hills. Hizaree spotted a small ravine, cutting through the red and black rocks and we made a beeline for it. Cal declared it perfect. Joffre immediately left us and flew back towards the town. He told me he was going for a recky. I had no idea what he was talking about.

Once we'd landed, Maraed pulled out Asher's bedroll and she and Cal made sure he was comfortable. Meanwhile, Tiffany, Alun and I collected scraps of wood to make a fire and Kieran cut vegetables up and put them in the pot.

Joffre returned. *I saw the nasty men on the road into the town,* he said. *I bet the old man shoots at them, too.*

I hope not, I said. *He's been hurt enough already. Those men could kill him.*

I shared the raven's report with the others. Tiffany gasped and grabbed Alun's arm. 'Don't worry,' he said. 'They won't have the first clue where we are.'

Cal said, 'We got out of there just in time.'

While we waited for the fire to get hot enough, Maraed, after giving Joffre a slice of dried goat meat, added the rest to the chopped vegetables and poured in a canister of water. We sat around the fire, keeping warm and watching the flames lick the sides of the cooking pot. Joffre settled in for the night, perched on Fitzee's head.

Cal found a bottle of brandy and gave Asher a swig of it. Then she poured a small amount in four picnic cups and added lots of water in each one before handing them around to us. Tiffany, much to her disgust, was given straight water. Cal drank straight from the bottle. I hated mine but didn't want to admit it in front of the others.

When the stew was ready, and we'd all received our serve, Cal helped Asher sit up and gently fed him one spoonful at a time. He didn't eat very much but at least he had some food in his belly. He was still a dreadful colour. Maraed told me that Ash had received a huge shock to his system and it would take him a while to recover.

'Don't fuss,' Asher said. 'Come morning, I'll be as right as rain. Kieran, help me get up so I can pass water before I sleep.'

Kieran and I both helped him stand up and then we walked either side of him, as he limped behind some of the rocks. I could hear Hizaree and Fitzee having a quiet chuckle at our strange behaviour. Shadreer said he'd become used to the weird ways of the two legs.

We helped Asher back to his bedroll and then unrolled our own. Cal said we needed to make an early start in the morning. Hopefully, in Wulverstane there was still a healer who could help Asher.

'I'll be a new man in the morning,' Asher said.

Tiffany, of course, threw a tantrum because we wouldn't be staying in a hotel. Cal told her to grow up and to stop being a whiny little madam. No one felt like chatting. The atmosphere was chilly and it wasn't all because the sun had sunk below the hills. When Tiffany was upset, she generated her own force field of ice and gloom. Despite the tension and the hard ground, the brandy did its job and I didn't take long to fall asleep.

When we awoke the next morning, Asher was hot and sweaty. Cal made us break camp and mount the dragons as quickly as we could. We lifted the old man up onto Fitzee's back and Cal sat with her arms around him, holding him tight. Asher's head flopped back against Cal's right shoulder. The rest of us then climbed up onto the dragons and we set off towards the Mac Tire Ranges.

Seventeen

Kane

On Seventh Day, Riva came with Fee and me to the temple. She said that she would have liked to attend more often but Riff wasn't interested. We'd already noticed that, and it was the cause of some heartache to Fee, but we acted as if we were surprised to hear it.

Jonathen was in fine form. I even enjoyed his preaching and I usually tend to drift off during that part of the proceedings. The choir were magnificent. The new director, Corban, had done a good job with them. He was a fine figure of a man: tall, with sandy-coloured hair and a beaming smile. I could see why Seeger was a little jealous that Maraed was having singing lessons with the fellow.

Towards the end of the service, I saw Talia the Well-Keeper sitting in the back row of her section. I was surprised to see her there. She wasn't known for her regular attendance at worship. I wondered if she was changing her ways.

Riva wasn't feeling well and Fee was keen to get her home. I had intended to see if I could catch up with Talia, while the girls were involved in the usual talkfest that Fee gets into every Seventh Day. However, Riva wasn't a good colour and it wasn't that important to speak to the Well-Keeper. She'd probably just give me a mouthful of cheek for my trouble.

However, the next morning at the stables as I was working on the accounts, I was surprised to see her wander in.

'Morning, Kane,' she said.

'Good morning, Talia,' I said. 'What brings you here today?'

She fiddled with the pens on my desk. 'Oh, nothing special,' she said. 'Have you heard anything from Riff and the others?'

I shook my head. 'I'd have thought you'd be the first to hear from your well-keepers. When do you expect to see them back?'

'Not for a few days.'

She lined up the pens but they weren't in any proper order. Everyone knows they should go from shortest to longest! She used no recognisable pattern and she kept picking them up and putting them down again. I could feel the irritation rising in my chest.

'Any news on Asher and company and their great search for the elusive wolf?' she said. I shook my head. 'As if that's really why they're out there.'

I sighed. 'What else would they be doing?'

'I expect Seeger is taking good care of the Commander's daughter.' She winked. 'She's a pretty thing.'

'I'm sure Seeger and the others are making Tiffany feel welcome. They work well as a team.'

'He'd do himself a bit of good if he could charm the girl. I'm sure it'd give him some status in the Citadel.' She wiggled her eyebrows.

Why does her mind always drop into the gutter? 'Seeger isn't interested in status and he's too much of a gentleman to do anything that isn't proper.'

She smiled. 'It's lovely to see a father so supportive of his son. Do you go to temple regularly?' she said, changing the subject so fast I nearly had whiplash.

I took the pencils from her and put them in my desk drawer. 'Please sit you down, Talia,' I said, stretching my hand out towards the chair opposite me.

She didn't sit. Instead, she wandered about the room idly picking things up and then putting them down somewhere else.

'We go practically every Seventh Day to temple,' I said. 'Fee is very devout. What brought you there, yesterday? You don't usually attend the services.'

'I've been taking my mother for the past two lunar cycles. She's getting old and she thinks her days here are numbered, so she wants to be on good terms with Sed before she dies.'

I said, 'I hadn't noticed you before yesterday.'

'We've sat down near the front so you wouldn't have seen me. Yesterday, we were running late, which meant we had to make do with the back row.'

'It's good of you to take her.'

She shrugged. 'She's my mother so what am I going to do?' she said. 'What do you think of the choir?'

'I loved what they did with the hymn of the birds yesterday,' I said.

She walked over to the window and stood staring outside. 'That new choir director seems to know what he's doing. What's his name? Cobalt? Corner?'

'Corban.'

'Yes, that's him. Good looking fellow, too. Don't you think?'

I shrugged. 'I suppose so. I don't pay much attention to that sort of thing.'

'He's about my age, isn't he?'

I shrugged. 'I don't think you've ever told me your age, so …'

She swept her fingers along the windowsill and made a clicking noise with her tongue. Then, she wiped her hand down the length of her tunic. 'Do you happen to know if Corban is married or romantically involved with anyone?'

I gave up trying to sort out the accounts and pushed the papers to one side. 'You're asking the wrong person, Talia. Fee is far more observant about that sort of thing.' I rubbed my chin and thought for a moment. 'I'm fairly certain that he isn't married. Why do you ask?'

'Oh no particular reason,' Talia said. 'Just being nosy.' She studied her fingernails. 'I heard he's been seeing that girl your son is so fond of.'

I felt a shiver run down my spine. I sat up straighter in my chair and studied Talia's face. 'What are you implying, Talia?'

'Settle down, Kane. I'm just repeating some gossip I've heard floating around the barracks.'

'Who was spreading this gossip?'

'Perhaps Randi, Boyd's brother, suggested something.' She stared out the window as if she were looking for the rumour monger out in the yard. 'I'm not sure.'

'You don't want to believe everything Randi says about my family. It won't be the first time he's got the wrong slant on things.'

She turned away from the window. 'But Maraed *is* seeing Corban on a regular basis.'

'She's having singing lessons with him,' I said. 'She's a very talented young lady.'

'Really?' she said. 'I hadn't heard that. She's done well for herself, hasn't she?'

'What do you mean by that?'

She wandered back to my desk and sat down. 'Well, she's just a little slave girl and there she is mixing with the likes of Corban and the temple crowd.'

'She's not a little slave girl.'

She smiled. 'Oh no, not now of course, but that's what she was before. Didn't Asher steal her from her owner?'

I frowned. 'Did you get that from Randi, too?' She inclined her head. 'As it happens, she was stolen from her family and Asher and her brother, Kieran, rescued her. There's a difference, Talia.'

She nodded slowly. 'Of course.'

'Jonathen heard her sing,' I continued, 'and offered her the opportunity to be trained by Corban. There is no suggestion of any impropriety on her or Corban's part.'

She sniffed. 'I didn't mean to cast any aspersions on Corban's good name.'

'I should hope not.'

She slowly nodded. 'In any case, Corban is much too old for her. I suppose everything is above board.'

'You say true,' I said. 'Maraed has become an important person in our family. We think very highly of her.'

'That's nice,' Talia said. 'Well done, Maraed.' She stood up. 'I won't keep you from your work, Kane. I was just passing and thought I'd pop in and pass the time of day with you.'

'You're always welcome,' I said, even though I didn't mean it.

She nodded and began to move towards the door. When her hand was on the doorhandle she turned around and grinned. 'I expect I'll see you at the Citadel when you next try to convince the Commander to purchase some of those animals you have your eye on. Enjoy your day.'

She walked out as I answered, 'And good day to you, too.'

As soon as she had gone, I got up and hurriedly put everything back in its proper place. Once my nerves were no longer jangling, I sat back down and re-played Talia's visit in my head. Could she be the one who sent the mercenaries after Seeger and the others, or was she just playing her usual game of watching people squirm? I wasn't sure what to make of it.

Darn Randi and his sense of grievance! You'd have thought that after all this time, and with Boyd now home, he'd have let that go.

I took the pencils out of my drawer and lined them up across the desk in order of their height. That felt much better!

Later, as we shared the evening meal, I told Fee and Riva about the conversation I'd had with Talia. The two of them shared a smile.

'Well, well,' Fee said.

Riva giggled. 'I had no idea!'

Fee raised her eyebrows and they grinned at each other again.

'What?' I asked. 'What aren't you saying that I'm supposed to already know?'

'It's rather obvious, dear,' Fee said, reaching for the bowl of salt.

I put my fork down. 'It's not obvious to me.'

Fee passed the salt to Riva, who sprinkled some on her red fish and roasted tubers. 'Just think about it, dear,' Fee said. 'It'll come to you.'

I frowned and thought about it for a while. Then I shook my head. 'I've got nothing.'

Riva picked up her cup and had a sip of water. She put it down carefully and looked at me. 'Do you truly not know what we're talking about?' I shook my head. 'Talia's got her eye on Corban.'

'What do you mean?' I asked. 'Is she watching him? Why? Surely she doesn't suspect he's a spy!'

The two women laughed. 'Oh Kane,' Fee said. 'For goodness sake! Talia is romantically interested in Corban.'

I stared at the two of them, with my mouth hanging open. They smiled and nodded at me. 'I don't believe it,' I said. 'Not her!'

'And why not?' Fee said. 'She's a healthy, unattached young woman, who's not getting any younger. I'm happy for her. I just hope the feeling is mutual.'

'I doubt he's even met her,' I said.

'Perhaps you could introduce them?' Fee said.

'Oh no you don't. I'm not playing matchmaker.' I picked up my fork and pushed some of the fish around the plate. 'What of her questions about Maraed?'

Riva said, 'She's heard about the singing lessons and she wants to be sure she doesn't have any competition.'

'But Maraed is a lot younger than Corban and she's involved with Seeger!'

Fee smiled. 'Love isn't always rational, dear.'

She and Riva looked at each other and giggled again. It hadn't even occurred to me that Talia was attracted to Corban! I was more worried that she was the one who'd set the mercenaries onto Asher and the group. Talia in love? I'd never thought of her like that. I suppose she had as much right as the next person but she'd never struck me as the romantic sort. She was always making sly suggestions that were inappropriate. Still, that didn't mean she didn't have a tender side … I suppose.

Poor Corban. I wondered if he had any idea of the sort of trouble he was in.

Eighteen

Seeger

The flight seemed to take forever but eventually we could see a valley nestled between the hills. The town of Wulverstane spread out below us. There was a large lake between it and the mountain range.

Fitzee was worried about Asher. *I can feel the heat in his body, Seeger. This is not normal.*

Hopefully, this town has a healer who can help him.

We love the funny old man.

So do we, Fitzee. So do we.

The dragons circled around and landed in a space between the lake and Wulverstane. There was a path leading from the water down into the town. I guessed the townspeople made regular trips to the lake to collect water and, perhaps, to fish.

As we landed, Shadreer said to me, *Someone is watching us from those hills, Seeger.*

Is it the men who were following us?

I do not sense any danger but there is something strange about the watcher.

What?

I cannot tell. We will have a soak in the water and then we will find a safe place to wait in the forest on the hills. We will then concentrate on the place where the watcher is and if we can find out anything more, we will tell you. Be safe in that town. It also feels strange. Call me if you need help. You did not call us at the other place and now Asher is hurt.

So, you blame me as well!

I do not blame you. I was simply stating the facts.

Kieran and I helped lift Asher down off Fitzee's back and placed him in Cal's arms. He was lost to the fever and unable to walk. If we'd been further out in the hills, away from the town, we'd have tried to make a stretcher for the old man. However, we could already see the outskirts of Wulverstane from the top of the path so it wasn't far to go.

I shared Shadreer's warning about Wulverstane with the group. Maraed moved up next to me and took my hand. I squeezed it with gratitude. Tiffany bombarded me with questions.

'How do you know what the dragons think? What's wrong with the town? Should we be going in there? Are we in danger? Have those slave-hunters got here before us?'

She would have gone on with more if Cal hadn't told her to be quiet. I repeated that all Shadreer said was that there was something about the town that made him uneasy, so we should be alert.

Joffre, who was still perched on my shoulder, said, *I don't know why they're worried. I'm here.*

Alun said, 'They could be feeling a little nervous after our visit to Ballyfaol.'

I shook my head. 'Shadreer just said that it felt strange. That could mean anything.'

Kieran backed me up. 'Maybe there are some wolves nearby and their scent is messing with their perception. Or maybe some of the townspeople have wolves for pets. Delia had one.'

I'd forgotten about that. 'That could well be it,' I said. 'The important thing is to find a healer for Asher.'

Joffre squawked his agreement.

'Quite right,' Cal said. 'Stay alert but remain polite.' She looked at Tiffany. 'Especially you.'

Tiffany's face turned red. 'I don't know what you're talking about. I'm always polite.' She sniffed and glared at Cal. Alun looked at me and grinned.

'Anyway,' Tiffany said, 'I don't know why we're worrying about what a bunch of dragons think. When we needed their help, they didn't do anything.'

'To be fair,' Alun said, 'Seeger didn't ask them to help.'

I sighed. Joffre rubbed his head against my cheek. Maraed squeezed my hand. Before I had a chance to defend myself she said, 'He didn't need to ask. You dealt with the shooter in Ballyfaol and the dragons flew us to safety. There's nothing to complain about.'

'They'll come when we really need them,' Kieran said. 'I've seen them in action. You haven't.'

Tiffany sniffed again and this time she glared at me. 'Just don't hesitate next time. My Pa's life could depend on it.'

'I didn't hesitate,' I said through gritted teeth. 'I assessed the situation and I made a judgment call. I know what's at stake.'

'Let it go,' Maraed said to Tiffany. 'Your attitude isn't helping.'

Tiffany gasped and opened her mouth to say something else but Cal interrupted her. 'That's enough, Tiffany. Shut it!'

Eighteen

The girl's mouth puckered up as she squeezed her lips together. She gave me her version of the death-stare and then moved up next to Cal. I decided not to mention the watcher in the hills. I didn't need the extra drama. Joffre ruffled his feathers but then settled down again. We continued walking towards Wulverstane.

As we entered the town, people stopped still in the street and stared. No one gave a greeting or spoke to us, they just watched as we walked by. Once we'd passed them, we could hear whispering behind us and then the soft footsteps of people following us. It was all rather unnerving.

Just tell me when, Joffre said, *and I'll sort these people out.*

They're just curious, I said. *I don't expect they get many visitors up here.*

Shadreer is correct, the raven said. *There's something a bit odd about these people.*

We moved further into the town, scanning the buildings for any sign of a healing centre but without any success. When we reached the General Store, there were a couple of benches outside it on the veranda, so Cal headed over to them. We all sat down, Asher still cradled in Cal's arms, and we stared at the crowd who were assembled in front of us. After a brief awkward silence, Asher moaned. That prompted Cal to action.

'Good citizens of Wulverstane,' she said, 'as you can see, our companion is ill and urgently needs the services of a healer. Will you help us?'

The people murmured softly amongst themselves but no one spoke to us. Some of them elbowed each other and pointed at Joffre. Alun reached up to swing his bow around to the front but I stopped him.

'Not yet,' I whispered. 'Stay alert but keep calm.' He nodded.

Someone came out of the store. He was tall, with a round belly and a long, grey-flecked beard. He turned towards Cal and Asher and studied the sick old man for a while. I swear, he even sniffed him! Finally, he spoke.

'I'm Tarryn, the storekeeper. What happened to your friend?'

Cal answered. 'An old man in Ballyfaol shot him.'

Tarryn stroked his beard and studied Cal for a bit. Then he said, 'Why?'

'Seeger?' Cal said.

I stood up, with Joffre firmly attached to my shoulder. The crowd shuffled and moved a little closer. I pointed to Ash.

'Asher there, and I, had gone into town to see if anyone remembered an old friend from the days of Asher's youth. She had originally come from Ballyfaol. She also moved up here with her father when she was a young girl. Her name was Delia.'

The crowd murmured and whispered to each other.

'The old man seemed to resent us asking any questions, even though we explained that Asher was an old friend of

Delia and was researching her life, so he could eventually write it down. He's the Record-Keeper of Seddon.'

Tarryn nodded, his eyebrows raised.

'We meant no disrespect. When the old man refused to answer us and told us to leave, we did so. However, he shot Asher in the leg as we were moving away. We took out the arrow and bandaged his leg but now he has a fever. We're very worried about him. Please, can you help?'

Tarryn moved a little closer toward me. 'What's with the bird?'

I reached up and patted Joffre. 'He's my friend.'

Tarryn stroked his beard again. 'How did you get here?'

I hesitated. What should I tell him? I looked at Cal who gave me a little nod.

'We flew here on some dragons.' There was a gasp from the crowd and then some began to laugh. 'If you don't believe me then I will call them here.'

Tarryn grinned. 'You do that.'

Shadreer, I called. *Fitzee. Hizaree. Please circle over the town a few times, to let the people see you. Stay high enough to keep yourselves safe.*

We are on our way, Shadreer said.

'They're coming,' I said.

'I'm sure they are,' Tarryn said.

Tiffany stood up. 'For goodness sake, we're wasting time here. Asher needs help NOW!'

Cal glared at the girl and shook her head.

'They won't take long,' I said. 'In fact, here they come now.'

I pointed up. The dragons were swooping in from the direction of the lake. They soared and dipped over the street where the crowd was gathered.

'Go on,' I said. 'Look up.'

The people gazed up at the sight of three magnificent dragons circling high above their town. An old woman near us sagged to the street in a faint. Maraed hurried over to help her but the lady's friends waved her away. One of them even bared her teeth and growled! Maraed raised her hands in surrender and sat back down on the bench.

I thanked The Flight and told them they could return to their roosting place. I said to the storekeeper, 'Well?'

Tiffany folded her arms across her chest and glared at Tarryn. 'Well?' she said.

Joffre squawked, *Well?*

Tarryn called to another man in the crowd. He came up to the veranda and stood next to the storekeeper. Tarryn said to Cal, 'We'll take him through to the back room. There's a cot in there, so he can lie down.'

The other man held the door open and Tarryn went in, followed by Cal carrying Asher. The rest of us shuffled along behind, nodding and murmuring a greeting to the man at the door as we edged past him.

When we got inside, Kieran whispered to me, 'He was sniffing us, Seeger. Sniffing! What the blazes is that all about?'

I shrugged and whispered back, 'Shadreer did say the town was a little strange.'

'He got that right,' Kieran said.

Nineteen

The back room was quite cosy. There was the cot alongside one wall, a carpet on the floor, a lamp, some shelving, a couple of chairs and a small kitchen area. However, with all of us in there, I would have had to go outside to change my mind.

'This isn't going to work,' I said. 'There's not enough room.'

Joffre flew off my shoulder and perched up on a shelf that was above the cot. From there he kept a watch on both Asher and the strangers who were in the room with us.

Cal had laid Asher down on the bed and was untying his sandals. She said she'd slide the old man's trousers down, so that Tarryn and the other man could see the wound. We couldn't just cut the pants off, like we did before, as these were the only ones that Asher had left in his kit.

Kieran said, 'I think that Cal and Seeger should stay with Asher and the rest of us can wait outside.'

Cal nodded. 'Good idea. Leave the first aid kit with me and wait out on the veranda. I'm sure the crowd have dispersed by now.'

'Can't we have a look around the store?' Tiffany said.

Maraed put her arm around the girl's shoulders. 'Now's not really the time for shopping. Perhaps once Asher is taken care of, we can have a look then.'

That seemed to mollify the young lady. Alun led the way and the rest followed him, squeezing past Tarryn and his friend who stood in the doorway.

Nineteen

I helped Cal remove Asher's trousers and then I sat on the chair at the end of the bed, out of the way. Cal stayed next to Asher's head. Tarryn and his friend moved up for a closer look. The un-named man pointed to the red streaks that were creeping out from the edges of the bandage. He shook his head and then whispered something to Tarryn.

They don't like what they see, Joffre said.

'I have a small bottle of iodine in the store,' Tarryn said.

'We'd be happy to pay you for it,' Cal said.

'I'll get it,' the other man said and he hurried out of the room. A few moments later he returned with a small brown bottle. Tarryn said the price, Cal took the money out of the small purse she had attached to her belt and gave it to the storekeeper. The other man then handed the iodine to Cal.

'Remove the bandage please Seeger,' Cal said. She went to the sink and washed her hands.

I got up off the chair and went to Asher's leg. As I began to unravel the bandage, I could see that the wound had bled quite a bit. There was a lot of red seeping through the cloth. I could also feel the heat in his leg.

Poor Asher, Joffre said. *Are you going to cut his leg off?*

'I don't like the look of this,' I said. I rolled up the soiled bandage and put it on the chair.

Cal poured some of the iodine on a wad of cloth and smeared it over both wound sites. 'I'm hoping this will deal with the infection,' she said. 'I don't know what we'll do if it doesn't. Strap his leg up with the remaining bandage.'

I god-spoke to Sed while I was washing my hands before tending to Asher. *Please don't let him die.*

Cal turned to the men who were still staring at the patient. 'Our friend needs to rest. Can you recommend anywhere we can stay while he recovers?'

While the two men had a whispered discussion, I went to the small kitchen and put the soiled bandage in the sink to soak for a while. There were four cups hanging from hooks on the wall. I carried a cup of water back to the old man and held his head while he took a few sips.

Cal began to pull his trousers back up and was struggling on her own, so I put the cup down and went to help her. Tarryn's friend picked up the cup and took it back to the kitchen. He then began to wash the soiled bandage.

'You don't have to do that,' I said.

'No trouble,' he said. 'I'm not as bothered as some by the smell of blood.'

'Thank you, sir.'

'Call me, Ralf,' he said.

What did he mean by that stuff about smelling blood? Joffre said.

I have no idea. Do you sense any danger?

He turned his head to the side and stared at the men. *No but there's something a bit odd about those fellas.*

Once Asher had been re-trousered and his sandals were back on, I sat down on the chair again. Joffre fluttered down and perched on my shoulder.

Nineteen

'He's a chatty little thing, that bird,' Tarryn said. He smiled at Joffre. 'We like ravens up here in Wulverstane but I've never seen one so tame before.'

Joffre immediately raised his hackles. 'He's not tame,' I said. 'He's chosen to be with me and he's free to leave at any time.' Joffre settled his feathers back down.

'Good to know,' Tarryn said. 'But the dragons…you've got them well-trained.'

I shook my head. 'I realise it's hard to understand but I don't tame or train any animal. The dragons are my friends.'

Tarryn and Ralf exchanged glances. 'That's very unusual, young man,' the storekeeper said. 'Most people like to dominate their animals.'

'We're not most people,' I said.

One of those fellas is trying to talk to me, Joffre said. *Should I answer him?*

I smiled at Tarryn and Ralf. 'Which one of you is talking to the raven?'

'I am,' Ralf said. 'I hope you don't mind.' He wrung out the bandage and draped it over the back of one of the chairs.

'Not at all, I said. 'He's his own bird.'

Tarryn said, 'I told you we like ravens in this town.'

Joffre rubbed his head on my cheek. *I think I'm going to like it here. Sensible people.*

Cal gave a polite cough. 'Does this town have an inn?'

'I live above the store,' Tarryn said. 'I'd be happy to bunk down in here and you and your crew can stay upstairs.'

'That's too kind of you, sir,' Cal said. 'We don't want to cause you any trouble.'

'We could camp out near the lake,' I said. 'Just as long as Asher is comfortable.'

Ralf shook his head. 'It's not safe to sleep outdoors up here. We like folk to stay inside once it's dark.'

I frowned at Cal and she looked puzzled. 'We've done it plenty of times, sir,' I said. 'We're not worried.'

'I'm sure you're not,' Tarryn said, 'but you've not camped out in these hills before. Trust me. It's not safe. If you all stay here, we can keep an eye on Asher during the night. I'm sure the young ladies would be happier to sleep in a comfortable bed.'

Tiffany's face flashed into my head. I knew how she'd vote.

Cal said, 'What could be so dangerous in these hills that we couldn't handle it?' Tarryn and Ralf looked at each other and then at the floor. 'Is it the wolves we've heard about?'

The men stared at us. 'Are you questioning my advice?' Tarryn said.

Be careful, Joffre said.

I stood up and held out my hands in a peaceful gesture. 'Please, sir. We're tired and very worried about old Asher. We're used to camping under the stars and have never had any trouble before.'

'You live here and know the area,' Cal said. 'We won't question your wisdom. We'd be very grateful to accept your generosity. Thank you.'

The men relaxed. Ralf nodded at me and smiled. 'I'll call the others in and show them the way upstairs,' he said.

Joffre fluttered over and perched on Ralf's shoulder. *Just thought I'd get to know this bloke a bit better.*

You go right ahead.

Tarryn still seemed a bit on edge so I said, 'We didn't mean to be impertinent. We're a bit wary of staying in a town we don't know, especially after what happened back in Ballyfaol.'

He grinned. 'Old Rupert is a grumpy old fool. He should have moved up here with us a long time ago but he prefers his own company.'

Cal smoothed Asher's hair back from his forehead. 'I don't understand why he's so sick. It was a clean wound.'

Tarryn grimaced. 'Not exactly. Rupert has the nasty habit of dipping his arrow heads in cat poo.'

Cal gasped. 'That'd do it,' she said.

Tarryn nodded. 'You two collect your friend and follow me.'

Cal lifted Asher up off the bed and into her arms. She made it look easy, as if he weighed less than a feather.

I picked up the first aid kit and went to collect the still wet bandage. 'Leave it there,' Tarryn said. 'It'll be dry in the morning.'

I did as I was told. We followed the storekeeper into the store and across to the far corner, where there was a staircase. The rest of our group were already making their way up it.

Joffre fluttered down the stairs, swooped over Cal and Asher and perched on my shoulder. *I hope they feed us.*

We'll get something once we've got Asher settled.

At the top of the stairs, we entered a wide passageway with rooms going off it on both sides. At the far end, there was an open room in which I could see the end of a table and some cupboards. That had to be the kitchen.

Tarryn told us that the first two rooms on each side of the passage were bedrooms. We could choose for ourselves who went where. Cal took Asher down to the bedroom nearest the kitchen, on the left. I agreed to sleep in there with the old man. Cal had the room opposite. Kieran and Alun took the other room on the left and Maraed and Tiffany had the one on the right; the nearest one to the stairwell.

The others put their bags into their respective rooms and then went down to the kitchen. Once Cal and I had settled Asher into bed, supervised by Joffre, we joined them. They were seated around a long table and were watching Tarryn stirring something in a huge pot on the stove.

'This is a big place,' Cal said.

'It's the family home,' Tarryn said. 'We've lived here for several generations. I'm one of six children but the only one still living. I never married, so now it echoes a little.'

'I'm sorry to hear that,' Cal said.

He shrugged. 'That's life.' He stirred the pot again. 'I was cooking some lentil soup when you walked into town. It seems to be all right. I'd moved the pot to the side of the oven so that it kept warm. It won't take long to add some extra vegetables and broth. If you're willing to wait until it's heated up, there'll be plenty here for everyone.'

Tiffany, Alun and Kieran perked up. 'That sounds good,' Alun said.

'You don't have to cook for us,' Maraed said. 'We've got provisions.'

Kieran bumped her. 'What she meant to say was, thank you.'

Joffre said, *Ask him if there's an open window I can use and I'll go hunting.*

'Could we open a window and let the raven go foraging for himself?' I asked. 'He's not a fan of soup.'

'Of course,' Tarryn said. 'The room that's between Asher's bedroom and the kitchen is the washroom. You could open the small window that's in there. I'd like it closed once he's back, though.'

'Not a problem,' I said, getting up from the table. 'Let's go, Joffre.'

We found the washroom, which was resplendent with a large bath; a privy surrounded with screens, so that the person in the bath couldn't see the privy-user in action; a cupboard, and a large towel rack. There was only one towel on the rack but I assumed there'd be some more in the cupboard. A bath would be good for Asher and it'd been a while since any of us had had a proper wash.

There was a small window high up on the outside wall, facing the foot end of the bath. I had to stand on tiptoe to push it open. Joffre perched on the windowsill, the night air ruffling his feathers.

You be safe out there, I said.

I'll have a quick recky while I'm at it.

I've been meaning to ask you, what's a recky?

A strategic look around.

Oh. Right. Stay in the town.

You don't believe all that guff about the dangerous hills, do you?

It's their town. They should know. Come back to the kitchen once you've eaten.

He took off and I went back to the others. The soup was beginning to smell amazing!

Cal finished her soup first and took a cupful to Asher. When she came back, she said he was still feverish but he was awake and knew who she was. Maraed and Tiffany shared a smile. Alun tapped the table with his fist and then shoulder bumped Kieran. I wasn't happy that the fever hadn't broken yet, and I could see that Cal felt the same, but at least he was more alert.

As the rest of us were finishing our meal, Joffre flew into the kitchen and landed on my shoulder. I excused myself and went to close the washroom window. I had to balance on tiptoe to reach the darn thing and, even then, I couldn't quite grasp hold of the latch. I should have brought a chair from the kitchen with me. Once again, I found myself wishing I were as tall as Riff and Father.

Nineteen

The raven described his foray into the town to scavenge for food. He'd found a couple of rats in the back of a neighbouring building. They were on their way out of the rubbish bins and, sadly for them, met Joffre while they were poised ready to jump down from the bin's lip. One made it to the ground but the bird soon caught him. He then enjoyed his dinner of two plump rodents, while he listened to the sounds of the night around him.

He told me all this as I stretched and jumped. I had just decided to go fetch a chair when Tarryn came in.

'I thought you might have a bit of bother with the latch,' he said. 'Here, let me.' He reached up and pulled the window shut. 'If you like,' he said, 'I can open it up again at first light and I'll leave the door ajar.' He looked at Joffre. 'Would that be to your liking, young raven?'

Joffre tilted his head and squawked. Tarryn laughed.

'That's kind of you,' I said.

He smiled. 'Has the bird told you what he saw out there?'

'Only that he caught two plump rats and is now full and happy.'

He nodded and walked towards the door. Then he turned around. 'He didn't say anything else?'

I frowned. 'Just the rats. Why?'

He stood and stared at me. I felt a tugging in my mind. I put my hand up to my forehead and sat down on the edge of the bath. He couldn't be trying to mind-speak with me. That could only happen with animals.

He moved forward a couple of steps, still staring intently. For a few seconds I saw the face of a huge animal. I shook my head and then kneaded my forehead again. Joffre rubbed his face on my cheek. I jumped a little because I'd forgotten he was there.

What's the matter? the raven said.

I thought I saw a sand devil. No, a wolf! *That can't be right.*

I looked around the room but couldn't see any other creature in there with us. I looked at Tarryn again, whose face was strained with effort. Once again, I saw the wolf and felt the tugging sensation in my head.

'What's going on?' I asked. I was now feeling slightly dizzy and sick.

Maybe he's one of them, Joffre said.

One of who?

Those wolfish humans who were prowling around the edge of town, Joffre said. *I bet he's one of them.*

Suddenly it felt as though something had ripped apart in my mind. I slid to the floor and cradled my head in my arms. I don't know what happened to Joffre. I tried not to moan out loud but I couldn't help myself. The pain was overwhelming.

Tarryn hurried to me and put his hand on my back. 'Seeger?' he said. 'Are you all right? What have I done?'

I couldn't answer him. I tried to make myself as small as possible and held on to my head so that it wouldn't explode. My gut began to churn and I was worried I'd vomit all that delicious soup onto the washroom floor. I heard Tarryn call for Cal and then she and Maraed were there.

Maraed lay down next to me and wrapped herself around me. I whimpered. I heard Cal say, 'She knows what she's doing.' I heard the door close. Maraed said, 'I've got you.'

I don't know how long we lay like that but eventually the pain subsided and my head was almost back to normal. There was just a dull ache behind my eyes and at the top of my neck. I carefully stretched my legs out and, when nothing terrible happened, I slowly opened my eyes. Joffre was standing in front of my face, staring intently at me.

You all right, pal? he said.

Maraed gently squeezed me and whispered in my ear, 'I'm going to let go now. Do you think you can get up?'

I answered both with, 'Mmm.'

I felt Maraed move away from me. She walked around to where I could see her and stood waiting. I rolled over so that I was in a sitting position and then, as I heaved myself up, she reached down and helped me. Between the two of us, we managed to get myself perched back on the edge of the bath. She sat down next to me. Joffre stayed on the floor, his head tilted, staring up at us both. I gently rubbed the back of my neck.

'What happened, Seeger?' she said. 'The last time I saw you like this you were caught up in the emotions of the dragons. Surely there was nothing like that this time?'

'I…' I cleared my throat and started again. 'I'm not sure. There's something strange about our host.'

Her eyes flashed. 'Did he do this to you?'

I shook my head and winced. I decided not to do that again for a while. 'He didn't do anything to me. At least, nothing I can put my finger on.'

She gasped. 'Did he use magic?'

'Nothing like that,' I said. 'I thought he was trying to mind-speak with me like I do with animals and birds but that can't be right. Besides, I kept seeing the face of a wolf and there's none of them here.' I rubbed my forehead again. 'Maybe there's one nearby?'

There's plenty nearby, Joffre said. *Tarryn is one of them. You should ask him.*

'You can't be both,' I said to the bird.

'Pardon?' Maraed said.

'Joffre is saying that Tarryn is a wolfish human or a human wolf. It's crazy talk.'

She folded her arms across her chest, as Joffre clucked his disappointment with me. 'Since when have you ever not been able to trust what this bird says? Has he ever told an untruth to you?'

'Well…'

'You owe him an apology.'

Joffre tapped my foot with his beak.

'Sorry, bird,' I said. 'But you have to admit, Maraed, that what he's saying sounds crazy.'

She smiled at me and put her arm around my shoulders. 'Seeger, sounding crazy and being crazy are two different things.' Joffre tapped my foot again. 'Besides, our life is full of things that other people would call crazy. You talk with dragons, for goodness sake.'

'You say true.' I smiled at her sweet face and kissed her. 'I'm so glad you're with me.'

She kissed me back and then said, 'Tarryn seemed genuinely concerned for you. I think you should talk with him.'

'You say true,' I said. Joffre landed on my shoulder. 'If nothing else, I need to work out what affected me so that it doesn't happen again. It was awful.'

'I could see that,' she said. She kissed me on the cheek, stood up and reached out her hand. 'Let's go.'

Twenty

Kane

It was the fourth day since Seeger, Asher and the others had left Seddon. It was at least six days since they had first met with the Commander. I had to trust that they were still safe and doing their best to complete their mission but my heart chewed on worry like it was a fine meal.

I took Riva to the stables and then headed on up to the Citadel. The guard on the door to the Commander's private quarters said, 'You must really want those donkeys, Kane!'

I smiled and nodded. 'You say true, Ivor. I know it seems as though I'm nagging the Commander but I think it's important. And we do talk about other things as well.'

'Of course, Beast-Master.' He held the door open for me. 'Go in. He's expecting you.'

Inside, I found the new Boroni healer, Sarosh, smearing ointment up the Commander's blue arms. I didn't say anything and took the opportunity to study Sarosh's face, in the hope that I could solve the mystery of why he seemed so familiar. As he turned side on to me, to put the tubes of ointment back in his bag, I had a sudden thought flash across my mind but it was gone as quickly as it came. I had to trust that one day things would click into place and I'd finally remember but, nevertheless, it was irritating! It was like trying to grasp soap bubbles as they floated past.

Once the procedure was over and the healer was wiping his hands with a cloth, I greeted the men. Sarosh merely nodded at me, shoved the cloth in his bag, picked it up and hurried past me to the door.

The Commander was more polite. 'Greetings, Kane,' he said. 'No, you can't get any donkeys.'

The healer snorted as he left the room. When he'd gone I said, 'I see the colour is progressing.'

The Commander pulled his sleeves down and slumped a little in his chair. 'It's past the elbows now, Kane, and it's nearly up to my knees.'

I walked over and sat down opposite him. 'That ointment isn't doing much good, then.'

He shook his head. 'I don't think so but Sarosh insists on it. He says the infection would move a lot faster without it.'

I studied his face. There were shadows beneath his eyes. 'How are you feeling, sir?'

The Commander shifted in his seat, sitting up a bit straighter. 'I'm tired, Kane. I'm tired all the time. By the way, you never call me by name.'

I thought about what he said, rubbing my chin. I always called him Commander or sir. In fact, I don't think I'd heard anyone call him by name. He had been Commander for so long that I didn't think I could even remember it. It's not as if we were close in our youth.

'Err…' I said.

'You don't remember it, do you?' he said, smiling.

'It's been a long time, sir,' I said. 'Besides, I would never call you by name unless you invite me to do so. It's not right.'

The Commander nodded. 'Well, I'm inviting you now. We've been friends for a very long time. Your son and his friends are trying to save my life. I think it's time we forego some of the formalities, don't you?'

I rubbed my chin. 'The others – Talia, Mika, Arken – won't like it.'

The Commander chuckled. 'You mean, Talia won't like it. The others won't care.' We sat in companionable silence for a while. 'If you prefer, you can use my personal name when we meet in private and you can persist with my title when others are present.'

'Very well … Keaten,' I said. 'Thank you.'

He grinned. 'Well done! I thought you were going to ask me what it was.'

I grinned back at him. 'I nearly did.' The grin slid off my face and I leaned forward. 'I'm concerned for you, sir. The poison is taking its toll. Do you plan to keep working?'

He rubbed his forehead and sighed. 'I don't know what else I can do. If I don't attend my appointments, hiding away here in my home, then rumours will spread like butter on hot bread. My enemies will take advantage of my weakened state.'

I could see his point. It wasn't as though he was an ordinary citizen. He was our leader. The order and peace of Seddon depended on him being strong and in charge.

'I'm sorry, Keaten. If only I could wish it all away.' I reached over and gently patted his gloved hand. 'Tell me how I can help.'

'Just having a true friend that I can confide in, does more for me than you could ever know.'

He turned and looked over at the cupboard up against the far wall. There were portraits of his late wife and his daughter, Tiffany, on the top shelf. His eyes were wet with salt water. He turned back to me.

'Promise me that if I don't make it, you'll take good care of Tiffany?'

'Truly I will,' I said, 'but you're going to make it. I trust in the goodness of Sed and the perseverance of my son.' He nodded slowly and I immediately knew he didn't agree with me. 'Pace yourself, Keaten,' I said. 'Give yourself time to rest up between appointments.'

'As you wish, Kane.'

I thanked Ivor as I left the Commander's private quarters. He grabbed my arm as I began to move away.

'He's not well is he, sir?' the guard said.

I studied the man's face. He seemed trustworthy but one could never tell. 'He's just tired, son.'

'But the healer is here every day.'

'Oh that. Nothing to worry about.' The guard frowned. 'He's got a bit of a rash. The healer is using somc ointment to clear it up.' He still frowned. 'What? You've never had a bad rash before?'

Ivor pursed his lips as he thought. 'Well, yes. Nearly drove me crazy with the itching.'

I nodded. 'I expect it kept you awake at night.'

'I didn't have a healer come every day to fix it.'

'You're not the Commander,' I said. 'It's different for someone in his position.'

'I suppose you're right,' he said. 'I love him, sir, like I love my father. I'd give my life to keep him safe. Promise me that if he ever needs my help, you'll just shout.'

I patted his arm. 'You're a good lad. Thank you.' I started to walk away but then I thought I needed to say one thing more. 'By the way, keep your concerns to yourself, please. We don't want damaging rumours circulating about the Commander. All right?'

'Very good, sir,' he said.

I left the Citadel feeling heartened that Keaten had some good people around him. At least, I hoped they were good people. I was growing heartily sick of being suspicious of everyone. It's not in my nature to question other people's intentions. I just wasn't used to it.

As Karmal and I headed out of the Citadel's gate, we passed Talia going the other way. She called out a greeting as she rode past. I wondered why she was going there, again. I guessed she was up to some sort of political manoeuvring. Then I reprimanded myself for being so quick to judge the woman. After all, she could just as easily be wondering what I was doing up there again.

Why did I let Talia get under my skin? She did a good job in her role as Well-Keeper. In fact, after she'd gained that important position, she made some good innovations to the system that guaranteed our water supply in Seddon. Over time, her keepers had replaced many of the old and rusted leaden pipes with new ceramic ones. The supply was now more reliable and the water came cleaner and fresher, while at the same time she'd provided work for several of the ceramicists in the city. She was the first Well-Keeper in many, many turns of the sun to have sent out search teams to find new water supplies, which were essential considering how much our city had grown.

She was doing a great job, so why did she have an uncanny knack of irritating me.

Twenty-one

Seeger

I held Maraed's hand and, with Joffre perched on my shoulder, we slowly walked to the kitchen. I was still a bit unsteady on my feet. The others were seated around the table. They all stared at me as we walked in. Kieran smiled sympathetically. He'd seen me have a similar problem once before. The others, not having witnessed a previous episode, were frowning with concern.

Kieran said, 'How do you feel now, Seeger?'

'Fine.'

'We heard you moaning,' he said. 'Was it as bad as last time? What set it off?'

I shrugged. Joffre rode the movement like a small fishing boat cresting a wave.

'Last time?' Tiffany said. 'Are you mentally unstable, Seeger?'

Cal gasped as Kieran gave her a shove. 'Have a bit of respect,' he said. 'You've no idea the sorts of things he has to deal with.'

Tiffany sneered at him. 'Perhaps not but we need someone a bit better than a halfwit to lead us.'

'Tiffany!' Cal said. 'That's uncalled for.'

Maraed and I sat down. I could feel her shaking so I squeezed her hand and smiled at her. She was staring at Tiffany. Her free hand was clenched in a fist and she looked as though she wanted to tear the girl limb from limb.

I leaned on her shoulder and whispered, 'She's just a young girl.'

Maraed muttered, 'She's just a young brat. Stop squeezing my hand so tight.'

'Don't be rude,' Cal said, glaring at Tiffany. She turned to me. 'Is there something we should be concerned about?'

So far, I hadn't looked at Tarryn who was busy cleaning up after our meal.

Kieran said, 'Was he lying on the floor, clutching his head?' Cal nodded. 'He's done that before. After we'd rescued Maraed, we met up with some new dragons and the animals began the mating dance. Seeger somehow got overwhelmed by the creatures' emotions. But the dragons are off in the hills so I can't think what would have set him off this time.'

Tiffany's nose scrunched up as though there was a bad smell in the room. 'Eww,' she said. 'That's disgusting.'

Maraed stiffened. She leaned forward and said through clenched teeth. 'Shut your mouth before I shut it for you.'

Tiffany's eyes widened. She began to reply but Cal put her hand on her shoulder and said, 'Enough.'

For a while all we could hear was Tarryn stacking the clean plates. Alun broke the silence. 'What happened this time, Seeger?'

'I'm not sure, Al,' I said. I flicked a glance at Tarryn's back. 'I need to think about it. Don't worry, I'm all right now.'

'Fair enough,' Alun said. 'I'm going to the privy.' He turned to Cal. 'Would you like me to look in on Asher on my way back?'

She said, 'Yes, please.' Alun left the room. Tiffany tapped her nails on the kitchen table.

Kieran stood up. 'I'll make us a hot drink if that's acceptable to you, Tarryn?'

The storekeeper nodded.

'Would you like one as well?' Kieran asked

Once again, the storekeeper nodded as he placed the stacked plates up on a shelf. When he'd put the dishes away, he started putting out mugs on the countertop.

Joffre said, *He knows what happened. When are you going to ask him about it?*

I'm giving him a chance to speak first.

The raven cawed and fluffed his feathers. Tarryn whipped around. 'That's enough from you!' he said.

Everyone turned to stare at him. 'I beg your pardon?' Cal said.

Joffre, I said, *can he talk with you?*

Didn't I tell you? Lots of humans in this town can do it.

'You can speak with the raven?' I said to Tarryn.

He nodded.

'I think we need to talk,' I said. 'Will we do it here, or would you prefer somewhere private?'

Before Tarryn could answer Cal said, 'I don't think this is a good time to be having secrets. You can speak in front of us.'

Twenty-one

Maraed and I looked at each other and then at Cal. Maraed said, 'Really, Cal? No secrets? Perhaps you'd like to tell Tarryn why we're here.'

Tarryn sat in Kieran's empty chair and folded his arms, resting them on his ample belly. 'What a good idea,' he said.

Cal glared at Maraed. 'I was waiting until we could be sure he's trustworthy. We have no idea who these people are or what they're like.'

Kieran came back to the table and handed Maraed and Tarryn a hot drink each. 'I think we've found out they're kind and hospitable, Cal. That's a good start.' He went back to collect two more mugs.

'Tarryn was the only person in the room with Seeger when he took ill,' she said. 'We need to know if he had anything to do with that.'

The storekeeper looked down at his folded arms and shifted in his chair.

'Tarryn,' I said, 'if you tell us what happened in the washroom, then we'll tell you why we've come to Wulverstane. Agreed?'

He looked up and the left half of his mouth curved up into a half-smile. 'What, so I tell you, you tell me and then you'll have to kill me?'

Tiffany exploded. 'For mercy's sake! If we were going to kill you, we'd have got the dragons to do it for us. Stop fiddle-faddling about!'

For once, she made sense! I'd never heard the term 'fiddle-faddling' before – I think she made it up – but we all had a good idea of what she meant. We looked at Tarryn and he slowly nodded. Kieran gave a mug each to Cal and Tiffany.

'It's a bit complicated,' the storekeeper said. 'I was trying to mind-speak with Seeger.'

'I didn't think people could do that,' Cal interrupted.

'As I said,' Tarryn replied, 'it's complicated.'

Joffre said, *I told you.*

My mouth dropped open. Tarryn nodded. I studied his face but he looked perfectly normal. I said, 'The wolf I saw …?'

'Indeed,' he said.

'Wait. What?' Tiffany said. 'There's a wolf in the house?'

I rubbed my head. I heard Maraed sigh and then she said, 'Could you for once not interrupt?'

Tiffany sniffed. 'We were all thinking it.'

Cal put her hand on Tiffany's shoulder. 'I'm sure we'll find out in time.'

I shook my head. 'This is difficult to understand. I need to speak with Shadreer for a moment.'

'Who's he?' Tarryn said.

Maraed leaned across the table. 'He's the head dragon. Seeger can speak to him across quite a distance. Clever, hey?'

Tarryn nodded, his eyebrows disappearing in the flop of his fringe. Joffre left my shoulder and flew across to the storekeeper, and Kieran handed out the rest of the drinks. I focussed on connecting with the Flight.

Shadreer, I called, *are you there?*

I hear you, hatchling, he said.

Is it possible for a man and a wolf to live in the one body?

It is a rare thing, hatchling. I had thought that such a creature no longer existed. The two-legs killed most of them a long time ago.

What are they, Shadreer?

Have you heard the name, werewolf? No? It is a two-legs who can change into a wolf and back again. Most of the time they choose when to shape-shift from one to the other. However, when it is a full moon they have no control and are then at their most dangerous. Have you encountered such a creature?

I think we may be in a place that has many of them. I'm looking at one now.

Is he in human-form or animal?

Human.

Then you should be safe. If he begins to turn, call me and run. The change takes a short while, so you have some time to escape.

Thank you, Shadreer. Sleep well.

Stay safe, my friend.

I looked at Tarryn who was staring intently at me. Joffre tilted his head. I said, 'It's a good thing the moon isn't full.'

'You say true,' he said. 'However, if it were full, I'd have stayed away from the house. I'd not willingly place you in danger.'

He's a good man, Joffre said.

I nodded and smiled at him. 'I believe you, sir.'

Cal thumped the table. 'Stop speaking in riddles, you two!'

I pointed at Tarryn. 'Our friend the storekeeper is a werewolf.'

Cal leaned back and fingered the knife on her belt. Maraed gasped and Kieran said, 'Well I never.'

'You've heard of them?' I asked.

'In the Outer Islands, there are stories shared by the old folk when the village gathers for a dance and a drink or two. I thought they were just legends told to frighten us.'

'What are they?' Tiffany said.

'Shape-shifters,' Maraed said. 'They can be a man or a wolf.'

Of course, the girl shrieked and fluttered her hands in front of her face as if she could simply push the werewolf away. She shoved her chair back and leaped up. 'We're all going to die!'

Joffre squawked and spread his wings, ready to take off.

Cal pulled Tiffany back down onto her seat. 'Calm down. I don't think we have much to worry about.' She looked at Tarryn. 'Are there are more of you in this place?' He nodded. 'That's why you wouldn't allow us to camp near the lake?' Again, he nodded.

Kieran sat down next to Tiffany and slurped some of his drink. She glared at him and he grinned.

'How did this cause Seeger so much pain?' Maraed said.

'I think I know,' I said. 'It's because he tried to mind-speak while he was human but I could also sense the wolf in him. My mind was torn between the two beings that reside in Tarryn's body. If he had spoken to me while he was a wolf, I doubt that there would have been a problem.'

'I didn't want to frighten you,' he said. I nodded. 'Now, please tell me why you're here.'

'Of course,' I said. 'It's because –'

Alun rushed into the room. 'Cal. Seeger. Come quick. It's Asher.'

We all ran to Asher's room. He was trying to climb out of the bed but kept falling back. He was muttering to himself and sweat ran in rivulets down his face.

Cal shouted, 'Kieran, go get a cup of water.' Kieran ran back to the kitchen. 'Maraed and Tiffany, please stand back. Alun, grab the first aid kitbag. Seeger, help me with the old man.'

I ran to Asher and stroked his head. It was as wet as if he'd stuck his head in a barrel of rainwater. 'He's burning up,' I said.

Cal lifted the blanket off the old man and started to pull his trousers down. I moved to help her. 'Maraed,' she said, 'could you and Tiffany soak some cloths and bring them here. We need to cool him down.'

'Very well,' Maraed said. She took Tiffany's arm and led the girl out of the room.

Joffre flew over onto Tarryn's shoulder.

Kieran passed the girls in the doorway, carefully carrying a cup of water. He tried to get Asher to take a few sips but the old man flailed his arms about and nearly knocked the cup flying. Kieran placed it on the window ledge and stood back with Alun and Tarryn.

Cal and I got Asher's trousers down. I folded them neatly and placed them on a chair. She started to unravel the bandaging but Asher began to thrash about again. Without being asked, Alun held the old man down. Kieran kept reassuring Asher that he was in good hands and we were taking care of him.

Cal gasped as she saw the state of his wounds. She turned around and said, 'I don't think the iodine is working.'

'When one of the dragons had a serious infection,' I said, 'I cured it by washing the wound with alcohol and then covering it with honey. Why don't we try that?'

She rolled her eyes. 'Are you trained in the healing arts, Seeger? I thought not. He's a man, not a dragon. He needs a healer.'

The girls came back with the wet cloths and placed them across Asher's forehead and around his neck. There was one left over and Cal used it to wash the old man's wounds.

I turned to Tarryn. 'We've heard there's a skilled healer in this town, or nearby. We came searching for them because Tiffany's father, the Commander of Seddon, is seriously ill and needs their help.'

Tarryn rubbed his chin. 'Who told you there was a healer here?'

I pointed at the red-faced, sweating, gasping man lying helpless on the bed. 'Asher believes that Delia was mentored by a gifted healer,' I said. 'He's hoping that there's someone in the town who was also trained by Delia's teacher. Is he right?'

Tarryn didn't answer. Joffre squawked. When Tarryn didn't respond, the bird poked the man's cheek with his beak.

Joffre! I said. *Don't antagonise him. We want him to help.*

I didn't hurt him, the bird said. *I was just giving him a gentle nudge.*

Tarryn finally spoke. 'There's a healer nearby but he lives up in the hills. It's too late to take your friend there tonight. We can go first thing in the morning.' Cal smiled her thanks. 'I'm afraid it's a bit of a hike.'

'Don't worry,' I said, 'the dragons will fly us there. It won't take long at all.' The man's eyebrows were getting quite a work-out.

'Meanwhile,' Cal said, 'we must make him more comfortable.' She smeared more iodine on Asher's leg. 'Do you have anything that would help him sleep?'

Tarryn grunted and hurried out of the room.

'Girls, you might as well go to bed,' Cal said. 'There's no need for all of us to stay up all night.'

Tiffany began to protest but I interrupted her. 'We'll do it in shifts. Kieran and Alun, why don't you go to bed as well? I'll come wake you when it's your turn.'

All four left the room. We could hear Tiffany arguing with Maraed all the way down the corridor.

Tarryn hurried back in with a small packet in his hand. He tipped the contents into the cup of water and then sat on the edge of the bed near Asher's head. He gently coaxed the old man to drink the concoction down, a sip at a time.

I took the cup from Tarryn and we waited. Eventually we could see Asher's arms and legs become less stiff and finally he began to snore. Tarryn grinned. 'Thank you for not questioning me about the medicine,' he said. 'I would have understood if you were suspicious.'

Cal shook her head. 'If Seeger vouches for you, that's all we need to know. I suggest you get some sleep as well. We'll see you at first light.'

Twenty-two

None of us, except Asher and Tiffany, got a lot of sleep that night. Kieran said that Maraed did a shift on her own, in the early hours, because she couldn't wake Tiffany. Not that it mattered in the end because, whatever the potion was that Tarryn gave the old man, he slept like a log. However, his fever was unabated in the morning so the storekeeper agreed we should still take Asher to see the healer.

I called for the dragons and they met us in a paddock behind the store. Tarryn thought that would be better than in the main street. All three dragons were very concerned for Asher but Fitzee, in particular, was most anxious about the old man.

As we began to climb up onto the dragons' backs, Tarryn called for our attention. 'Excuse me,' he said. 'There's something I need to tell you before we head off.'

We had just handed Asher up to Cal and they were settled comfortably on Fitzee's back. Joffre was hovering over the pair of them, keeping an eye on things. The rest of us had yet to mount up.

'It's about the healer,' Tarryn said. 'He's not like other men.'

That is correct, Shadreer said. *I am glad he is preparing you.*

What do you know, Shadreer?

Tarryn will tell you. I assure you that you do not need to be afraid.

'What do you mean?' Cal said. Joffre landed on her shoulder.

Tarryn scratched behind his ear and screwed up his face. 'I don't really know how to explain it.'

'Just spit it out,' Tiffany said. For someone who had got the most sleep during the night, she was still grumpy as though she'd barely slept a wink.

I went to stand next to Tarryn and put my hand on his back. 'If it helps at all, Shadreer said we need not be afraid.'

'We're not quite sure what he is,' Tarryn said. 'The early settlers in Wulverstane thought he was like us – a werewolf – but that he'd somehow got stuck halfway through the transition.'

Alun interrupted him. 'Old Jeb was right! I owe him an apology.'

Tarryn continued, 'Or, perhaps, he'd learned how to master the change and was superior to us. However, we've come to realise he's something else again. I don't know the name for it and no one has dared to ask him.'

We looked at each other, as if we'd find the answer written across one of our foreheads.

Maraed said, 'What made you think he'd got stuck halfway?'

Tarryn scuffed his toe in the dirt. 'Err … Well …'

'Come on,' Tiffany said. 'Out with it!'

Shadreer suddenly showed me an image of the healer, standing outside a cave. For a moment, I reeled in shock. What kind of a creature was that? 'He has a wolf's head!' I said.

Tarryn's head whipped around. He grabbed my arm. It hurt! 'Are you telling me you've known all along. What kind of a game are you playing?'

I pulled his hand off my arm and rubbed the place where it had been. 'Shadreer has just shown me.'

'What?' the storekeeper said, frowning.

'The dragon has just shown me an image of the healer standing in front of a cave. He's dressed like us but he's far hairier than any man I know.'

'What, even hairier than Old Thomas the butcher?' Maraed said.

I nodded. 'And he had the head of a wolf but he didn't have a tail.'

From up on Fitzee's back, Asher croaked. 'A wulver.'

'Asher?' Cal said. 'You're awake?' The old man's head flopped back and he began to snore again. 'We're wasting valuable time,' she said. 'We'll see for ourselves soon enough.'

'Please keep your weapons sheathed,' Tarryn said. 'He deserves your respect.'

We all agreed, although Alun did so reluctantly. We climbed up onto the dragons. Tarryn sat with me and Alun on Shadreer. I heard the storekeeper gasp as we lifted up off the ground and he hung on to my waist with a grip of iron.

I was keen to meet the person/creature that Shadreer had shown me. I wondered if Asher was correct in calling it a wulver. I knew that the old man was usually right about these things but because of the fever he wasn't in a good state of mind. He might have been trying to say something else and wulver is what came out.

We landed in front of an opening in the cliffs on the far side of the lake. Cal stayed on Fitzee with Asher, while the rest of us climbed down from the dragons' backs. Joffre flew down and landed on me. Then Kieran and Alun took Asher from Cal, until she'd dismounted and could carry him again. We waited in silence. I could hear stealthy movements from inside the cave but couldn't see anything.

Tarryn called out, 'Mac, would you meet with us, please?'

From the depths of the hills a deep voice with a strong, strange accent rumbled out, 'Why should I? I'm busy. Come back tomorrow.'

Maraed gasped. 'That accent! It's like Calder's!'

'Who's Calder?' I asked.

'He's a friend of Corban's from the northern islands,' she said. 'He's been teaching us some of the old songs and the old language. That's how I knew that Mac Tire means wolf. I wonder if the healer knows the song that Calder taught us?'

'Give it a try,' I said. 'We've got nothing to lose.'

Joffre flapped and cawed. *Singing is always good,* he said.

We all looked at Tarryn, who nodded and grunted his approval, so Maraed took a deep breath and began to sing a sweet lilting song in very strange words.

Starka virna vestalie, obadeea, obadeea, Starka virna vestalie, obadeea, monye.

Stala, stoita, stonga raero. Whit saes du, da bunshka baero?

Twenty-two

From somewhere inside the cave the deep voice joined in with Maraed's singing, adding a delightful bass to the tune.

Whit saes du, da bunshka baero? Litra maevi, drenghie.

Saina papa, wara, obadeea, obadeea, saina papa, wara obadeea monye.

A strange figure walked slowly out of the cave and into the sunlight. Tiffany gasped and then said, 'Bleedin' heck' under her breath. I heard her because she was moving back behind me when she said it. Cal cleared her throat and tightened her grip on Asher. Maraed seemed transfixed by the hairy, wolfish man in front of her.

Kieran said, 'Wow.' Alun shook his head. The lad's eyes were wild. I saw his hand move slowly towards his bow and I muttered, 'No, Alun. Steady.' Even though I'd seen the healer's image, it was still a shock meeting him in the flesh. He was taller than I expected and I could see the ripple of muscles under his tunic.

He moved closer to Maraed and bowed deeply. I was so proud of her. She didn't move back; not even one step.

'Greetings, songstress,' he said. 'I haven't heard that old tune for many a hundred turns of the sun. It takes me back to my early days up in the northern islands. How do you know it?'

She bowed in return and said, her voice wobbling at first but gaining strength as she spoke, 'Greetings, healer. I learned the song from a man named Calder, who comes from those same islands. I've been told it's a boating song.'

The huge wolf head nodded and the jaw stretched into what must be the wolfish equivalent of a smile. He showed an extraordinary amount of teeth. 'It is out of place up here in the ranges.' He chuckled.

'What does it mean?' Tiffany said, standing well back. You must give her credit: she never stayed over-awed for long.

The wolf-man turned to her and said, 'It speaks of strong winds coming from the west and causing trouble for the men out on the sea. They wonder if their boat will be strong enough to withstand the damage caused by the weather. They ask the Holy Father to watch over them.'

'Oh,' Tiffany said. 'Nice.'

Then he turned to the Flight and bowed to them as well. 'Greetings, oh ancient ones. It does this old heart good to see you gracing the skies once more.'

The three dragons dipped their heads. Shadreer spoke for all of them and I was shocked to realise that the wolf-man could understand them.

Greetings, wulver, Shadreer said. *We did not know that any of your kind still walked the earth. The lad who is listening intently to our conversation is a dragon-friend. He and the bird can speak with us but none of the others are able.*

How very interesting, Mac said. *What brings you here this fine morning?* He turned and smiled at me. Those fangs!

I answered out loud so that the others would know what we were talking about. 'We're here for two reasons,' I said. 'The first is to see if you can help our friend, Asher, who has been wounded and is now in a bad fever. The second is to ask for your help in another matter, which is even more serious.'

The healer nodded. Joffre fluffed his wings. *I told you that singing helps.*

It most certainly does, servant of Rafnagud, the healer said.

He spoke raven as well! And why could he mind-speak with me? It didn't work for the werewolf. I had so many questions swirling around in my head.

'You'd best bring him inside,' the wulver said. 'Give me a moment to light a lamp or two and then come in. However, I must ask you to leave your weapons outside.'

We will wait here, Shadreer said.

Fitzee said, *Make sure he takes good care of the old man.*

Mac led the way into the cave and, once we could see some light ahead, Cal went first carrying Asher and then the rest of us followed. As we walked into the healer's home, Tarryn whispered to me, 'He must have really liked that song. I've *never* been in here before.'

Once we'd got past the entrance, which was all rocks and lichen, we turned down a short passageway that led into a wide space which was simply but beautifully furnished. It had all the necessities of life: a small table; a wood oven with a pan and other cooking instruments hanging on hooks above it; a small trough; one small cupboard and one enormous one; some chairs and a lamp on a stand. There was an opening in the back corner, which I assumed led to other rooms.

There was a large bed up against the far wall and Cal laid Asher down on it. The rest of us made ourselves comfortable as best we could. Maraed, Tiffany and Tarryn each got a chair and us lads sat on the rug on the ground.

Mac smiled but only with his lips. I think he'd noticed that everyone jumped when he flashed his teeth. 'Let me look at your friend's wound,' he said.

Cal pulled Asher's trousers down and then Mac took over, unravelling the bandage and staring intently at Asher's leg. He turned to Tarryn. 'Is this some of Rupert's work?'

'Unfortunately, you say true,' the storekeeper said.

'Dear oh dear.' The healer nodded. 'I see you tried some Iodine on it.'

He walked over to the big cupboard and opened the double doors. There were six drawers and above them were three deep shelves. He got some scraps of cloth out of the cupboard's top drawer and gave them to Cal. He handed her a bottle and said, 'Wipe the wounds down with this.'

She placed the cloths over the mouth of the bottle and tipped it upside down. 'This is good whiskey,' she said.

'That's right,' the healer said.

She rubbed the wounds with the alcohol-soaked cloths and Asher twitched and shouted. I remembered Azree doing something similar when I treated him in the caverns of Midrash. Thank goodness Asher couldn't breathe fire! Then Mac lifted an enormous jar down from the larger, deeper middle shelf. 'You're lucky I have plenty of this in stock,' he said. 'Smear it on the clean wounds.'

'What is it?' Cal said.

'Honey, of course,' Mac said. 'It's the best thing for this sort of infection.'

Maraed grinned at me. Cal did as she was told, without saying a word. Alun nudged me with his elbow.

'Honey?' Tarryn said, winking at me. 'Fancy that!'

Twenty-three

Kane

I woke up the next morning with a name on my lips that I hadn't said in several turns of the sun: Balash. The General was the leader of the Boroni troops when we attacked Midrash to rescue the stolen children. Sadly, he was killed in a swordfight while leading his men into the city. I hadn't thought of him in a very long time. Why would he be haunting my dreams? I shook it off and went down to breakfast.

It was an uneventful morning at the stables. Riva seemed unwell at first but, as the day progressed, she perked up and by late morning she was back to her old self. Just as we were sharing the midday break and a light meal of bread, cheese and fruit in my office, Talia stopped by. She'd received a messenger bird from Riff with a note saying that he and the others were on their way back to Seddon and would probably arrive within a few days. That news put a smile on Riva's face that could have lit up a whole house.

Riva said to Talia, 'I saw you at the Temple last seventh day. I didn't know you were a regular attender.'

Talia blushed! 'Just lately I've begun taking my elderly mother. It makes her happy. Anyway, things to do. Can't stop and chat.' She hurried out of the office, slamming the door as she went.

Riva grinned at me. 'Did you see that? I must have struck a nerve.' She giggled.

'You're a tease,' I said. 'As you're in such good spirits, would you like to come with me up to the Citadel? I thought you might be willing to do a quick check of the camels and griven up in the Citadel's stables, while I meet with the Commander.'

'Well ...'

'It won't be a long meeting and if you do the check for me, that'll save even more time. Fee will be pleased to have us come home a little earlier for once and it'll be all the sooner that she'll hear the good news about Riff coming home.'

Riva smiled. 'You say true. She'll be so happy. How will Stable-Master Simpson feel about me checking up on him?'

I stood up and scooped the crumbs off my desk into a little box. I intended to sprinkle them outside for the sparrows. 'Don't worry,' I said. 'You'll just be spending some time with the animals. Nothing official. Sometimes we learn more from the casual, unofficial visits than we do from the formal inspections. Just let the animals do the talking.'

She stood up and straightened her tunic. 'Very well. Just give me time to pay a quick visit to the privy.'

I frowned. 'Are you not feeling well?'

She closed her eyes, took a deep breath and then looked at me. 'I'm fine. I just need to pass water.'

'Right you are,' I said. 'I'll get the camels saddled and meet you in the mounting yard.'

The ride up to the Citadel was uneventful. It felt good to feel the afternoon sun warming my face. I told myself I needed to leave the stables more often. I spent far too much time inside my dark, cold office. When I mentioned this thought to Karmal he said, *You don't have enough fun, mate. When's the next lot of camel races? You and me could enter them and see how we do.*

I assume that's a joke, I said.

I left Riva, Karmal and Shirra at the stables and walked down to the palace's front entrance. One of the guards kindly held the door open for me.

'Greetings, Beast-Master,' he said. 'Back again? You're certainly persistent.'

'Greetings, Rory,' I said. 'I don't give up easily.'

He grinned and waved me inside. 'The Commander is in his office. You might have to wait for a while. There's a line-up outside his door.'

I headed towards the staircase. 'I'm married, Rory. I'm used to waiting.' I could hear him chuckling as I went up the stairs.

He was right about the queue. There were seven people standing outside the office door. They all turned to stare at me as I drew near. I recognised a couple of them and nodded a greeting. I said, 'Hello, Ivor' to the guard and then I took my place at the end of the line, preparing myself for a long wait.

I would like to say that I used the time thinking about Riva and her strange illness and god-speaking to Sed on her behalf; or pondering on why I'd woken up thinking of Balash; or going through the stable's accounts, but that would be a lie. I leaned against the wall and thought of nothing at all.

When I finally made it into the Commander's office, I hurried over to get a chair while waving at him saying, 'Don't get up.'

I pulled the chair over to his desk and studied him for a moment. There were dark smudges under his eyes and his mouth drooped downward. His shoulders were slumped.

'You're exhausted, Keaten,' I said. 'Perhaps you should rest. There's no one else waiting out there.'

He rubbed his face with his gloved hands. 'That's a good idea. I'll try to take a few moments once you've gone.'

'Take the rest of the day and go up to your quarters,' I said. 'No one will question it. They'll just assume you're busy elsewhere.'

He shook his head. It wobbled slightly as he made the movement.

'I don't know how you can keep on like this. You've been poisoned, man. You're ill!'

He closed his eyes and took a few deep, slow breaths. 'Perhaps you're right.'

'I know I am!' I said. 'Has Sarosh seen you today?'

He tugged at his gloves. 'He was first in the queue. He seems to think the ointment he smears on me every day is helping but I can't see it.'

I straightened his pile of pens on his desk. 'I can't see any improvement, either. In fact, you seem to be getting worse. Perhaps you should try one of the other healers?' He wearily shook his head again. 'Or at least tell Sarosh you won't be continuing with his treatment.'

He sighed. 'I don't know what to do. I'm too tired and ill to give it much thought.'

I stood up, pushing my chair away from the desk. 'Come along. I'll escort you up to your quarters. If anyone sees us, I'll tell them we've got important things to discuss.' I walked around the desk and helped the Commander get up. 'If you need support, lean on me.'

He sighed and gave a brief nod. 'Very well. Thanks, Kane.'

With Ivor following close behind, I escorted Keaten to his personal quarters. I made sure he was comfortable and then instructed the guard not to let anyone in for the rest of the day. He was worried but I assured him that it was simply because the Commander had some important issues to work through and didn't want any interruptions. I'm not sure he completely believed me but I knew he'd do his duty without question.

Down in the foyer, the crowd that had been there when I'd arrived had dwindled to just a few so I had a chance to admire the tapestry on the main wall. I remembered Seeger commenting on it, the first time I'd taken him there. It was a masterful piece of art depicting life under the sea and was a beautiful reminder that Seddon was a seaport. It would have taken a long time to make the thing – the stitches were so fine – and it was a shame that on most days it went unnoticed.

Twenty-three

As I was standing there, Sarosh came alongside me. 'It's beautiful,' he said. 'Are all those creatures real?' Of course, he was from landlocked Boron so the sea was unfamiliar to him.

'They're all real,' I said. 'What's more, there are many more kinds of creatures than are shown here. These are just a few.'

'I never knew there was such an abundance of life under the water.'

'It's a whole other world,' I said.

He nodded and we continued to study the tapestry for a few moments longer. Then he turned to me. 'You are the Beast-Master, yes? That means you can converse with animals, the same as our Beast-Master can. Can you speak with sea creatures?'

I smiled. 'I would love to talk with the dolphins and the whales but I can't. Like most beast-speakers, I can only converse with some animals.'

He nodded. 'That's a shame.'

'I often wish I had my son's abilities.'

He frowned inquisitively. 'What do you mean?'

'He's a Dragon-Master,' I said. 'That means hc can talk with any living creature. He's still developing his skills but, with every turn of the sun, he becomes more and more adept.'

Sarosh took a step away from me. 'He consorts with dragons?'

'They're his friends,' said a voice from behind us. Riva must have got tired of waiting for me down at the stables.

'Don't I know you?' she said to Sarosh. He shook his head. 'You look familiar.'

Again, he shook his head and picked up his healer's kit that was lying on the floor near his feet. 'We've never met,' he said. 'I've things to do and –'

'No, wait,' Riva said. 'Are you from Boron?' He nodded. 'Are you related to the late General Balash?'

'He was my father.'

As soon as he said it, I could see it. My sub-conscious had been trying to tell me, hence my dreams.

'I can see the family resemblance,' Riva said, 'can't you, Kane?'

I nodded. 'He was a wonderful leader and a very brave man.'

'Thank you,' Sarosh said, tucking his kit under his arm. He turned away. 'I'm sorry but I'm extremely busy. Good day.'

He hurried out through the front door, which Rory held open for him. We soon followed him. Riva didn't care for the tapestry. She said the blue and green made her feel seasick.

Twenty-four

Seeger

After giving Asher a powder mixed with water to drink, the wulver disappeared into the recesses of his cave and eventually re-emerged with some fishing poles. He handed them around saying, 'Go fishing. Bring us back enough for our midday meal.'

When I stood up Mac said, 'Not you.' Cal protested but he held up his hand. 'Your patient is sleeping.' Asher snorted right on cue. 'When he wakes, he'll need to eat. He and the lad are perfectly safe with me.' When she continued to resist, Mac said, 'I'm sure the dragons would deal me a savage blow if any harm came to them.'

I nodded at Cal. 'We'll be fine.'

Joffre, I said, *you should go with them. Find something to eat.*

Call me if you need me.

As they were heading out, Tiffany suddenly confronted the wulver. 'Before I go,' she said, 'could I please ask a favour? May I feel your arm?'

He held out his right arm and Tiffany gently stroked it. The wulver smiled.

'Come along, Tiffany!' Cal called.

'It's soft,' the girl said. 'Almost like cat fur. Thank you.'

'You're welcome,' he said.

She giggled and ran outside to Cal, who was tapping her foot. We watched them as they walked past the dragons and headed towards the narrow pathway that led down to the lake.

I could hear Tiffany telling Cal about Mac's soft fur as they walked. Alun took her fishing pole and carried it for her.

The dragons also went down to the lake. Shadreer said they were going to have a nice soak. I told him not to scare all the fish away.

'That was gracious of you,' I said to Mac.

The wulver shrugged and walked over to a fallen log lying not far from the entrance to his cave. 'At least, unlike so many, she doesn't recoil in fear. Neither do you. Why is that?'

He sat down and patted the space next to him. I quickly complied.

'When I only had thirteen years,' I said, 'I was stolen from my home by a Midrashi agent. He was collecting children to serve in their army. While I was there, I soon discovered that there are monsters in this world.'

He shifted a little away from me and turned his attention to some obscure point in the surrounding hills.

I continued. 'A lot of people think that if something is ugly, or fierce-looking, or just a different species, then they should be afraid. They call the strangest, monsters.' He nodded. 'That's what most people think of the dragons.'

Mac sighed. 'And of me.' He turned to look at me. 'But you don't.'

'Midrash taught me that the real monsters in this world aren't dragons, or wolves and, although the camels would disagree, not even spiders. The real monsters are people with wicked hearts.'

He smiled. 'That was wisdom gained. How did you befriend the dragons?'

'They befriended me. In the end, it was Shadreer who rescued me when I was about to be burned at the stake for the crime of speaking with animals. He and the other dragons brought me home. They also helped to overthrow Midrash and to rescue the stolen children. I owe them everything.'

'That is quite a tale,' he said.

I nodded. 'It's all true.'

'I believe you.'

'Tell me, Mac, what are you exactly?' I smiled at him. 'Obviously, you're not the same as me but you're not a werewolf, either.'

He sighed. 'I'm neither one nor the other and a bit of both.' He turned to look at me. 'I've lived a very long time but I'm not immortal. Eventually this body will return to the earth.'

I frowned at him.

'I can see you're not satisfied.' He scratched his chin. 'My purpose in life is to help the world live. I look after the trees and the lake and all the beings that live here. I help the lost find their way home. I help the sick regain their strength. I'm a helper.'

'But you're not a god or a spirit?'

He laughed. 'Unfortunately, you say true. The world is full of mysteries and my existence is one of them. Is that a problem for you?'

I shook my head. For a while we sat in companionable silence and watched the dragons soaking in the sunlit waters of the lake. It was the most peaceful I had felt in a very long time.

Eventually, Mac said, 'Now, what is the real reason you have come here?'

I told him the story, beginning with my first visit to the Commander and learning of his condition. When I got to the part where the Commander had seen the same problem on a friend of his father's, and how they had sent some men to Wulverstane on the advice of Delia the healer, he gasped and stood up.

'Delia sent some men here?' he said, staring out across the valley.

'That's right. She said that if anyone would know how to help him, it would be you.' I shrugged. 'Sadly, the men never came back. The general died and shortly after that so did Delia. Asher thinks she may have been killed by the person who had poisoned the general.'

He tilted his head upwards and howled. I was shocked to see saltwater coursing down his cheeks, making tracks in his fur.

Shadreer called to me. *Hatchling, do you need my help?*

I'm not in any danger. Something I said has made the wulver sad.

I saw Cal sprinting back up the hill, closely followed by Alun and Tarryn. Kieran held Maraed, and Tiffany stood close to them. I went to the head of the track, cupped my hands around my mouth and shouted, 'I'm fine!' I looked at Maraed and blew her a kiss.

They stopped their run and Cal shouted back, 'Are you sure?'

'I say true!'

She nodded, turned around and all three headed back down to the lake. It did my heart good to see how quickly they had rushed to help me. Meanwhile, Mac had stopped howling. He wiped his face with his hands.

'I'm sorry if I upset you,' I said. 'Are you all right?'

He sat back down on the log and I perched next to him. 'I failed my apprentice,' he said. 'It's my fault that she died. They arrived carrying weapons. I was afraid. The wolves of the village killed the men. They were protecting me. The soldiers had mentioned something about someone being ill but I neither trusted them, nor believed them. It's all my fault!'

The saltwater began to drip down his cheeks again. He wiped it away with the back of his hairy hand. 'Oh Delia. What have I done? The death of so many is too big a burden to carry.'

I put my hand on his shoulder. 'The general probably would have died anyway. Delia wrote that she thought it was too late. As for the men who came here, you and the townspeople made a tragic mistake. For many years, you've learned to protect yourselves from the prejudice of others. It doesn't excuse your mistake but it explains it. I think that fear often pushes us into wrong decisions.'

He sat in silence for a while. Then he sighed deeply and looked at me with eyes that were deep pools of grief. 'For such a young man, you have a lot of wisdom. Tell me again the symptoms of your Commander's illness.'

'When we left Seddon, the Commander's fingertips were blue. From what Delia wrote in her notes, we know that it will gradually spread up his limbs and then onto his back and chest. Scabs will form and he will have trouble breathing, and then he'll die. Delia called it, Dead Man's Fingers. Have you heard of this?'

He nodded. 'It's a rare malady caused by the poisonous bark of a tree that grows in the north,' he said. 'It's surprising to hear of it so far south so I don't think the poisoning was accidental. It's similar to the fungus called Dead Man's Fingers, having both the colour of the mushrooms and replicating their growth pattern, with the skin and organs gradually becoming more and more wooden. It's a horrible way to die.'

'The Commander is Tiffany's father,' I said.

'Poor child,' he said.

'Is there anything we can do about it?'

'How long has he had the symptoms?'

'This is about the seventh day.'

He stood up. 'Still time but not much! This will take some hard work.'

I looked up at him. 'We will do whatever it takes.'

He smiled. 'I'm sure you will. We'll need the help of some of the villagers. I must speak with Tarryn.'

He looked down the hill towards the lake and then towards the town. 'There is a small problem.'

'What?'

'We'll need to go into the old copper mine and they won't want to do that.' He smiled at me. 'They've heard the singing stone, so they think the tunnels are haunted. I could not convince them otherwise. They might refuse.'

'We must try,' I said. 'We have no choice. It's a matter of life and death for the Commander. Tiffany has already lost her mother. I'd hate to see her become an orphan.'

'You say true.' He walked back into the cave.

I sat for a while, watching the others fishing, and wondered what the blazes a singing stone was.

When Cal and the others began walking up the path, carrying their catch, I slipped back into the cave to tell Mac they were on their way. He began loading wood into the oven. I sat on the side of Asher's bed and studied him. He seemed to be breathing a bit better.

'Can I do anything to help?' I said to Mac.

He pointed to the small cupboard. 'There are plates in there. You could get them out and put them on the table.'

While I got out a stack of plates and looked for knives and forks, he fussed with the fire until it was burning to his satisfaction. Then he pulled a sharp knife out of a block of wood that had several knives sticking out of it. He said, 'This'll do for scaling and gutting' and then he went back outside to wait for the others.

I heard a cough behind me. I turned and saw Asher trying to sit up. 'Ash!' I said. 'You're awake.'

I ran over to him and put my hands on his shoulders, gently pushing on them to get him to lie down again.

He said, 'I want to sit up for a while, Seeger. Can you help me do that?'

'Wait,' I said.

I looked around the room but couldn't see any spare pillows. I went to the big cupboard and opened the drawers. Finally, down in the bottom right-hand side, I found a couple of cushions. I helped Asher lean forward and held him there with one hand, while I shoved the cushions in behind him. He sank back against them with a grateful sigh. He wasn't sitting up straight, but he was at least halfway there.

'What's going on?' Asher said.

'Cal and the others have caught some fish. Mac's going to clean them and then cook them for our lunch. Are you hungry?'

He flapped his hand. 'Yes, yes but what about the Commander? Do we have a cure?'

'Don't worry,' I said. 'Mac says he knows what to do. The only thing is it's going to take some hard work, which means it won't be quick.'

Asher frowned. 'What is he going to do?'

I shrugged. 'I don't know but there's a singing stone involved.'

He blinked several times and then said, 'What –?' but he was interrupted by the sound of everyone talking at once about their fishing expedition. Kieran was first into the cave.

'Asher!' he said. 'It's about time you joined the party.'

I patted Asher's hand and went to get him a cup of water. The others came in to greet the old man and the moment passed. I lifted down the biggest, heaviest frying pan that was hanging over the oven and put it on the stove top to warm it up. Then I searched the cupboard's shelves to find something that could be used for cooking fat. I found a bottle of nut oil close to the huge honey jar and took it over to the table.

The good thing about fresh fish is that, once the cleaning's been done, they don't take very long to cook. We were all soon tucking in, picking out the bones and licking our fingers clean.

As Maraed collected our dirty plates and Alun handed round cups of water to everyone, Asher asked Mac, 'Can you heal the Commander?'

Tiffany leaned forward. 'Yes, can you?'

Mac nodded. He looked at Tarryn. 'I will need the help of some of the townsfolk. We must go into the old mine.'

Tarryn shook his head. 'You know that won't happen.'

'It's the only way,' Mac said. 'I need to get a good supply of copper and I can't do it on my own.'

Tarryn rubbed his forehead and moaned. 'Isn't there another way?' he asked. Mac shook his head. Tarryn continued, 'Can't we get it from somewhere else?'

'It'd take too long,' Mac said. 'The Commander only has a few more days at best. We can't let him down. We got it wrong the last time people came here for help and many men died. Delia died, too. That was all on us. This is our time to make amends.'

Tarryn sighed. 'I can ask but I doubt that anyone will help. They won't go into a haunted mine.'

'It's not haunted,' Mac said. 'I guarantee it.'

'But the moaning!'

'It's the singing stone,' Mac said. 'It's a work of nature. It's not a departed spirit.'

Tarryn shook his head. 'I don't believe you. Singing stone, my fat eye!' He stared at Mac for a moment and then said, 'Thank you for the meal. I've got things to do.' He hurried out of the cave.

Alun, who was standing near the entrance, watched him go and shortly called out, 'He's heading down towards the town.'

Mac stood in the middle of the room with his hands holding his enormous head. Then he sighed and sat down on the end of Asher's bed. 'I'm sorry,' he said.

Tiffany leaped up. 'What? That's it? You're just going to let my father die?'

Mac looked at her. 'I'm sorry my dear but it's a big job to mine the ore and crush it and bag it. It will take more than just me to get it done in time.'

She said, 'There's five of us in this room.'

Alun moved up next to her. 'She's right. I'm willing to work. Just tell me what you need me to do.'

Kieran joined in. 'Me too. I'm not scared of ghosts.'

Cal and Maraed also murmured their support. I said to Mac, 'At least we can try.'

Mac stood up. 'Very well. I've kept the miners' abandoned equipment, so there's plenty to go around. We can begin straight away. Follow me.'

He headed towards the doorway in the back of the cave and we all followed him.

'Wait!' Asher called. He had one leg over the edge of the bed and was trying to heave himself up.

'You can't come,' Cal said. 'Focus on getting better.'

He sank back against the pillows, looking miserable. 'Go on then,' he said, flapping his hand at us. 'Don't let me keep you.'

Twenty-five

Mac gathered a few lamps and lit them, while Cal and the girls refilled our water containers. Tiffany took one back to Asher. She said he was still sulking so she gave him a kiss on the cheek, which seemed to cheer him up a little.

As we left Mac's cave, Kieran said, 'It must have been a nuisance having the villagers come through your home every day, when they were mining here.'

Mac shook his head. 'No, son,' he said. 'This is the back way in. They never came here.'

Cal, Kieran, Alun and I carried the lamps as the wulver led us down a winding passageway. At first it took us through a few more spaces that were part of his home. Then it took a sharp turn to the right and became a dark tunnel through the rocky hill. We seemed to be walking for ages. Finally, we reached a wooden door that had huge planks of wood and some stony boulders piled up against it.

We three lads handed our lamps to the others. We lifted the wood and stone away and cleared a space in front of the door. It opened into a small room, with shelving full of picks, shovels and buckets.

'When the miners quit,' Mac said, 'I collected up the gear they'd abandoned and stored it here. I haven't been back in many turns of the sun.'

We could see the truth of what he said in the thick coat of dust on everything. Cal found some old rags on one shelf and we used them to clear away the dirt. Then we lads each chose a pick and Cal carried two. Tiffany and Maraed carried some buckets stacked one inside the other. Mac carried two shovels.

We hung the lamps on the handles of the picks that were balanced on our shoulders. Mac tucked the two shovels under one arm, held his lamp in the other and led the way through another doorway, which opened into the mine itself. I waited to hear the moaning that had frightened Tarryn but it was deathly quiet.

'Where are the ghosts then?' Tiffany said.

'There aren't any,' Mac said. 'I told you, it's just the singing stone.'

'Is it close by?' Kieran asked.

'It's at the other end of the mine,' Mac said. 'Follow me. You'll see it soon.'

I settled my pick more comfortably on my shoulder and followed the rest of the crew down the mine tunnel. Occasionally, in the lamp light, I caught glimpses of colours – mainly red, blue and green – but for most of the time it was dark, damp and boring.

As we walked, I heard Shadreer calling me. *Hatchling, where are you? I have a very worried raven sitting on my shoulder. He tells me that the old man is sleeping but there is no sign of the rest of you.*

We're in the old mine, I said. *We're going to dig for copper. The wulver says it's what is needed to cure the Commander.*

But you are not miners! Shadreer said. *You must be careful in there. Is there no one to help you?*

Tarryn said that the townspeople won't come in here because they think the mine is haunted, so it will be up to us to do the work. We can't come this far without trying to get help for the Commander. Please tell Joffre not to worry but we will be down here a long time. We might not emerge until nightfall.

Very well, Shadreer said. *We will stay nearby so that we may fly you back to town when you are finished for the day.*

Thank you.

We walked on for a very long time. I thought, *At least the slave-hunters won't find us down here.* A couple of times Tiffany asked us to stop for a while and we'd then slump down on the ground. I was always grateful for the rest but there was no way I was going to admit it. For once I was glad she wasn't afraid to speak up if she was uncomfortable because we all benefitted from it.

Finally, just as we could see a faint glimmer of daylight in the distance, Mac called a halt to our march. 'Tomorrow morning,' he said, 'have the dragons bring you to the opening of the mine that you can see up ahead. Then you can get to work a lot quicker.'

All of us, apart from Cal, were already tired so we just nodded. I took a quick swig of water and some of the others quickly copied me.

'Before you begin work,' he said, 'rest your picks here and follow me.'

Twenty-five

We did as we were told and followed him towards the signs of daylight. Then he turned down a side passage and eventually came to a halt in front of a huge boulder. It was as high as the wulver and as wide as three of him.

'Bring the lamps closer,' he said.

Once all the lamplight was aimed at the giant rock, we could see how stunning it was. It had an undercoat of midnight black, which was criss-crossed with traces of red, blue, yellow and green. I thought it was one of the most beautiful things I'd ever seen.

'This is the singing stone,' he said.

'It's beautiful,' Maraed said, 'but I don't hear anything. Does it really sing? How does that work?'

'When the weather is changing, especially if rain is on its way, the stone absorbs the moisture and then releases it back into the air. As it does that, it makes a humming sound. When the miners heard the stone singing, they thought it was the voices of miners who had died in the tunnels. They were afraid and refused to work here any longer.'

Cal said, 'I could imagine how unnerving that would sound if you didn't know what was causing it.'

'Quite so,' Mac said. 'Now we must get to work.'

He led us back into the main tunnel and placed us several paces apart, facing the tunnel wall. He lifted his lamp and showed us a vein of red in the rock.

'This is the colour that we're looking for,' he said. 'This is natural copper.'

'What makes the blue and green colours?' Kieran asked.

'The blue is azurite and the green is malachite,' Mac said. 'They're good indicators that copper is near.'

I rested my pick on the rock face. 'How will we know what we're excavating?' I asked. 'It's so hard to see in here.'

Mac smiled and his teeth flashed in the glow of his lamp. 'Just hack away and hope. Tiffany and Maraed will scoop up the pieces and carry them closer to the mine entrance. There is an old sorting table up there and they can pick out any red pieces that turn up. I'll show them what to look for. I warned you that it was a big job.'

Cal hefted her pick and struck the rock face with it. 'Come on,' she said. 'Time is a-wasting.'

Kieran, Alun and I joined in and I developed a good steady rhythm within a short space of time. Once the flakes of rock had piled up near our feet, Tiffany and Maraed would come with shovels to scoop it up into a bucket and then carry it all back to the sorting table. After Mac had shown the girls what to do there, he joined us in the pick work.

For most of the time we were working, all you could hear were the grunts of the pick wielders, the smack and scrape of the picks on the rock face, the falling shards and all of us breathing heavily.

That is how the afternoon progressed. The only rest any of us had was when Tiffany or Maraed would ask us to stop for a moment and we'd move out of the way so they could get closer with their buckets, or when we crept back up the mine to pass water in private.

Twenty-five

Finally, as the light near the mine's mouth grew dim and the lamps began to flicker, Mac called a halt to our work. 'That's enough for today,' he said. 'Go back to town, rest up and return here first thing in the morning. Leave your tools here. No one will disturb them.'

We propped our picks up against the tunnel wall and began to slowly walk towards the opening of the mine. Everything hurt: my shoulders, my legs, my hands, my stomach and even my head. I had a new and deep respect for those who worked every day in a mine. It was hard, hard work. I had to put my arm around Maraed to help her walk outside and Alun helped Tiffany.

Shadreer! I called. *We need the Flight now.*

We are on our way.

When we got outside, we could see the sun sinking behind the hills. All I wanted was to get back to Tarryn's house and to soak in a deep, hot bath.

'Tomorrow, as well as using the picks again, we must begin to crush the rock that holds the copper,' Mac said. 'I'm so sorry my friends. This has been a difficult day for you but it is only going to get worse. Make sure you eat well and go to bed early. Don't worry about the old man. I will look after him tonight.'

Cal shook his hand. 'Thank you, Mac. We will see you in the morning.'

The dragons arrived and we began to climb up onto their backs. Cal and Alun helped the rest of us. I don't know about the others but my legs had begun to shake. Tiffany moaned as they lifted her up onto Fitzee. She had worked the whole time without making one complaint so I called out to her, 'Well done, Tiffany. Your father would be proud of you today.'

She smiled at me and salt water threatened to overflow from her eyes. 'I hope so,' she said.

Once we were all mounted securely, the dragons lifted up and away. Within a very short time they landed in the yard behind the General Store and we then had to climb down again. This was done slowly and carefully. We thanked and farewelled the Flight and then painfully made our way to the back door of the store. It was closed and locked, so Cal knocked on it.

As we waited for Tarryn to let us in, I looked around at our little group. We were all covered in dirt and holding ourselves up with some difficulty.

Cal knocked again, harder and more insistent. Finally, the door creaked open. Tarryn stood there but he didn't look welcoming.

'Is there a problem?' Cal said.

'I thought, seeing as you were this late returning, that you'd stayed up in the hills with the wulver,' he said.

'He doesn't have the beds,' Cal said. 'Would you please let us in? We're all exhausted from working in the mine.'

'You what?' he said. 'In the mine?'

We all nodded. Then Maraed said, 'Please, sir. We're dirty, we're sore and we're exhausted. Please, let us in before I fall down?'

Twenty-five

The raven swooped in over our heads and landed on Tarryn's shoulder. *They've been working hard*, he said. *Be nice!*

Tarryn stood to one side, holding the door open, and we all trooped past him, through the downstairs room and towards the staircase.

Tiffany began to cry. 'I'm so sorry,' she said, sniffing and wiping her face. 'I don't think I can climb up there.'

Tarryn picked her up and ascended the stairs. Joffre flew on ahead. I stood watching the storekeeper, wishing and hoping he'd come back down to carry me. Cal began to slowly climb up, one step at a time. Maraed nudged me in the small of my back and whispered, 'Seeger, please help me?'

I put my arm around her shoulders, realised it would be too awkward that way, so then I simply held her hand with my left, grabbed the banister with my right, and pulled her up behind me; one step at a time. I expected Alun to tell me to hurry up, or Kieran to tease us about stopping on every stair, but they didn't say anything. The only sounds I heard were all four of us huffing and puffing, and occasionally letting slip a short groan.

When we'd finally made it upstairs, Tarryn called us into the kitchen. 'Come and eat first,' he said. 'You can clean up afterwards.'

We staggered down the passageway into the kitchen and flopped down on the chairs around the table. Tarryn poured ladles of soup into bowls and handed them around. 'Get this into you,' he said.

As we picked up our spoons and began to sip the warm chicken and pea soup, he stood watching us shaking his head. 'What possessed you?' he said. 'Apart from Cal, the rest of you are children. Just look at you! You must be mad.'

Joffre fluttered and squawked. Tiffany began to cry again. Maraed put her arm around the girl's shoulders. Alun's face said he'd like to give Tarryn a good thumping if he could muster the strength to stand up. Kieran put his spoon down and glared at the storekeeper. Cal kept eating her soup.

I guessed it was up to me so I said, 'We're trying to save the Commander's life. Tiffany's father, remember? Today's work was more demanding than we expected but we'll be back up there tomorrow because it's the only hope we have and we're running out of time. Thank you for the soup.'

Kieran thumped me on the back, so I assume he approved. We all kept eating. Tarryn sullenly watched us, with his arms folded across his chest. After a while, he fetched a jug and poured tapanj juice into beakers and gave one to each of us. I remember staring at the big jug and thinking, *That's a lot of juice. He must have been squeezing the fruit all afternoon.*

Cal was the first to finish. She stood up, handed Tarryn her empty bowl and beaker, thanked him and said she was going to prepare the bath. She told the girls to join her once they'd finished.

She stopped in the doorway and looked back at us. 'I'll bid you all a good night now, as I'm going straight to bed once I'm clean. The last girl out of the bath will give you boys a call. All right? Good.' She left the room.

Tarryn muttered something about having to visit a friend, plonked Cal's crockery down on the countertop and then left. Maraed told us to leave our dirty dishes in the sink and she would do them in the morning. I pushed my unfinished soup to one side and lay my head down on the table while I waited for a bath. Joffre helped himself to the bits of chicken that were left on the bottom of the bowl.

Twenty-six

Kane

I was becoming increasingly worried about Seeger and the others. We'd had no news from them, so only Sed knew what was happening. Had the slave-hunters caught up with them and taken Maraed away? Did they fight back? Were they lying injured somewhere out in the Eastern ranges? The worry gnawed at me, day and night.

Fee knew something was bothering me but I refused to give in to her badgering. She was also worried about Seeger. She often said, 'I have a strong feeling that he is in difficulties.'

Riva seemed quite at home with us. She still had occasional bouts of not feeling her best but I was certain that her strange malady would soon disappear once Riff was home again. I told Fee that and she laughed. She said, 'You're so wise, Kane' and then laughed again!

I was even more worried about the Commander. When I next saw him, he was much worse. The skin on his arms was blue right up to halfway between his elbows and shoulders. On his legs, the blue was now above his knees. What was more, he was getting some scabby formations on his hands and feet. Thank Sed it hadn't reached his torso yet but, at the rate it was growing, that was only a matter of days away.

After some urging from myself, he called the other leaders to his office and showed them the predicament he was in. He bared his arms and legs, so they could see the damage for themselves.

Twenty-six

Brick, the Captain of the Watch said, 'Bleedin' heck!' Arken, Sed's Mouthpiece, made the sign of the sword on his chest. Talia gasped and then stood gaping at the sight of all that blue skin. Mika was her usual inscrutable self.

'What is this?' Brick said, pointing at the Commander's arm.

'Dead Man's Fingers,' he said. 'It's a type of poisoning.'

Talia pulled her chair closer to the desk and said, 'What's the cure?'

The Commander stared at the desktop and sighed. 'I don't know.'

'What?' Arken said. 'You've no idea? What do the healers say? What are you doing about it? How did this happen?'

The Commander looked at Arken and smiled ruefully. 'I have a healer visit me every day.'

'Are they helping you?' Arken said.

The Commander shook his head. 'Not for want of trying. Asher and company are on their way to a healer who lives in the Mac Tire Ranges. Ash found some records in his collection that talk about a cure for this … this thing. And, of course, I god-speak every day.'

Arken nodded. 'I shall do the same.'

Mika leaned back in her chair, her arms folded and her legs crossed. I could see her foot jiggling and she was scowling.

'Spit it out, Mika,' Talia said.

'Why weren't we told sooner?' Mika said.

The Commander sighed again. I could see the fatigue etched on his face. 'I'll answer that,' I said. 'The problem is, the Commander doesn't know how he was poisoned. He doesn't know who has done this to him. He couldn't trust anyone.'

Arken and Talia nodded. Brick grunted. Mika sniffed.

'He chose Asher to confide in and our Record-Keeper has found a possible solution,' I continued. 'Ash and a small band of helpers, including my son, have gone to get the cure and bring it back. We're waiting for their return.'

Talia smirked. 'I knew they weren't going on a wolf hunt.'

'The trouble is,' I said, 'we know that they're being followed by some slave-hunters, who are a dangerous band of mercenaries. We've no idea if they've escaped their attention or even if they are still alive.'

Talia's cheeks flamed and she shifted a little in her chair. 'Surely you exaggerate?' she said. 'They'd only be interested in finding runaway slaves.'

Brick turned to Talia. 'Don't kid yourself,' he said. 'Those men will do anything to get their prey, even if it means killing anyone who gets in their way. I've met their kind before.'

Talia frowned and chewed at her lip.

Arken said, 'And if they can't find a cure?'

The Commander looked at Sed's Mouthpiece. 'I'll die.'

All the leaders started denying it. 'No, no, sir! You're wrong' and so on.

Twenty-six

The Commander held up his hand. 'Let's not waste time,' he said. 'I don't have the energy to argue with you. I've called you here today because time is running out for me and you need to be prepared in the event of my death.'

'Surely there's something we can do?' Talia said.

'Mika will take over until a new commander has been chosen by the people,' the Commander said. 'Don't leave it too long before holding the assembly.' His gaze swept across the rest of us. 'I expect the rest of you to help Mika do the right thing by the city.'

She huffed and uncrossed her legs. 'I'm quite capable of being a leader!'

Talia patted her shoulder. 'Power is so tempting, dear,' she said but, just as Mika's eyes flashed, she added, 'However, we know you will do an excellent job.'

'I've asked Kane to take care of my daughter, Tiffany,' the Commander said. 'I know that he and Fee will treat her as if she were their own.'

They all turned to stare at me. Then Brick said, 'Are you telling me that he's known about this before the rest of us?'

The Commander rubbed his forehead. 'Don't do this, Brick. I had to trust someone and Kane's son, Seeger, is a member of the search party.'

I smiled, trying to look far more confident than I felt. 'I'm sure they'll get back in time.'

'As long as those slave-hunters don't catch them,' Mika said. 'Do you think they're tied up in all this?'

'It's possible,' the Commander said.

'I wouldn't think so,' Talia said. 'Surely not.'

I turned to her. 'You must admit, it's an odd coincidence. I wouldn't be at all surprised that whoever set the slavers onto Maraed, also poisoned the Commander. The hunters would be a handy way to get rid of any hope of a cure reaching Seddon.'

Talia stood up. 'I think that's a bit far-fetched, Kane.' She turned to the Commander. 'If there isn't anything else you want from me today, I'll bid you farewell. I've lots to do back at the barracks.'

'You're excused,' the Commander said.

'Sed's blessings to you, sir,' she said. She nodded at the rest of us and then strode out of the room.

'That was interesting,' Mika said. 'She seemed a bit twitchy.'

'That's Talia for you,' Brick said. 'Still, she's doing a good job with our water.'

Twenty-seven

Seeger

The next morning, when I tried to get out of bed, every muscle in my body screamed. I'm not ashamed to admit that I screamed with them. Immediately, Joffre leapt from his perch on the windowsill and hovered in front of my face.

What is it, pal? he said. *How can I help?*

'You can't,' I said. 'I think I'm going to die.' I lay my head back down on the pillow and groaned.

You can't die! Not now, he said. *You've got to save the Commander first.*

This may surprise you but, just for a moment, I seriously considered leaving the Commander to his fate.

You've come this far, Joffre said. *You escaped the nasty men. You didn't drown in the creek. You didn't get shot by the horrible old man. You worked so hard in the mine. You can't waste that.*

I knew the bird was right but I still didn't want to move. Then there was a sharp rap on the bedroom door and Cal strode into the room. 'Not up yet?' she said. 'Get a move on. We've got a lot to do today.'

'I can't move,' I said.

She grabbed my arm and yanked me up and out of the bed. I screamed again. 'Right,' she said. 'Now you're up, keep moving. It'll get better.'

She hurried out of the room. I stood there thinking about putting my trousers on. I heard a short yell and a couple of rude words from the room next door. Obviously, Kieran and

Alun were receiving the same treatment. Those army types can be rather pushy.

I grabbed my trousers and dropped them on the floor in front of me. I sat on the bed, put a foot into the gap in each pant leg and then slowly pulled the trousers up. When they were nearly at the top of my legs, I heaved myself upright and tugged them up the rest of the way.

Joffre said, *I don't know why you don't keep your feathers on, like I do.*

I wiped the sweat off my face and then dropped my tunic over my head. I god-spoke to Sed for strength and then, one at a time, put my arms into the sleeves. After that, I desperately wanted to lie down again but Cal called out, 'Hurry up!' from the kitchen door. So, instead of returning to bed, I shuffled along to the washroom to use the privy. Joffre flew on ahead of me.

In the kitchen, Kieran and Alun were already seated at the table. They both had dark shadows under their eyes. Maraed and Tiffany were yet to make an appearance. Joffre landed on Kieran's shoulder and he winced. Cal was busy toasting bread. There was no sign of Tarryn.

When the girls joined us, they didn't look well. For the first time since we'd left Seddon, Tiffany's hair wasn't smoothly braided or tied up in some fancy arrangement. She'd just dragged it to the back of her head and tied it with a band. There were stray strands flapping about her face. I thought it suited her a whole lot better than the twiddly stuff.

Twenty-seven

Cal plonked a plate of toasted buttered bread in the middle of the table and said, 'Eat.'

So that's what we did. It was the quietest meal we'd shared on the whole trip. I cleared my throat and Tiffany burst into tears.

Maraed said, 'What's the matter now?'

Tiffany sniffed, sucked in her breath and then said, 'He's my Pa and I want to save him but I don't think I can do it because it's going to kill me and then it'll be my fault that he dies and I don't think I could live with myself if that happens but I don't even have the strength to do my hair let alone carry one more bucket of rock out of that flipping mine so I just wanna die!'

'Oh, right,' Maraed said. 'Eat your breakfast.'

We finished eating and then made our way downstairs. The dragons were already waiting in the backyard. I'd sensed their presence while I was in the washroom so I knew I didn't need to summon them.

'I'm not sure I can get up there,' Kieran said, pointing to Hizaree's back.

The dragons stretched flat out on the ground so that they were as low as they could go. Kieran and Alun climbed onto Hizaree, using his leg as a steppingstone. Cal helped the girls up onto Fitzee and then she pushed me up onto Shadreer before climbing up behind me. The dragons stood up and then leaped into the air.

Are you in pain, hatchling? Shadreer said.

Yes, I said, *and it's only going to get worse.*

I wish we could help you dig, he said.

I think the rock would be too hard for your talons, I said. *It would wear them away. Also, you wouldn't fit into the tunnel.*

I am very sorry. If you or the wulver think of a way in which we could be of use, please tell us.

Of course, I said. *Thank you.*

The dragons landed at the entrance to the mine and once again stretched out flat on the ground to make it easier for us to dismount. Cal was the only one who seemed unaffected by the previous day's work. I'm sure she was feeling it too but she was a very tough lady.

The wulver was waiting for us and hurried out to help us dismount. He kept shaking his head and muttering to himself. Once the dragons had moved off to have another soak in the lake, he gathered us together and said, 'I don't think you can do it.'

'We *have* to do it,' I said. 'It's now day eight.'

He studied our faces as we all stared at him. Then he said, 'Very well. Your equipment is where you left it.'

Kieran said, 'Before we get started, how is Asher this morning?'

Mac put his hairy hand on Kieran's arm. 'He's doing much better.'

Kieran smiled and nodded. 'Good,' he said. 'He might be a bit of an old windbag but he's our windbag and we love him.'

We trooped into the mine, found our equipment and then studied the rock face. I didn't know if I had the strength to lift my pick, let alone wield it. Once again, I god-spoke to Sed begging him for help and then I sucked in my gut, took a deep breath, heaved the pick and with divine help swung it at the rock. The others did the same and soon we were back into some sort of rhythm. Deep in my chest I could feel the cold tendrils of despair entwining my heart. We were never going to do it in time.

I don't know how long we worked before Kieran laid his pick down and then sat on the ground next to it. It felt like half the morning but I suspect it was nowhere near as long as that. I stopped hacking away at the rock and looked at him. He had saltwater coursing down his cheeks. Then I heard Alun groan. He too had put his pick down and was leaning against the wall of the mine.

'Come on fellas,' I said. 'We can't stop now.'

Kieran stared at his up-turned hands and said, 'I can't, Seeger. My hands are a mass of broken blisters. There's blood on the pick handle.'

When I saw the mess his hands were in, I said, 'Why don't you go help Maraed and Tiffany with the sorting?' I turned to Alun. 'What about you?'

'I just need a breather, Seeg,' he said. 'I'll get back to it soon.'

Kieran heaved himself up and slowly walked down to where Maraed and Tiffany were searching through the spoilage, looking for the red copper.

Alun rubbed his hands down the sides of his trousers. 'Any time now, Seeg,' he said. 'I'll get right back to it.'

Cal hadn't broken her stride the whole time we were talking. Halfway through the next swing, she looked at me and nodded. I dragged a short smile from the depths of my straining body and shared it with her. Then I swung my pick again. I pretended that I couldn't hear Alun sobbing.

Mac, who'd been putting the sorted rocks into a container, came up to us. He told Alun to join Kieran and the girls, grabbed Alun's pick and began to swing. Alun walked away. Neither Cal nor I said anything.

Just when I could feel my legs shaking so hard that I was afraid that I wouldn't be able to stand any longer, there was a commotion at the entrance to the mine.

'What now?' Mac said, as he put his pick down.

He hurried down to see what was happening. Cal and I kept hacking away at the rock. I tried to lock my knees so they wouldn't buckle. We could hear voices but we couldn't make out what they were saying. Then a miracle happened.

Mac shouted to us to stop working but Cal ignored him so I did too. The next thing we knew people were streaming down the tunnel, lit candles attached to their helmets. The person leading the charge was Tarryn.

'That's enough, you two,' he said. 'Wulverstane will do the rest. Off you go.'

Cal kept swinging her pick. I stared at him with my mouth hanging open. I couldn't believe what I was hearing. 'What?'

'You've done a good job, lad,' he said, 'but this sort of work is best left to the professionals. Off you go.'

Twenty-seven

I looked at Cal. She nodded at me. 'Go before you fall down, Seeger,' she said.

'What about you?'

'I'm good for a bit longer. Why don't you get a dragon to fly you around to Mac's cave and see Asher?'

I handed my pick to Tarryn, who patted me on my arm. I wobbled my way down towards the mine entrance, thanking the townspeople as I went. They were already hard at work. Halfway down the tunnel, my legs buckled and down I went. Mac ran up to me, hoisted me up and over his shoulder and carried me the rest of the way. It was very undignified but I was past caring about such things.

Mac put me down near the sorting table. He said, 'Keep out of the way. I've got to get the crusher started up.'

He then hurried over to the men who'd begun putting the copper into the big container and beckoned for them to follow him down a passage that branched off to my left.

Maraed nudged me and pointed back up the tunnel. 'Have a look at that,' she said. Many of the townsmen were taking their clothes off and putting them into neat piles on the other side of the tunnel. 'What do you think they're doing?'

Tiffany said, 'Perhaps they don't want to get their clothes dirty.'

Alun shook his head. 'Doubt it.'

We continued to watch and then we saw something I have great difficulty describing to you. The men's backs curved and twisted and elongated, while their legs shortened but somehow thickened, and their jaws stretched. Hair begun to sprout out of their skin. It was horrifying but fascinating. Within a short time, the townsmen had become huge, man-wolves. You could see they weren't real wolves; for a start, they didn't have tails. The wolf-men went back to their picks and hacked at the rock, faster, stronger and more effectively.

'Now that's something you don't see every day,' Kieran said.

'I hope Cal will be all right with that lot,' Tiffany said.

Alun said, 'I'm sure she can look after herself.'

A few of the non-wolves ran back and forth collecting the rock shards and carrying them down to be sorted. Some women told us to move out of the way and then they took over picking out the red copper.

We moved outside of the tunnel and slumped down on the ground, leaning up against the side of the hill. We didn't speak for quite some time. We just sat in the sunshine, looking out over the valley. Eventually, Joffre flew up and landed on my shoulder.

Are you all right, pal? he said.

I soon will be, I said. *I wonder what made them decide to help us.*

That'd be Tarryn, the raven said. *He gathered the town together last night and told everyone how you'd all worked so hard in the mine that you had trouble standing up. He said you were trying to save the Commander from a deadly disease that Delia had tried to find an answer for many, many turns of the sun ago. He reminded them that the wolves killed the soldiers who'd come from Seddon. He really put the guilts on them, Seeger.*

How do you know all this?

I went to find him while you were in the bath. I saw the lights on in the town hall and listened outside the window. Some of the people said the mine was haunted and it wasn't safe but he said it hadn't stopped you kids from working in there. Then he asked them if they were more afraid of the dark than a few kids were. He didn't tell them about the singing stone. I don't blame him. They'd have laughed at him and gone home.

I just hope there isn't a sudden change in the weather, I said. Why didn't you tell me?

I stopped listening before they stopped talking so I wasn't sure what they'd decided to do. I didn't want to get your hopes up.

I looked at the others slumped against the dirt. 'Listen everyone,' I said, 'why don't I get the dragons to fly us to Asher? We could have a better rest there and we won't be in everyone's way?'

'I don't know,' Tiffany said. 'I feel I should be doing something to help.'

Mac spoke from the mine entrance. I have no idea how long he'd been standing there. 'You've done plenty. Let the townsfolk do the rest. They know what they're doing. At the rate they're working, we should have enough copper crushed and bagged by the end of the day.'

Tiffany said, 'But he's my Pa.'

'Yes, dear,' Mac said. 'He'll be very proud of you. Now go to my cave, make yourselves and Asher a hot drink and have something to eat. You're welcome to raid my larder. Cal and I will come to you when we're done.' He went back into the mine.

'Sounds like a plan to me,' Alun said.

I called to Shadreer and the Flight immediately flew up the hill to us. When they landed, they flattened themselves on the ground again but the girls couldn't climb up. I could see the saltwater gathering in Maraed's eyes and Tiffany sunk groaning back down to the ground.

Then Shadreer spoke. *Do not worry, hatchling. We will carry them there.*

I shared the dragon's plan with my friends. Alun and Kieran climbed onto Fitzee, once more using his front leg as a halfway step. They were both a little annoyed that they wouldn't be carried like the girls.

Maraed and Tiffany were unconvinced. Tiffany said, 'But their claws!'

I said, 'I'll go first so you can see how safe you'll be.'

Joffre left my shoulder and fluttered up onto Shadreer's back. The Flight leader cupped his front feet and I stepped onto them. The girls could see how careful and gentle the dragon was. He closed his talons around me so that I sat on the palm of his left foot, while the right formed a wall around me. My feet dangled down between his talons and my head poked up at the top. I rested my arms along the nearest claw of his right foot.

'I suppose it'll be all right,' Tiffany said.

'Are you comfortable, Seeger?' Maraed said.

'I'm fine. Fitzee will look after you and Hizaree will carry Tiffany. Don't be frightened.'

The dragons carried us around the hill to where Asher was. Tiffany laughed and squealed the whole way there.

Twenty-eight

The Flight let us down at the entrance to Mac's cave and then headed off to the lake once more. Hizaree was keen to do some fishing.

Asher was sitting up and he even got out of bed to greet us. I think that once he'd started to feel better, he'd got bored very quickly. I wish we'd thought to bring his kit up to the cave so he could at least do some reading.

'Oh, it's lovely to see you all,' he said. 'Lovely, lovely! Put the kettle on, Kieran. You can't? What happened to your hands? Alun, get the kettle on. Let's have something hot to drink, there are mint leaves in the cupboard, and Kieran can tell me about his hands. Are you hungry? I helped Mac make some honey drops last night. I'm sure there are plenty left. Let me just look for them.'

Asher hurried over to the cupboard and started searching for the sweet treats. Maraed went over to him and put her hand on his back.

'I'll look for them after I've sorted Kieran out,' she said. 'Then I'll change your bandages. Go, sit.' She gave Asher a little hug and then gently pushed him away.

I pulled out a chair for him and said, 'Over here, Asher. I'll tell you all about it.'

'I've been out of my mind with worry,' he said. He yawned and closed his eyes for a moment. Then he shook his head.

'Don't mind me,' he said. 'I still tire easily.' He looked at me. 'You were saying?'

Alun took the kettle to fill it up from Mac's water barrel and then set the fire and got a nice blaze going. Maraed gently washed Kieran's hands and carefully patted them dry before wrapping them in bandages. While she was doing that, Tiffany collected the beakers and set them out on the table, ready for the drinks. Then she said, 'Don't worry, Maraed. I'll look for the honey drops.'

Asher was shocked to see the broken blisters on Kieran's palms and kept murmuring, 'You poor, poor boy.'

He'd stare at Kieran's hands and then he'd shift in his chair and tug at his tunic. When I asked him what the problem was, he said he wasn't comfortable with the idea of the ladies seeing him with his trousers off. I didn't have the heart to tell him they'd already seen his naked skinny legs several times. Instead, I offered to take care of him while the girls were still busy.

I sat him on the edge of the bed and then stood in front of him, with my back to the others. It gave him a little privacy. I wiped his wounds with Mac's whiskey and then wrapped his legs in clean bandages. The redness had gone and everything looked much better. While I worked, I gave him a short account of the previous day's work in the mines. He listened intently, murmuring his concern over how hard we'd worked, and gasping and clapping his hands when he heard how the town were helping us now.

'That's wonderful,' he said as I helped him pull up his trousers, 'but there's something I need to know. What is a singing stone? Did you see it? Did you hear it?'

He pulled the chair closer to the table and sat back down. Tiffany put down a plate of honey drops and everyone grabbed one. I confess, I was hungry enough to eat the entire plateful by myself.

Tiffany said, through a mouthful of crumbs, 'It's just beautiful, Asher. It's black and red and green and yellow and blue and it shines, even in the dark tunnel.' She swallowed the honey drop and flicked her hair back. 'But it didn't even squeak so I'm thinking the wulver might be exaggerating that part of the story.' She picked up another drop and took a bite.

Kieran said, 'Mac explained that it doesn't happen all the time. He said it's when the weather is changing. Something about sucking in wet air and then breathing it out or something.'

Asher nodded. 'Ah yes. That makes perfect sense.'

'It does?' Kieran said.

'It's science, my dear boy,' Asher said. 'I wish I could hear it.'

Alun poured the mint infused drink into the beakers. 'He said it was singing up a storm the night it rained in the hills and sent the flash flood down Disappointment Creek.'

Asher nodded again. 'Yes, of course it did. Marvellous.' He sipped his drink. 'Simply marvellous. Eat up. I'm sure we can find something else that's edible if you're still hungry.'

Twenty-eight

Kieran said, 'I'd like to do some fishing but –' He looked down at his bandaged hands. 'It could get awkward. Anyone want to come with me?'

Alun nodded, put another honey drop in his mouth and then stood up. 'I'll help. You can unhook the fish.'

He went to get a fishing pole and a bucket, and then they both set off to catch us a feed. Tiffany watched them go, clasping and unclasping her hands.

Maraed said, 'You can go with them if you want. The dragons are down there so nothing's going to happen to you.' Tiffany grabbed a honey drop and ran out of the cave after the lads. 'I sometimes forget she's still young,' Maraed said, sitting down next to Asher.

'Oh yes,' he said, winking. 'After all, you have a whole three and a half turns of the sun more than her, you old thing, you.'

He laughed but when Maraed and I didn't join in, he stopped. I actually thought that what he said was funny but there was no way I was going to let Maraed know it. Not when I saw the stink-eye glare she gave Asher.

While the others were fishing, Maraed and I tidied Mac's home. Asher spent the time peppering us with questions. It was a relief when the fishers came back with their catch. We enjoyed the fish for lunch and then we all took the chance to have a long nap. Maraed and Tiffany shared the bed, Asher and Kieran slept in the chairs and Alun and I lay on the rug. Despite the hardness of the ground, we were both so tired that it didn't take us long to drift into sleep.

Later in the afternoon, as Maraed searched the wulver's larder for ingredients for the evening meal, we speculated as to how Mac was going to use the copper to cure the Commander. Alun, Kieran and Tiffany thought he might have to drink it and Asher and I thought it might be made into a paste that'd be spread over the skin.

Maraed said, 'Who cares, just as long as it works.'

At twilight, Joffre flew back into the cave. He'd spent the day foraging for food. The dragons flew up with him and parked themselves outside.

When a big pot of mushrooms, tubers, onions and assorted herbs were bubbling away on the fire and Alun was getting the bowls out, Mac and Cal turned up. They staggered in through the back of the cave; the same way we'd originally left to go mining. They both carried a bulging sack with them.

'What's in the sacks?' Tiffany said.

'Crushed copper,' Cal said. 'It's now a red powder.'

Kieran rolled his eyes at Tiffany and then leaped up to surrender his chair to Mac. The wulver put his sack down between his legs and sank gratefully down. Cal leaned her bag against the wall and then collapsed onto the bed.

'Can I get you anything, Cal?' Maraed said. 'A cup of water? A hot mint drink?'

Cal wearily shook her head. 'Just give me a few moments to recuperate.'

'The evening meal is almost ready,' Maraed said. 'You rest there and I'll bring you a bowl shortly.' Cal nodded. 'What about you, Mac?'

'I'll wait for the meal, thank you,' the wulver said.

Maraed went to check on the food. The wulver rubbed his face with his hands. Joffre flew over and perched on his shoulder.

I turned to Asher. 'I forgot to tell you, Ash! Some of the townsmen turned into werewolves right in front of our eyes. It was amazing. You'd have loved it.'

Asher's bottom lip pushed forward. 'I seem to have missed all the excitement. All because of some silly, crabby old man who had no manners and should have known better.'

Tiffany put her arm around his shoulders and gave them a squeeze. 'We're just thankful you're still with us.'

Kieran looked at me, his eyes wide and his mouth open in a silent, 'Oooh'. I raised my eyebrows in reply. Joffre said, *I told you she was nice!*

'What do we do now?' Alun said.

A loud snore came from the vicinity of the bed. Cal's right arm was dangling down towards the floor and her left arm was draped across her face. I don't think any of us were surprised that she was asleep. Quite frankly, I have no idea how she had pushed herself so hard for so long. She was one tough lady. We smiled at each other and lowered the volume of our voices, so that we wouldn't disturb her.

'I suggest we first eat the delicious meal that Maraed has prepared for us,' Mac said. 'Then, we fly to Seddon tonight.

We're running out of days. The sooner I can see the Commander, the more possible his cure becomes.'

'We can't all go straight to Seddon,' I said. 'Someone has to collect the camels from Pederson's farm.'

'Let's think about it while we're eating,' Asher said. 'Maraed, put a bowl aside for Cal and we'll let her sleep a bit longer. She can eat while we're cleaning up.'

Maraed and Alun served out the food and, for a while, we ate in companionable silence. Joffre wasn't interested in any of it, so he fluttered over to the big cupboard and perched there preening his feathers. Mac was the first to finish. He said he wanted to pack a small bag to take with him. He hurried into the next room and we could hear him moving things around with the occasional thump or scraping sound.

While he was busy, I said to Asher, 'What will the Commander and others make of Mac? Will he be in any danger?'

Asher shrugged. 'It's hard to say. He's certainly an unusual sight when you first meet him. However, we'll be flying in at night and I'll be with him, so that should help.'

Tiffany said, 'I'll vouch for him, too. Surely that should carry some weight?'

Asher slowly nodded. 'I think Tiffany and Cal should accompany Mac and me to the citadel. We can drop you boys off at Pederson's and you can bring the camels home. Maraed, what do you want to do?'

I watched her as she thought about it. She looked at Cal and Tiffany and then at Kieran and me. Then she looked at Asher and bit her lip. While she was still thinking, Mac came back into the room wearing a cloak, a long scarf that was wrapped around the bottom half of his face and a large floppy hat. From a distance, you would be hard pressed to distinguish him from other men.

'Great disguise!' I said.

'Thank you, young man,' Mac said. 'I've had a bit of practice at this sort of thing.'

Maraed stood up and began stacking the dirty bowls. She told Tiffany to wake Cal up and get her to eat. I helped carry the bowls to the sink and found a cloth to wipe them dry once she'd washed them. Joffre flew down and settled on my shoulder.

I whispered to Maraed, 'What are you thinking?'

She whispered back, 'I'm not sure what to do. It would be good to get back to the city that much sooner and to help look after Asher. However, I'm tired of being with that spoiled little madam and I'd like to keep an eye on Kieran's hands.'

I dried the bowl in my hands and put it down on the adjacent shelf with all the others. I leaned closer to her and whispered in her ear, 'I think you've already decided. You just feel a bit guilty about it.'

She whispered back, 'It's not seemly for a young woman to travel as a lone female with three men.'

'One of them is your brother,' I said.

She nodded. 'There is that.'

And there's me as well, Joffre squawked. *I'll look after you.*

'Come on you two,' Asher said, 'stop your whispering and tell us what is going on.'

We turned around. Cal was sitting on the edge of the bed, eating her meal. She looked at us and, before putting the next spoonful in her mouth, said, 'Don't worry about your reputation, Maraed. Kieran's your brother. Anyone with eyes will be able to see that. Go home with the lads.'

So that was that. Once Cal had finished eating and we'd all visited the privy, Mac blocked the entrance to his cave with a large boulder, seeing as he wasn't sure when he'd be returning. The Flight flew us down to Wulverstane and waited behind the store while we collected our kitbags from Tarryn's place. We bade the storekeeper a fond farewell and promised to return one day for a proper visit.

We then took off into the night, flying by moon and starlight. It was nearly a full moon so we could see the landscape slipping past below us. Joffre said it was a good thing we left when we did, considering where the moon was at in its cycle. *Another few days and I wouldn't be able to protect you from the man-wolves,* he said.

I'd forgotten about that. When the werewolves were working in the mine, it wasn't a full moon so they still had control. It would be a different story once the moon was full.

You forget, bird, Shadreer said, *that they could summon us. We are not frightened by wolves of any kind.*

Twenty-eight

The dragons set us down in the tuber field at Pederson's farm and, as Albert and the other geese let the farmer know we'd arrived, we said our farewells. There were hugs all round and many a pat on the back.

'All the best everyone,' I said. 'We should be back in two days if we get a move on tomorrow morning. May Sed go with you and bless your endeavours, Mac.' He inclined his head in thanks.

Maraed gave Tiffany a quick hug and said, 'I hope your Pa will be on the mend by the time we get back.'

We waved and blew kisses and the dragons leaped into the air and flew away. Shadreer called to me as they went. *Goodbye, hatchling! I will stay nearby so that I may fly Mac home when he has finished saving the Commander.*

Thank you, I said. *I'll listen for your voice when we near Seddon.*

Asher, Mac, Cal and Tiffany's goodbyes mingled with the Flight's farewells, as they flew across the face of the moon. We watched them for a short while and then turned towards the farmhouse where Pederson was standing, holding up a lamp to make us welcome.

Twenty-eight

Kane

I was heading up the stairs to go to bed when there was an insistent knocking on our front door.

Fee called out, 'Who's that?

'I'll go see,' I shouted up to her. As if I'd know who was there!

Ivor, the Commander's guard, stood with his hand raised ready to knock again. He lowered his arm and said, 'I'm sorry to disturb you, Beast-Master, but you must come to the citadel.'

'Is something wrong?'

'I'll explain on the way,' he said. 'Please, sir, you must come now!'

'Wait a moment,' I said. I walked to the bottom of the stairs and shouted, 'Got to go to the citadel, Fee. Don't wait up for me.'

She ran out of the bedroom, a shawl clutched around her shoulders, and stopped at the top of the stairs. 'What's going on?' she said. 'Is it Seeger?'

'I don't know, dear,' I said. 'I'll tell you about it when I get home.' I smiled at her and then hurried back to the front door.

'I'll just get my camel,' I said to Ivor.

'You can ride behind me,' he said.

'No, I'd rather be able to get myself home later. I won't be long.'

Twenty-eight

I ran around to the stables, saddled up a disgruntled Karmal, and then we set off at a brisk pace to the citadel.

'What's going on, Ivor?' I asked.

He glanced across at me and then focussed on the road again. I didn't blame him as the streets weren't that well-lit now that we no longer had the bonfires burning on the street corners.

'Asher, Tiffany and her bodyguard, Cal, have arrived at the palace on the backs of dragons.' He flicked another quick glance at me. 'I've never seen those beasts before. They're quite something, aren't they!'

'Oh yes,' I said.

'What's more, they've brought a stranger with them and two bags full of something heavy.' He paused for a moment. 'There's something rather odd about the newcomer and Asher is his usual vague self. Rory…you remember him?' I nodded. 'He's not happy about letting them into the palace so he called for me and Asher suggested I should come get you. Rory says he trusts your judgement. Meanwhile, Tiffany is throwing a fit and Cal is having trouble keeping her under control. She can be a right little madam, can Tiffany.' He shook his head and laughed. 'She's going to be a force to be reckoned with when she's older.'

'And the dragons?' I asked.

'They left as soon as their passengers had disembarked.' He shook his head again. 'They make a beautiful sight, flying across a moonlit sky.' He sighed. 'Really something to behold.'

I was going to ask him about the stranger and what Asher had to say and where the rest of the group were but I decided it'd be easier to wait until I got to the palace. Ivor was more interested in the dragons than anything else. Not that I could blame him. Also, he didn't know the purpose of Asher's trip, so the guard would have had no idea of the significance of the old man's sudden return in the night.

Karmal picked up his pace and the other camel followed suit, so it didn't take us long to reach the entrance to the palace. I could see Asher and company standing at the front door. There were two bulging sacks at the feet of the stranger. He was wearing a hat that drooped over most of his face and a long scarf draped over his mouth and chin and then hanging down behind him. Ivor was right; there was something odd about him.

Tiffany was pacing up and down in front of the building waving her arms in the air and demanding to be let into her 'own home, for Sed's sake!' Rory was stoically immobile, despite the young girl's ranting. He seemed pleased to see me.

'Ah, Beast-Master,' he said. 'Thank you for coming out at such a late hour.'

Ivor dismounted and led his beast to the corner of the front yard, where camels are hitched when their rider isn't staying very long. Karmal knelt to let me dismount and then he settled down next to Ivor's camel. *Good luck, Kane*, he said. *You'll need it with that lot.*

Twenty-eight

Asher turned around and stretched his arms out in greeting. 'At last!' he said. 'Someone to bring some sanity to the proceedings.'

'What's the problem, Rory?' I said, as Ivor and I walked up to the group. 'Surely you know the Commander's daughter, Tiffany? And Cal. And Asher, the Record-Keeper, has been here on numerous occasions.'

'Yes, yes,' Rory said, 'but then there's this chap.' He pointed to the stranger. 'They won't tell me what he's here for and I'm not letting him inside at this time of night without getting the proper information. I've already said they could go in without him but they won't accept that compromise. I'm just doing my job, Kane.'

The girl stood in front of me. 'Well, come on. Sort this out. Time is wasting.' She leaned forward and whispered, 'Please?'

I nodded at her. Then I said, 'Just a moment, please Rory.' I held Asher's arm and pulled him to one side and whispered. 'Is this the healer, Ash?'

Asher leaned in closer and said, 'Yes, his name is Mac. He's a wulver, Kane. Just wonderful! You'll be amazed when you see him without all the extra clothing on. We couldn't tell this guard what he's here for because we don't want to reveal the Commander's situation.'

I patted Asher's arm. 'You've done the right thing, Ash. Leave it to me.'

I had no idea who or what a wulver was – I guessed it meant he was from a place called Wulver or Wulve – but I trusted Asher's judgement. I walked over to the stranger and stuck my hand out. 'Welcome, Mac. It's very good of you to come all this way.'

I shook his hand and was startled at how hairy it felt. What on earth had Asher brought back with him?

I turned to the guard. 'Rory, this is an important visitor from quite a long way away. The Commander and I were expecting him. Normally, I'd take him home for the night and bring him back in the morning but his visit is a matter of some urgency. The Commander will want to see him immediately. There is absolutely no danger. So would you be so kind as to let us in?'

I picked up one of the bags and instantly regretted it. What on earth did they have in those things? I must have grimaced because Mac reached across and took the thing from me. Cal picked up the other one and made it look easy. Rory held the door open and in we all filed.

As we were going up the staircase, I asked Asher where Seeger and the others were and if they were safe.

'Yes, yes,' the old man said. 'They're bringing back the camels from Pederson's farm. Such a nice man. Makes an excellent pancake.'

I asked, 'Did you have any trouble with some slave-hunters?'

Cal said, 'They followed us for a while and seemed very interested in Maraed but we eventually lost them.' She rested the bag on the step as she caught her breath. 'The only other trouble was when Asher got shot with a toxic arrow but Mac took good care of him.' She heaved the bag up across her shoulders and kept walking.

'Oh yes,' Asher said, his head bobbing on his skinny neck. 'Marvellous. I was really ill for a moment or two but Mac saved the day.'

Tiffany snorted and said, 'A moment!' I'm sure I heard Cal stifle a laugh. We left the stairs and made our way down the corridor, with Ivor leading the way.

'There's lots to tell you, Kane,' Asher said, 'but now is not the time. First things first.'

We walked the rest of the way in silence apart from Asher's wheezing. When we reached the Commander's private quarters, Ivor greeted the fellow who was guarding the door. 'Good evening, Jorge,' he said. 'The Commander is expecting these people.' He turned to me. 'I'll be on duty in the morning, Beast-Master.'

'Thank you, Ivor.'

He and Jorge saluted each other and the fellow opened the door to let us in.

'Pa!' Tiffany called. 'I'm home, Pa. Where are you?' There was silence. Dread gripped my heart. Were we too late? 'He might have gone to bed early,' Tiffany said. 'Follow me.'

She hurried across the grand sitting room and through a door at the far end. Cal followed her, the weight of her burden slowing her down, and we men trailed behind. Mac held his head slightly tilted upwards and he seemed to be sniffing the air. The heavy bag didn't seem to trouble him at all. I wondered whether he was a man or whether he was some sort of creature dressed in human clothing.

I grabbed Asher's arm. 'Ash, who or what is Mac?' I muttered. 'Is he safe?'

The creature turned to me and spoke for the first time. 'I assure you, sir, that I'm very safe. I'm a wulver. I'm a mix of human and wolf and a little of something else. I wear the hat and scarf to protect me from those who might choose to react before getting to know me. Not everyone is as welcoming or accepting as your son.'

I stiffened. 'My son?'

'He is a wonderful young man,' the wulver said. 'He won my heart when he told me that the only true monsters in this world are people with wicked hearts.'

That sounds like Seeger, I thought.

'I consider him a good friend,' Mac continued. 'Do not worry. He is safe and well.'

A weight that I hadn't realised was there, suddenly lifted off my chest. 'Thank you for that.' He nodded and his floppy hat wobbled a little. For a fleeting moment I caught a glimpse of a very hairy cheek. Even hairier than Old Thomas the butcher!

We walked through a large dining room, then down a long passageway, flanked by many rooms. Tiffany explained the purpose of some of them.

'That's the reading room,' she said, pointing to the left. She waved her hand at several doors on her right. 'They're the guest bedrooms.'

Twenty-eight

We reached a T-junction at the end of the passage. She pointed to the left and said, 'Down there are the servant quarters and the kitchen. This way,' pointing to the right, 'are the family bedrooms, Pa's reading room, my room for Foundation studies and a smaller family dining room.'

'Does he have any personal menservants?' I asked. 'Should we expect any trouble?'

Tiffany shook her head. 'The day before Cal and I left, Pa gave Liam and Dara a full lunar cycle away from their duties. They've gone home to the Outer Islands. Usually, they get some time to visit their families at Sedmass but Pa said he was planning on inviting lots of special guests this year and he'd need them here, so he gave them a holiday now.'

I looked at Asher and he nodded. 'What?' Tiffany said. 'What does that look mean?'

'I expect he sent the men away before his condition became obvious,' I said.

Asher said, 'It would be difficult to hide blue patches on his skin from anyone who shared his quarters, or who helped him dress in the mornings.'

'Oh,' Tiffany said. 'Right. His bedchamber is just down here.' She called out, 'Pa? I'm home.'

A wavery voice called back. Tiffany opened the door to Keaten's room and we all filed in. Cal and Mac carried the sacks in and put them down against the wall. Asher and I were the last to enter.

Tiffany ran to hug her father and then sat on the bed next to him, her arm draped across his shoulders. He looked pale and weak. I think the meeting earlier in the day had taken its toll.

'Good evening, Commander,' I said. 'Sorry to disturb you but we didn't think this could wait. Asher has brought –'

'Allow me to introduce myself,' the wulver said, stepping forward. 'My name is Mac. I'm a wulver. You've probably not heard of my kind. We're a rare breed these days. Prepare yourself for a little surprise.'

He unwound his scarf and took off his hat. Keaten and I gasped at the same time. I couldn't help it. The man had the head of a wolf! That was just not normal.

Keaten turned his head to look at his daughter. 'Don't be afraid, sweetie.'

She squeezed his shoulders. 'Don't be silly, Pa. This is Mac. He's lovely and he's come to cure you.'

'I vouch for him,' Asher said. 'I was shot with an arrow that had been dipped in something putrid. It made me very ill. Cal did her best.' He bowed to the bodyguard. 'But it was Mac's ministrations that turned the tide for me. He's promised he can do the same for you.'

The Commander spoke to Cal. 'What say you?'

'If I didn't think he was trustworthy, sir,' she said, 'I wouldn't have allowed him to step into your chamber.'

Ash continued, 'I think we should give Mac some room to make his examination and then we'll do whatever he thinks is necessary.' He beckoned to the girl. 'Come along, dear.'

Tiffany kissed her father's cheek and then reluctantly climbed down off the bed. There was a chair on the left-hand side of the bed, so she walked around to it and sat down. Cal went to guard the door. As Mac moved forward, Ash and I stepped back from the bed. The old man looked a bit wobbly so I guided him over to some chairs that were next to a small cupboard with a mirror attached. I pulled him down next to me saying, 'Set you down here, Ash. We'll be out of the way but still able to watch what's going on.'

He sank down onto the chair and then reached over to pat my arm. 'It's good to be home,' he said.

The wulver had already pulled back the blankets and was studying the Commander's body. Ash turned to me with his eyes full of saltwater. 'I hope we're not too late.'

I looked across the room to Tiffany. She held a trembling hand over her mouth and was leaning forward in the chair, ready to leap up at a moment's notice. When she'd last seen her father there was only the faintest tinge of blue on his fingertips and I doubted that she'd even noticed.

'Oh Pa,' she said. 'I had no idea.'

The wulver asked Keaten to roll over, which he did. Again, we all gasped. There were streaks of blue shooting up from his waist towards the middle of his back.

'I have come just in time,' Mac said. 'We must begin treatment straight away.' He turned around and said to us, 'Will someone please fill a bath with warm water?'

Tiffany leaped up. 'I'll do it.' She hurried into the small washroom that led off from the main bedchamber. Soon we could hear the water gushing into the bath. She called out, 'Shall I add the bath salts?'

'No!' Mac shouted. 'I need one of the bags to be taken into the washroom. There is a scoop on top of the contents. Please sprinkle four scoops of copper dust into the water.'

Asher and I stood up. I grabbed a bag and dragged it into the washroom and put it at the foot of the bath, out of the way. Asher fumbled with the knot but finally got the thing open. He scooped out the red dust and poured it into the rising water.

'I hope he knows what he's doing,' I said. Asher nodded. 'Tiffany,' I said, 'I think you'd best leave your Pa alone while he has a bath. Let's preserve his dignity, yes?'

She nodded and left the room. Mac assisted Keaten into the washroom and then gently removed his sleeping garments. Keaten slid into the water. Mac turned the taps off and began to swirl the water and copper powder around so that the Commander lay in a consistent red mixture.

'Call me when the water turns cold,' Mac said. He left the room, so we did the same. Asher patted the Commander's shoulder as he walked past.

Back in the bedchamber, Mac was fiddling with his bag. He dug around in it and finally took out a small bottle of white powder. 'There it is!' he said. 'Tiffany, can you bring me the cup there on the bedside table? Thank you.'

He turned to Asher and me. 'Once he's had a thorough soak, I'll give him a drink of this and he should then have a good night's sleep.' He then lifted out of his bag a small bowl and a bottle of some sort of oil. 'I'm also going to make a paste to smear onto the scabs. I suggest that you go home to your beds and try to get some rest.'

He looked at Tiffany. 'You can see him in the morning.'

'He'll be better by then, right?' she said.

Mac shook his head. 'Why do you think I brought two big sacks of copper, if he only needed four scoops? No, it's going to take several days of regular baths, as well as washing his clothing in the same solution. You must be patient.'

Before she could say anything more than, 'But –', Cal interrupted her. 'He's right, Tiffany.' She turned to Mac. 'Will you remain here?'

Mac nodded. 'I promise I won't leave his side. And, of course, there's young Jorge guarding the main door. I'm sure we'll be fine.' He turned to Tiffany again. 'I will stay until he's better.'

She nodded. 'I trust you, Mac. Come on then, Cal, let's go.' She walked over to the washroom door and called out, 'Goodnight, Pa.'

Keaten called back, 'See you in the morning.'

She and Cal left the room. I looked at Asher, who seemed completely comfortable with the situation. 'I don't know,' I said. 'I'm not sure it's wise to leave the Commander alone with a stranger.'

Asher sighed. 'I'm not going to argue with you, Kane. I'm too tired. I'm recovering from a serious injury you know.' He rubbed his face with his wrinkled hands. 'Tell you what, there won't be anyone at my house, so how about I stay here with Mac? I'm sure we can get some bedding from one of the guest rooms.'

I grudgingly accepted the compromise. 'I'm sorry, Mac,' I said. 'I don't mean any disrespect. It's just that I've known Keaten all my life and I've only just met you tonight. I've been keeping his secret while looking after him and it's difficult to now trust a stranger.'

'I understand,' Mac said. 'Now if you'll excuse me, I'll put some water in this beaker and see how the patient is doing. Goodnight, sir.' He smiled.

I nodded to the wulver – those teeth! – and then shook hands with Asher. 'I'll be back at first light.'

Twenty-nine

Seeger

We went to bed early the night we arrived at the farm and slept the sleep of the just. All four of us were still sore and sorry from our work in the mine. Before we went to sleep, Maraed washed and rebandaged Kieran's hands so that we could make a quick start in the morning.

Pederson said that he hadn't seen any sign of the mercenaries and we were glad to hear it. I hate to think what they might have done to the old couple; especially if Bella had charged at them with her frying pan!

We left the next morning just as the sun had begun to climb over the treetops, hoping to make it to Zenda by nightfall. Although it took us a day to get from Zenda to Carrig on the way from Seddon, we'd left late the first morning and had walked half the way. We'd also travelled at a sedate pace on the way to Carrig, so as not to look suspicious to the slave-hunters. This time, we could go as fast as we liked, so we had high expectations.

The camels were happy to be back on the road, especially Lenny. Even though the others had reassured him, he'd been worried he'd never see Alun again. We made good time and, thankfully, Disappointment Creek was back to its usual dry state. This time Joffre didn't sense anything to worry about and we went straight across it with no drama. Even Lenny didn't make a fuss. I think he was still embarrassed about the last time we'd gone through there.

We reached Carrig by midmorning and stopped at The Bearded Man to rest the camels and to have something to eat and drink. That way we wouldn't have to stop again until we reached Alun's father's hotel, The Beggar's Arms. Joffre chose to stay in the stables with the camels.

The landlord came over to our table and shook our hands. 'I'm delighted to see you again,' he said. 'Where are the others in your party?'

Alun said, 'We had to separate for the return journey. They're all well. Thanks for asking, sir.'

The landlord thumped him on the back. 'No problem, young sir. I was just concerned for you because of those mercenaries. I'm glad you made an early escape. They weren't half fuming when they got up the next morning and discovered you'd already left. There was a lot of effing and blinding and other choice words being thrown around and they accused me of tricking them.'

He shrugged. 'I told their leader it was none of my business when you chose to leave and I didn't see how it was theirs either.' He chuckled. 'They tried to give me a hard time but the lads from the kitchen came out with meat hatchets and other sharp implements and stood with me. They soon backed down and they ran out of here like their butts were on fire. I was so worried they'd catch up with you and I'd have to explain Alun's demise to his old dad.'

'Have you seen them again since then?' Alun said.

The landlord shook his head. 'No and I'm not sorry for it. I'd be happy if they never cross the doorstep ever again.'

He gave an emphatic nod of his head. 'Well now, you eat up and enjoy yourselves.' He smiled at Maraed. 'Especially you, young lady.' He left us and went back behind the bar.

Maraed's shoulders loosened and she exhaled. I hadn't realised how anxious she'd been until then.

'Maraed, why didn't you tell us you were worried about coming back here?' I asked. 'We could have gone somewhere else, or even stopped for a break on the side of the road.'

She flapped her hand at us. 'Don't be silly,' she said. 'It's just I hadn't thought of those men for a few days and when we walked into the hotel, I suddenly remembered.' She smiled at us. 'I hope they're well on their way to Forabad by now.'

'Hear! Hear!' Kieran said.

'If we never see them again, it'll be too soon,' Alun said.

We laughed and then tucked into our late breakfast/early lunch and gave the men no more thought. When we were back on the road again, Joffre said he was going to do another recky for us just in case. I still don't know where he learned this word because it's not one I, nor any of my friends use. Perhaps he picked it up when we were in the land of the Xanthi, with Captain Grimm and the other soldiers.

We made excellent time on the road to Zenda. It was such a different journey to the one we'd made a few days before. We felt quite carefree, as if we were on a holiday. As we rode along, Alun told us his story of being a soldier in

Midrash and then how difficult it had been for him to adjust to life back home with his father.

'He expects me to take over the hotel one day, so he can retire and finally get to sleep in for a change,' Alun said.

'That's nice,' Kieran said.

'There's only one problem,' Alun said. 'I don't want to do it. I see how hard my dad works and there is no way known to man that I want to be trapped in a little country tavern.'

'What do you want to do?' Maraed said.

Alun grimaced. 'That's also the problem.'

'So, there isn't only one problem then,' Kieran said.

Maraed frowned. 'Don't be petty, Kieran. You were saying, Alun?'

He shrugged. 'There's a restlessness in my bones. I just can't seem to settle at anything. I'm plagued by nightmares, thanks to the Midrashi monsters. I don't trust myself. What if I hurt someone? I've done some awful things, Maraed. If you knew what they were, you wouldn't want to be anywhere near me.'

'It was a long time ago, Alun,' Maraed said.

He shook his head. 'It's as if it were yesterday.'

I nodded. I knew what he meant. I thought that Maraed and Kieran would never understand what it was like for those of us who had survived Midrash.

'Even so,' Maraed persisted, 'you must try to put it behind you and move on.'

'That's not easily done,' I said.

Twenty-nine

'I wasn't a child soldier,' Maraed said, 'but I was taken from my parents and tied up to a stake, having been told I was going to be eaten by a dragon. Can you even begin to imagine the fear that consumed me? Then foreign men took me to Forabad and put me on parade in a slave market. A fat-bellied, sleazy innkeeper bought me and kept me for more than a full turn of the sun, in a one-room hut in his backyard. I knew it wouldn't be much longer before the innkeeper forced himself upon me. I was surprised he hadn't already tried and I lived in dread of the day it would finally happen. He'd already threatened to allow his customers to pay for the pleasure. I thought that would be my life until I died. The only time I saw any other people was when I sang in the inn at night. I know a little of what it's like to suffer.'

'Yes, you do,' Alun said. 'I'm sorry. How did you put it behind you?'

She looked at us, one at a time, and then said, 'Well … I might have been exaggerating … a little. I can't forget, any more than you can forget what happened to you. But I god-speak to Sed every morning and ask him to get me through the day. I have people around me who care about me, and I concentrate on doing what I love.'

'What's that?' Alun said.

'Singing,' she said. 'I pour all my pain, fear and hope into every song I sing and trust that it will be a blessing to someone else.' She smiled at Alun. 'You must find what you love to do and go do that.'

He nodded thoughtfully. We rode on in silence. I was ashamed of myself. I'd never truly given much thought to what Maraed had endured. It was exciting to rescue her but then we had the expedition to deal with Blunt, so it never really featured in my thinking.

I thought you loved her, Bryan said. *You're a piece of work, Seeger. Shame on you.*

'I'm sorry,' I said to Maraed. 'I've never really talked with you about your time in Forabad.'

'You've never really talked with me about your time in Midrash,' Maraed said. 'One of the things I like about you, Seeger, is your ability to live in the moment.'

Errol snorted. *What's your problem?* I asked him.

She's too kind to you, matey. You've been a selfish poo.

I know, I said. *I've had a few other things on my mind. I'm trying to apologise.*

He snorted again and some of the others joined in. They were right, of course, but I wasn't going to have a bunch of camels tell me what to do.

Joffre came back from his recky and settled onto my shoulder once more. I thanked him for being so careful and he said, *Not a problem, matey. It's all part of my job.* Then he cocked his head to one side. *Why are the camels snotty with you?*

I haven't been as attentive to Maraed as I should have been.

Apologise!

I have.

He fluffed his feathers. *Well done. Those fleabags will have to get over it.*

Twenty-nine

Much later in the afternoon, we could see the wall of Zenda in the distance. It'd be good to have a decent meal and then sleep in a comfortable bed.

Alun said, 'Look, I was wondering … I mean, I'm hoping that …'

'Spit it out,' Kieran said.

'How would you feel if I came on to Seddon with you in the morning?'

Kieran and I looked at each other and then we both turned to Maraed who shrugged and smiled.

'I don't think there'd be any problem with that,' I said. 'What about your father?'

'It's not as if I'm much use at the hotel, so he won't be too concerned,' Alun said. 'Perhaps I could join the Seddonese army? I've already got some of the required skills and I really love using my bow.'

Kieran shook his head. 'It might stir up bad memories for you.'

Alun frowned. 'I hadn't thought of that.'

'I have an idea,' Kieran said. 'You could live at Asher's house with Maraed and me. You could share my room. You could be the bodyguard when we go on his knowledge-gathering missions. We're often setting out for places unknown and your ability with the bow would come in very handy.'

Alun brightened up at that suggestion. I was kicking myself that I hadn't thought of it. Kieran was right; he used his wits and I used the dragons. We rode in through the gates of Zenda and headed towards The Beggar's Arms.

Thirty

Kane

As I was cleaning my teeth before heading back up to the citadel, Fee cornered me in the washroom. She stood in the doorway, her hands on her hips and a very determined look on her face.

'Kane,' she said, 'it's time you told me what's going on. I'm sick of being kept in the dark. I know when you're not being honest with me. Speak up and speak true.'

At first, I considered denying that I was keeping anything from her but then I realised that ship had sailed. Was there something I could use to deflect her from the main issue? As I thought about that, she said, 'Don't try to muddy the scent with something else.'

In the end, I told her the truth. After all, the Commander was getting the cure and the crisis would soon be over. She kept peppering me with question after question so that eventually I had to say, 'Let me tell this in one sitting, please, without interruption or I'll stop right now. I don't want this to take all morning.'

She folded her hands in her lap and said, 'Please continue.'

I told her about the Dead Man's Fingers. I told her that the Commander had sworn me to secrecy and that up until yesterday Sarosh his healer, Asher and his crew, and I were the only people in Seddon who knew what was going on. I told her what Asher and Seeger had been doing on their latest trip, looking for an expert on the Commander's malady. I told her about Asher's arrival at the citadel last night. Then, I told her about the wulver.

She stared at me with her mouth open. Then she shook her head and frowned. 'Are you telling me that you and Asher have entrusted the Commander's welfare to a talking wolf?'

'He's a wulver, dear,' I said. 'There's a difference.'

'How do we know that Seeger and Maraed are all right?' she said. 'What if this creature has eaten them?'

I put my arm around her and gave her a gentle hug. 'Asher assures me that Seeger, Maraed and the others are fine. They're bringing the camels home, so they'll probably get here some time tomorrow.'

She left my arms and began to pace back and forth. 'Are you telling me everything? I still feel that Seeger is in danger.' She stopped and stared at me. 'What have you left out? Where are the dragons?'

'The dragons brought Asher, Tiffany, her bodyguard and the wulver here last night. They've gone now. I presume they've headed back to their mountain.'

She shook her head, her eyes closed and grimaced in pain. 'No, no, no! That's not good. They were his protection. He's in danger.'

'What are you talking –?'

'Seeger is in danger,' she said. '*I know!*'

I went to get my boots. 'I think you're over-reacting, dear.' I sat on the end of the bed and pulled my boots on.

'They're probably enjoying themselves now that their job is done. You worry too much.'

'Are you sure that Asher didn't mention any other danger or worry that they had on the mission?' Once more her hands were on her hips.

I frowned. Sometimes her instincts were rather unnerving! 'He did say something about some mercenaries who were following them, early on. They were slave-hunters who had their eye on Maraed.' She gasped. 'But they lost contact with them after a couple of days and they haven't seen them since. They've probably gone back to where they came from.'

'How did they know about Maraed?' she said.

'I've no idea.'

'Right,' she said. 'I'm coming with you to the palace.'

'That's not a good idea,' I said. 'Besides, Riff may be coming home today. Don't you want to be here for him?'

She flapped her hand dismissively. 'Don't be silly. Riva will make him welcome and they will need some time to themselves. She has something important she needs to tell him.'

I was going to speak but she cut me off. 'I'll come with you this morning. I'm sure I can be of help and I need to meet this wulver character for myself.'

I could see there was no point arguing with her, so I told her to hurry up as I was already running later than I'd intended. We said goodbye to Riva, saddled up Karmal and set off for the citadel.

Ivor was on guard at the door to Keaten's home, just as he'd promised. I introduced him to Fee. After greeting her, Ivor told me that no one else had come to see the Commander so far that morning and no one had left his private quarters. I told him not to let anyone in except Sarosh the healer, Brick, Mika, Talia or Arken, without first consulting me. Then we went inside and I used the walk to the Commander's bedchamber to worry about what he'd think of Fee turning up.

She followed me into the room and then took charge. First, she marched up to the wulver, studied his face for a moment and must have liked what she saw because she thrust her hand out to him.

'Good morning,' she said, 'I'm Fee, Kane's wife and Seeger's mother. How do you do?'

He smiled and she didn't even flinch! Then he bowed to her and shook her hand. 'It's an honour, fair lady.'

She nodded at him and then turned to Tiffany. 'You must be the Commander's daughter,' she said. 'How are you holding up dear?'

She walked towards the girl, with her arms outstretched, and Tiffany ran into them and burst into tears. Fee patted the child's back. 'I know. I know,' she said. 'You've been very brave. Don't worry. Everything's going to be all right.' She gave Tiffany another gentle hug and then let her go.

Next, she turned to Asher. 'Why are you limping?'

'I was shot in the leg.'

'Oh dear. That was careless,' Fee said. 'Are you on the mend now?' He nodded. 'Excellent,' she said as she looked at the remaining occupant of the room.

'And this must be Tiffany's bodyguard,' she said, walking towards Cal with her hand outstretched. The bodyguard looked a little bewildered. My wife can have that effect on people. Nevertheless, Cal shook her hand. 'Where's the Commander?' Fee said.

The wulver told her, 'He's soaking in the bath.'

'Good,' she said. 'I assume that's part of the treatment?' He nodded. She continued, 'I expect you'll be wanting to wash his bedding and clothing as well.'

The wulver nodded. 'How did you know?'

'A mother knows these things. I'll get onto that this morning but first have you all had breakfast?' Everyone shook their heads. 'I see. Tiffany, dear, why don't you show me the way to the kitchen and we'll soon sort that out.'

Tiffany held the door open and Fee sailed through it like a war galleon leaving port. Tiffany hurried out after her. When the door was shut, I immediately apologised. 'I'm so sorry. She figured things out somehow and gave me no choice.'

Asher smiled. 'Fee is a force of nature, Kane. It was just a matter of time.'

'You say true,' I said, 'but I promised the Commander I wouldn't tell anyone. What's he going to say about it?'

The wulver sat on the end of the bed and gave me a toothy grin. 'She's a remarkable lady.' He smiled again. 'I'm guessing that she's a good cook?'

I nodded but then groaned. 'There could be a diplomatic incident in the kitchen. Professional cooks don't take kindly to amateurs telling them what to do and how to do it. I hate to think what effect Fee is having on the staff.'

Cal said, 'I'll keep an eye on things.' She opened the door and then turned. 'They'll probably need another pair of hands in any case.'

'There goes a brave woman,' Asher said.

I needn't have worried. Fee charmed the cook and her staff and soon had them all focussed on helping the Commander. A simple but satisfying breakfast was later followed by a warm and hearty lunch and then, as the sun set, we were all served a delicious evening meal.

Ellen, Tiffany's personal maid, arrived shortly after breakfast carrying two jugs. One was full of water and the other contained tapanj juice. There were beakers stored in the small cupboard near the bed. Fee and the two housemaids stripped the Commander's bedlinen and replaced it with clean sheets and a quilt, while he was having his second bath after breakfast. They then gathered up all his clothing – even his fancy embroidered cloak – and took them away to be washed. Mac made sure they had a container of copper powder to be added to the water in which they were cleaned.

My wife swept through the palace like a whirlwind of brisk but kind efficiency. She was in her element. Asher kept out of her way as much as possible, especially when she threatened to 'pop him into the wash with the sheets'. Tiffany, on the other hand, followed Fee around like a lovesick calf. I hate to confess that it wasn't until late in the morning that I remembered the poor girl's mother had died when Tiffany had only a few years. It explained a lot.

Asher and I were both surprised that Sarosh, the Commander's healer, didn't attend his patient that day. Up until the day before, he had visited every day to check on his patient's progress and to administer ointment. When we mentioned this to Keaten, he told us that Sarosh had told him he'd be absent because he needed to prepare more ointment and other medicines, and he'd be back the next day. Mac said that he was looking forward to meeting him and comparing notes.

After the evening meal, Fee and I collected Karmal from the stable and rode home. We were heartened by the improvement we'd seen in the Commander. The streaks had already gone from his back. Also, we were both keen to see Riff again and to hear about the trip he'd been on.

Fee said, 'Riva should have told Riff her news by now, so we can celebrate with them.'

Obviously, I'd missed something important. 'What news?' I asked.

She smiled. 'Don't tell me you haven't figured it out.' I shook my head. 'We're going to be grandparents, Kane. Isn't it wonderful?'

'I'm not old enough to be a grandpa!' I said.

Thirty-one

Seeger

The next morning, we had breakfast in the kitchen with Stefan, Alun's father. He agreed to let Alun come to Seddon with us on the condition that if he wasn't happy, he would return to the inn. As a farewell gift, Stefan gave him Lenny.

'Let's face it,' he said, 'that young camel is a bit nervous and twitchy for my liking. He seems to like you, son, so you might as well take him.'

Alun promised to write to his father. They shook hands and then Stefan pulled Alun into a fierce embrace. 'Go with Sed, my son,' he said. He wiped his face with his apron. 'Well, off you go. Things to do.' He bustled back into the inn.

'Father hates a fuss,' Alun said.

Joffre squawked. *I think I'm going to cry.*

Ravens don't cry, I said.

Yes, we do. We cry on the inside!

We mounted our camels and took the road to Seddon. I told Joffre he wouldn't need to do a recky that morning as we were on the home stretch and the slave-hunters were long gone. At first, he complained about not doing his job but it didn't take long for his head to droop forward and to fall fast asleep.

As we rode along, we talked about the Commander, wondering what he thought of Mac and how the treatment was progressing.

Thirty-one

'It'd better work, is all I can say,' Kieran said. 'I don't want to have messed up my hands for nothing.'

'And we don't want poor Tiffany to lose her father,' Alun said.

'You say true,' Kieran agreed.

'It can't have been easy for her,' Alun said, 'worrying about her father and never having left the palace before, but she soldiered on and did a blazing good job.'

'She certainly held her own in the mine,' Kieran said.

'Exactly!' Alun said.

Maraed smiled and waggled her eyebrows at me. I decided to ask her what that meant when we had a chance to speak privately. In the meantime, I just smiled back at her.

The sun was warm on our backs and there was a light breeze blowing in from the sea. We told each other that after all we'd been through, to finish our journey in such a pleasant manner must have been Sed's reward to us for getting the job done.

When we neared the Great Sea Caves I wondered if Shadreer was there. I called to him but I could only just make out a faint answer. He must have chosen another place to wait until Mac needed his flight home.

Just past the caves, we found a sheltered spot amongst some needle trees and decided to give the camels a rest and to finish off the last of our provisions before going home. The trees were tightly clustered, which provided both shade and privacy. We all found a spot to relieve ourselves and then settled down in the shade to eat. The camels sat together not far from us.

Joffre had woken up and was stretching his wings, as he called it. He was a little show-off, doing acrobatics in the air for our amusement. At one point he even flew upside down for a while. We laughed and clapped as we watched his antics and, I swear, it was one of the happiest, carefree moments we'd had in a very long time.

Alun said, 'I wish that bird was with us in Midrash.'

Then Joffre croaked in warning and at the same time a deep voice, which had an inbuilt sneer said, 'It'd probably be as useless as it is now.'

Out from behind the trees stepped the slave-hunters! They'd crept up while Joffre was entertaining us. Of course, both the bird and our camels were deeply embarrassed that they hadn't warned us but we didn't blame them. Those men were masters at making no sound as they moved across the sand.

The camels heaved themselves up and bunched close together, while Joffre streaked towards the men, screaming, *I'll put their eyes out, Seeger.*

One of the men casually raised his bow and aimed at the bird.

'Stop!' I called. *Come to me, Joffre, please. I don't want to see you killed.* 'He'll do what I ask. I promise.' I raised my arm. 'Come, Joffre. Now.'

I could do it, Seeg. I could put that big one's eye out.

I know but then I'd have to watch his friend put an arrow through you. Please?

Oh, all right but just say the word and I'll get him.

He circled around, landed on my arm and then grumbled his way up it to sit in the crook of my neck.

'Well, ain't that something,' the leader said. 'Put it down for now, Shan.'

The fellow lowered his bow but I noticed he kept it loaded and ready. I took Maraed's hand, which was trembling like a leaf on the breeze, and pulled her closer to me.

'What do you want?' Alun said, pulling an arrow out of his quiver and notching it on his bow.

'Settle down young fella,' the leader said. 'No need for that. Just hand the slave over and we'll be on our way. No harm done.'

'There aren't any slaves here,' Kieran said.

'Now, now,' the slaver said, moving a few steps closer to us, 'we all know that's a lie.'

His men moved up next to him. All of them grinned at us. One of them pulled out a long knife. He had a few teeth missing. I thought, *Why hadn't I noticed that before?* Then I thought, *Not important, Seeger! Get a grip.*

We moved back a couple of steps and they moved forward. It was like a macabre dance. The camels moved a few steps forward behind the slavers, who didn't seem to notice.

I called to Shadreer, *Help! We're in danger*, but once again there was just the faintest of replies. *Where are you?* I called, straining to reach him with every fibre of my being.

'Come along, Red,' the slaver said. 'Your master at The Rusty Anchor wants you back, although I can't think why.'

Maraed whimpered and moved back behind me.

'You're not taking her,' I said. The camels moved a little closer. 'She's not a slave. You have no right.'

Alun raised his bow and aimed at the leader. The men laughed. The two archers raised their bows and pointed them at us. The one with the knife spat on the ground and then waved the blade around like he was trying to slice up flies.

'We don't get paid until she's back with her owner,' the leader said, 'so we ain't leaving without her.'

We moved back two steps, they moved forward two steps and the camels moved up three.

'If she doesn't come quietly,' the leader said, 'we'll kill you boys. Simple as that.'

Alun pulled back his arrow. 'Don't come any closer,' he said, 'or I'll shoot.'

The knife-wielder said, 'Oooh. Scary.' The other men thought that was a great joke. 'One arrow's not much use against four, kid,' he said.

'At least there'll be one less of you,' Alun said. He screamed as an arrow lodged near his shoulder. He dropped his bow and clutched his upper arm. It happened so quickly that I wasn't sure which of the men had fired the shot.

Maraed gasped, Kieran swore and I said, 'You all right, Alun?' He nodded but his face was drained of colour.

Shadreer, where are you?

I thought I heard a faint reply, *On my way, hatchling.*

The camels moved up even closer. They were now right behind the slavers. Lenny's nostrils were flared in anger. The men were so delighted to see Alun's misery that they didn't pay any attention to the animals. I think they were the sort of people who never paid much attention to animals unless they needed to use them for something.

Suddenly, Lenny yelled, *Now, fellas!*

The camels' heads lunged in a synchronised attack. Lenny, Errol, Bruce and Ajax all chomped down on the side of the men's necks. A couple of the men could only gurgle but the other two screamed. They all jerked their bodies and flailed their arms trying to get away but the camels held on. The slavers' weapons dropped to the ground. Blood streamed down the front of their tunics. Kevin and Bryan came around in front of the men and began to bite and kick them wherever they could make contact. Joffre flew across to the melee and joined in, darting in and out. It wasn't long before his beak and the feathers on his chest were red.

I heard Maraed moaning and Kieran swore like a drunk fisherman but Alun didn't say anything. He flopped down onto the ground, still clutching his arm. None of us could drag our eyes away from the horror in front of us.

Long after the screaming had stopped, the camels released the slavers' torn throats but all six continued to kick and trample on the men who were prone on the ground. Joffre pecked at their heads.

I'd never seen such a vicious and violent reaction from a camel before. I'd always thought of them as warm and, usually, friendly. From that time on, I decided I would never give a camel cause to use its huge teeth on me. I ran over to Alun and examined his wound. The arrow hadn't gone all the way through.

'They killed them,' he said. 'I didn't think camels were like that.'

'Stay here. I'll be right back,' I said. I ran over to the kitbag that had the last of our medical supplies. I looked at Kieran. He was busy being sick so I said, 'Maraed, come help me.' At first she didn't move. 'MARAED!'

She jerked as if waking up from a bad dream. 'Coming,' she said.

As Maraed and I worked on Alun's arm, the camels finally walked away from the bodies. They lay back down in the shade as if they'd just had a short stroll before bedtime. Joffre flew over to Lenny and perched on his back.

It was his idea, he said. *The young camel is a hero.*

I hope it makes up for my panic in the creek, Lenny said.

We owe you our lives, Len, I said. *You're a brave young camel. Thank you. Thank you, everyone.*

Kieran walked over to us and said, pointing back at what was left of the slavers, 'What are we going to do with them? Will we be in trouble for this?'

Alun shook his head and winced. 'I doubt it. They attacked us and it wasn't our fault that our animals went berserk.'

We all stared at the mangled bodies lying on the sand.

'Will the camels be under threat for doing this?' Maraed said.

We all stared some more.

'That could be a problem,' Kieran said, rubbing his chin.

'Father will look after them but we'll have to clean them up,' I said. 'We can't ride into Seddon with them looking like that. We could use the last of our drinking water to wash their muzzles but there won't be enough to clean the rest of their bodies.'

With Maraed's help, Alun stood up. He still looked pale. 'There's a small pond down near the shoreline,' he said. 'It's not far to go. We could rinse them off there. The water's brackish, no good for drinking, so most travellers don't bother with it.'

We nodded. 'That sounds like a plan,' Kieran said, 'but what about them?' He pointed at what remained of the slavers and we all stared some more. 'I don't think we could dig a big enough hole with just our bare hands. Especially not my hands.' He stared at his bandaged palms.

Then I heard, *I am nearly there, hatchling.*

'The dragon is on his way,' I said. 'Finally.'

You didn't need him, Lenny said. *You had us.*

Kieran said, 'Wait until we tell him the camels did his job for him.' Joffre croaked. 'Oh, sorry, I mean the camels and the raven.'

Maraed ran across to the camels and hugged each one around the neck, exclaiming, 'Thank you, thank you! You darling creatures. And you too, you clever bird.' They all looked very smug.

As Shadreer circled above us he said, *What has happened here, hatchling? Why did you not call?*

You were too far away, I said. *The camels and Joffre saved our lives.*

I have failed you, Shadreer said. *What can I do now to make amends?*

We don't know what to do with the bodies, I said.

I will take them out to sea, Shadreer said. *The fish will welcome them. What about the four camels tied up further back along the road? Shall I eat them?*

No, no! We'll take them with us.

We decided that Alun, Kieran and Maraed would lead our six to the brackish pond and get them clean, while I would walk back down the road to collect the slavers' camels. We'd meet up again at the needle trees and then travel on to Seddon together. After Shadreer had taken the bodies and before we split up, we scuffed sand over the splotches of blood on the ground.

Kieran said, 'I'd like to know who sent those men.'

'Wouldn't we all,' I said.

Thirty-two

We rode straight to the citadel and left the camels with Simpson, the Stable-Master. Shadreer perched on the palace roof. Kieran had to help Alun up the stairs. He was getting weaker.

We went to the Commander's private quarters. The guard told us to leave but when I said that the Beast-Master was expecting me, he said, 'Wait there.' He knocked on the door, Father opened it and his eyes lit up when he saw who it was.

'Let them in, Ivor!' he said.

The room was full of people. As well as my parents, I could see Cal, Tiffany, Talia, Mika, Asher, the wulver and, lying on the couch, the Commander. I noticed that Mika and Talia were both keeping the couch between them and Mac. They would occasionally flick him a wary glance.

As soon as we entered the room, my mother did her best to smother us. 'Darling!' she said. 'You're all right?' She kept me at arm's length while she checked me for injuries and then pulled me into her embrace. Joffre screeched, flew off and perched on a cupboard top.

Don't poop anywhere in here, mate, I said.

As if I would be so rude, Joffre said. *I'll go up the passageway if I need to do my business.*

'You were in danger, weren't you?' Mother said. 'I knew it! Thank Sed, you're home safe and sound.'

She then wrapped Maraed in an enormous hug. 'So glad you're home, sweetie.'

Then she turned to Kieran and Alun, both of whom nodded politely but leaned away from her. Alun staggered as he moved.

Mac hurried over to Alun, scooped him up in his arms and carried him off to tend to his wound. Thank Sed he was there. Later, Mac told us that if we'd left it much longer Alun might have lost his arm or, even worse, his life.

The Commander told us to sit down and tell everyone what had happened. It was soon obvious from my audience's reaction that Asher hadn't given many details of our trip. The only thing they seemed to know about were the slave-hunters. They all applauded our midnight escape. When I described the crossing of Disappointment Creek and the flash flood, my mother shrieked and Father turned to Asher saying, 'What the blazes, Ash?'

I said, 'Did you tell them anything at all, Asher?'

He shrugged. 'I thought it was more important to let the wulver get to work.'

Joffre flew down and settled on my shoulder. I felt better with the bird nestled up against my head. I went back to the tale, describing our visit to Pederson's farm, the trip to Ballyfaol and our encounter with the old man, Rupert.

When I got to the part when Asher was shot, Mika was outraged on his behalf. 'I'd have taught that old curmudgeon a lesson he wouldn't forget!' she said. Asher nodded and smiled his thanks at her.

Then I described our arrival at Wulverstane. Talia, who'd been fidgeting and shuffling about behind the Commander's sofa suddenly said, 'Those slave-hunters … err … did they follow you there?'

I shook my head. 'Not there. I'll get to them soon enough.'

She bit her lip and nodded. I described our meeting with Tarryn and our discovery that he, and many of the other townspeople, were werewolves. Talia snorted her disbelief but the Commander seemed impressed.

Father grinned. 'I'd love to meet them,' he said.

I told them about our meeting with Mac. The Commander insisted that Maraed sing the ancient boating song then and there. When she'd finished, everyone applauded. Talia said, 'That was lovely. I had no idea you could sing like that.'

Father said, 'I told you she was gifted.'

Mother said, 'Did you know that she's having lessons with Corban at the Temple?'

Talia didn't reply.

When I told them about our work in the mines, my mother leapt up from her seat and bustled over to Kieran. 'Show me your hands, sweetheart,' she said. He held them up and she tut-tutted over them. 'I've got some soothing ointment that'll do the trick,' she said.

'I'm fine,' Kieran said. 'They're on the mend.'

She patted his cheek. 'I'll take care of you.' He squirmed.

Then I told how the townsfolk had come to our rescue, digging the copper out of the tunnel walls and crushing it into the powder that Asher and Mac had brought back with them.

'We'd still be working down in that mine if they hadn't turned up,' I said.

The Commander said, 'Kane, when I'm better, you and I must visit Wulverstane to thank them for their help.'

Finally, I described the peaceful, happy day and a half we had riding the camels home. Then I got to the part where the slave-hunters returned.

As I told of their attempt to take Maraed from us, it felt as though the whole world was holding its breath. In the corner of my eye I could see Maraed's hands begin to tremble. Mother pulled her chair over next to her. Tiffany pulled her chair up to the other side of Maraed and put her arm around her shoulders. 'You must have been terrified,' she said.

Mika leaned forward expectantly. She always loved a fight story. Talia swore under her breath and began to pace again.

Cal said, 'I should have stayed with you!'

When I said the leader threatened to kill us all if we didn't hand Maraed over, Mika interrupted. 'Brick said they'd stop at nothing,' she said. 'I'd hoped he was exaggerating.'

I told them how Alun was shot, and they all gasped. 'What a brave lad,' the Commander said. 'Do go on, Seeger.'

I described the camels creeping up on the men and how, when Alun was shot, they'd attacked. I didn't go into every gory detail but they all got the picture. I even remembered to mention Joffre's part in the action. He fluffed his feathers in pride.

Mother sat with her eyes wide and her hands over her mouth. Father's face had gone pale. Asher stared at me with his mouth hanging open. Mika nodded in grim satisfaction and Talia looked as though she was going to vomit. She slumped down in a chair and ran her hands over her face.

Cal said, 'Well done, camels!' She turned to Tiffany, 'And you called them dumb.'

Tiffany flushed a deep pink.

Joffre said, *Who's the new fella?*

The Commander beckoned to the intruder. 'Come along in, Sarosh,' he said. 'We've been hearing a tale of great courage from these young people.'

The man walked hesitantly towards the couch. 'This is my healer,' the Commander said. 'He's from Boron. Just wait a moment, Sarosh, I've someone I want you to meet.' He looked at Mother. 'Fee, would you be so kind as to find Mac and bring him here? Thank you.' She hurried off.

'This should be interesting,' Asher said.

The Commander turned to Father. 'What will you do with the camels, Kane?'

Father looked at me. Kieran and Maraed got up and stood with me. They looked as determined as I felt. 'What do you recommend, Seeger?' he said.

'They need time to recover but then they should be fine,' I said.

'Yes, of course,' the Commander said, 'but can they be trusted not to be violent in the future?'

'It wasn't because they'd lost control,' I said. 'They courageously defended us against people who were determined to kill us. If they'd hesitated a few moments more, then Kieran, Alun and I would be dead and Maraed would be dragged back to Forabad. They should be honoured for that and so should Joffre.'

Father and the Commander stared at each other and then Father slowly nodded. 'Very well,' the Commander said, 'I trust your judgement but if they ever become unreliable or vicious I expect you, Kane, to take the necessary steps.' Father nodded again.

'The important question,' Mika said, 'is how the slave-hunters got on your trail in the first place.'

'Quite so,' Mac said as he entered the room.

The Boroni gasped and stepped back behind the sofa. 'What the –?'

Father said, 'This is Mac, the wulver, who is curing the Commander. Mac, this is Sarosh who was treating the Commander before you came.'

The wulver walked up to the Boroni, sniffing as he approached the young man. 'And what are you using to treat the patient, Sarosh?' he said. He smiled and the afternoon light, streaming in through the window, glinted on his teeth.

The healer twitched but answered, 'Just a soothing ointment.'

Thirty-two

Mac extended his hairy hand towards the Boroni. 'Pleased to meet you.'

The healer shook the wulver's hand. He started to wipe his hand down his trouser leg but then thought better of it.

Asher said, 'We must get Brick to call out the City Watch. Someone in Seddon was giving those slavers information.'

Sarosh said, 'You're in good hands here, Commander. If you'll excuse me, I'll take my leave.' He started to edge his way past everyone.

'No, no!' the Commander said. 'Stay for a while, Sarosh. I insist.'

The Boroni reluctantly sat down again. Father smiled at him and then leaned towards me and whispered, 'He's extremely shy.'

Meanwhile, Talia had almost reached the door when the Commander called to her, 'You too, please Talia. Don't rush off.' She stopped dead in her tracks and then turned and slowly made her way back. The Commander said to her, 'Are you able to shed some light on the mystery of the slavers?'

'What!' Mika said, standing up to stare at Talia, who was slumped back down in her chair.

'Surely you jest?' Asher said.

Kieran, Maraed and I looked at each other in bewilderment. Talia, the Well-Keeper? But she was one of the city's leaders! I'd never warmed to her but I never expected she'd have anything to do with such men.

Cal moved up to stand next to her, her sword unsheathed. Talia now had salt-water streaming down her cheeks.

Tiffany said, 'Someone tell me what's going on?'

Mother went to Talia and draped her arm around the Well-Keeper's shoulders. 'I expect it had something to do with the Choir Director,' she said. 'Your reasoning was swept away by jealousy. Am I right?'

Talia nodded. She looked across at Maraed and, her cheeks flaming with heat, said, 'I had no idea it would turn into something so awful. I'd been told you were a runaway slave. I figured if you could be returned to your owner, you'd no longer be a distraction for Corban. I'm so sorry!'

She began to sob. Mother squeezed her shoulders and said, 'There, there.'

Maraed frowned. 'But Corban's just my teacher.'

Kieran stood up and shouted at Talia, 'You stupid woman!'

Mika strode over to Talia. 'So, you poisoned the Commander?'

'Nooooo!' Talia wailed and began sobbing even harder. She furiously shook her head.

Mother said, 'No, this was a simple case of irrational jealousy aimed at Maraed. I'm certain it had nothing to do with the Commander.'

'Well then, who?' Asher said.

Mika turned towards Sarosh, the healer. 'Isn't it obvious? Who's here every day, smearing so-called ointment on the Commander?'

Thirty-two

We all turned to stare at Sarosh, who was shaking his head. 'I'm a healer, not a poisoner.' He turned to the Commander. 'Surely you're not going to allow this person to falsely accuse me?'

'He's a foreigner,' Mika said.

'He's General Balash's son,' Father said.

'Why would the son of Balash want to poison the Commander?' I asked. 'He was an honourable man and a brave soldier.'

Sarosh nodded at me. 'Thank you.'

'He was the Commander's friend,' I said.

Mika said, 'He was *my* friend. The Commander didn't go to Midrash.' She sniffed.

'It isn't him,' Mac said.

'How do you know?' the Commander asked.

The wulver replied, 'The poison that causes Dead Man's Fingers comes from a tree that grows in the north. It smells of the eucalyptus bark from which it's derived. Sarosh's ointment is harmless. It's lavender, honey, aloe vera, chicken fat and tapanj oil. Am I right?' Sarosh nodded, his mouth agape.

'Who else would know about this poison?' Asher said.

Mac smiled and said, 'It's rare but not that difficult to find if you ask the right people. Traders or soldiers, those who've travelled in the north, would hear about it.'

He pulled a long, fancy glass bottle out of his trouser pocket and held it up. It was about a third full of what appeared to be bath salts. He asked the Commander, 'Who gave you this?'

The Commander reached out for the bottle. Most of us leaned forward to stare at it. Mika stood up and began to move towards the door. I guessed she was keeping guard. Cal went with her. The Commander studied the bottle.

'This was given to me at my celebration of life party. I only began using it a short time ago. It has a refreshing scent. Why do you ask?'

Mac said, 'That refreshing scent comes from the bark of the bleeding eucalypt, which gets its name from the red streaks on its trunk. It's the source of your poisoning.'

We all gasped. Mother said, 'How diabolical!' and Tiffany said, 'Oh, Pa!'

The Commander lifted his head and looked towards the two women guarding the door. 'Mika?' he said.

The general shoved Cal away and reached for the doorknob but Father called out, 'IVOR!' The guard swung the door open, knocking the general to the floor. He immediately began to apologise to her but Cal, who'd already leapt back up, grabbed Mika.

Father called out, 'Mika's poisoned the Commander!'

Ivor drew his sword and held it at the ready as Cal, and Talia who'd run to help, secured the general, who was putting up a fight. They used Cal's belt to tie Mika's hands behind her back. Talia removed the general's weapons.

Asher stood up. 'I don't understand, Mika. Why?' She glared at the floor. Asher said, 'Mika?' She looked up and practically spat out her reply. 'Seddon needs a new leader!'

Joffre ruffled his hackles and hissed at her. I couldn't believe it! 'The Commander is a strong and fair leader,' I said. 'I don't understand.' Kieran, Maraed, Tiffany and Mother all nodded in agreement. 'What's your problem?'

She sniffed again. 'When was the last time he led a force from Seddon? He didn't bother going to Midrash. That was all done by me!'

Asher shook his head. 'There were also a few others involved in that fight, Mika.'

The Commander slowly stood up and walked towards the general. Halfway across the room, he staggered. Sarosh and Mother ran to support him. Mac hovered just behind them, ready to intervene if he had to.

'Mika,' the Commander said, 'my wife had just died. I had her funeral to arrange as well as a grieving child to comfort. I trusted you to represent Seddon and you did so, admirably.' He shook his head in sorrow. 'I can't believe I've misjudged you so badly.'

He sagged a little more so Mac gently scooped the Commander up and carried him back to the couch.

'Seddon needs a strong leader,' Mika said. 'Someone like me!'

Father shook his head. 'The people of Seddon make that choice, not you.'

'Take her to the cells,' the Commander said.

Ivor and Cal began to lead the struggling, cursing general away but Tiffany called out, 'Wait!

She ran up to Mika, her hand raised ready to strike, but then she slowly lowered it saying, 'I'm almost sorry for you. You nearly killed Pa because you love yourself and you're jealous of him.' She shook her head. 'Take her away.' She walked back to us with her head held high but her eyes were brimming with salt water.

Joffre said, *I never liked her!*

Once Mika and her guards had left, the Commander said, 'The leadership will meet first thing tomorrow to decide her fate.' Mac coughed and then smiled at the Commander. 'Ah, yes,' he continued, 'I mean, first thing after my morning soak.'

'What about Talia?' Asher said.

We all looked at the Well-Keeper, who went an even deeper shade of red and began to sob quietly again.

'Talia,' the Commander said, 'your reckless actions put these young people's lives at risk. You are relieved of your command for four lunar cycles. Rog will be Acting Well-Keeper. I also order you to pay Maraed what you would have earned in those cycles. No,' he said, holding up his hand, 'don't argue. I could give you time in prison but I don't think that's necessary. Do you, Maraed?'

She shook her flaming red hair. 'No, sir,' she said.

Kieran snorted. 'I do! Why she –'

Maraed put her hand on his arm and told him to stop. She turned to Talia. 'I'm sure you feel deeply ashamed.' She breathed deeply. 'So, I forgive you.'

Joffre flew over to Maraed's shoulder. *I'm so proud of her, Seeg.*

Talia bowed her head. 'Thank you, Commander. I'm very sorry, Maraed.'

Mac grinned, his teeth flashing. 'I'm glad that's all sorted,' he said. 'Keaten, why don't you show them your arms?'

The Commander pulled up his sleeves. The blue was almost up to his elbows. However, Asher said, 'Lovely! Lovely!' Father said, 'Oh Keaten, that's amazing' and Sarosh shook his head in wonder.

Kieran said. 'They look horrendous to me.'

Father smiled. 'The last time I had a good look at his arms, the blue was almost to his armpits. This is so much better.'

'I'll take your word for it,' Kieran said. He looked at me and raised his eyebrows.

Mac patted his patient's shoulder. 'It won't be much longer before I can ask Shadreer to fly me home.'

Mother suddenly spun around. 'Oh Seeger, I almost forgot to tell you. You're going to be an uncle!'

Maraed squealed with joy and ran over to hug me. 'What?' I said. 'How?'

'Riva and Riff are having a baby, silly!' Maraed said.

Mother excitedly clasped her hands and jiggled on the spot. Father looked … wary. 'You'll be grandparents!' I said. He winced.

END

CPSIA information can be obtained
at www.ICGtesting.com
Printed in the USA
BVHW050953200623
666145BV00003B/115

9 781666 754070